GLENN ICKLEI

To Laura -
Best wishes and enjoy

ARSENIC and OLD MEN

Glenn Ickler
9/14/19

A Mitch and Al MYSTERY

outskirts press

Arsenic and Old Men Title
A Mitch and Al Mystery

v4.0

Outskirts Press, Inc.
http://www.outskirtspress.com

ISBN: 978-1-9772-0481-3

PRINTED IN THE UNITED STATES OF AMERICA

Also by Glenn Ickler

One Death Too Many

Camping on Deadly Grounds

Stage Fright

Murder by Coffee

A Deadly Calling

Out at Home

A Deadly Vineyard

A Carnival of Killing

Murder on the St. Croix

A Killing Fair

Fishing for a Killer

A Cold Case of Killing

A Doomsday Killing

Dedication

To Jan, who kept nagging me to bring Mitch and Al out of Minnesota for an adventure in Massachusetts.

Acknowledgments

My thanks to Dr. D.P. Lyle, for his expert advice on the effects of certain sleep-inducing and life-terminating substances.

1

ON THE BEACH

Where does a guy dressed modestly in shorts and a T-shirt look when he's shaking hands with a naked man?

That was my dilemma as I reached for the outstretched hand of the nude sunbather who was introducing himself to me on the clothing-optional section of Lucy Vincent Beach on the island of Martha's Vineyard.

"Richard Rylander," the naked man was saying. "But you can call me Dick. I don't believe in formalities."

Or swimsuits, I said to myself. And as for Dick ... well, after taking a quick glance at waist level to intercept his hand, I raised my gaze to the level of his eyes and kept it there.

"Warren Mitchell," I said. "Better known as Mitch."

At six-foot one in height, I was looking down at Dick Rylander, who stood about five-foot-seven, with a sagging pot belly that thankfully was obscuring all objects between his navel and his knees. He was somewhere in his mid to late fifties, with a soft, lumpy body and a pudgy round face under a shiny bald dome that was surrounded by a ring of stringy gray hair. A deep brown suntan coated every inch of slightly-crinkled skin that I could see.

This was not a casual meeting with a bare-ass beach bum on a sunny, summery October morning. Rylander had invited the three of us to meet him on this beach without mentioning that we'd recognize him by what he was *not* wearing. By the three of us, I mean myself, Alan Jeffrey and Dave Jerome. For the record, Al and Dave were as conventionally clad as I was—in shorts and T-shirts.

Rylander was a lawyer representing the estate of the late Walter Jerome, Dave's 78-year-old uncle, who had become late quite unexpectedly a few days earlier in his expansive Victorian-style home in Oak Bluffs. Rylander had called Dave, who was Walter's only living relative, with a request to come to the Vineyard to take charge of Walter's body, take a look at Walter's will and take possession of Walter's 19th-century dwelling, which was called a cottage even though its size far exceeded the dictionary definition of the word.

Merriam-Webster says a cottage is (1) "a small single-storied house" or (2) "a small summer house." The people who live in New England say a cottage can have two stories, four bedrooms, two and a half bathrooms and an enormous wraparound porch, and be occupied summer, winter, spring and fall if the occupier so chooses. Curious folk, these New Englanders.

Dave did not want to make the trip from Minnesota to this famous island in Massachusetts all by himself, so he asked Al and me, his closest friends, to "take a few days" off work and accompany him for emotional and physical support. The three of us had worked together for many years at the *St. Paul Daily Dispatch*, where I am an investigative reporter, Al is the paper's best photographer and, until recently, Dave was the staff editorial cartoonist. Dave had been one of those reduced in a staff reduction, but he had survived by becoming nationally syndicated and was happier working at home in his jammies and bathrobe than he had been in his closet-size office at the *Daily Dispatch*.

Al and his wife and I (and my longtime feline companion, Sherlock Holmes) had joined Dave and his wife for a Martha's Vineyard vacation at his Uncle Walt's cottage nine years earlier. Although it had not been an altogether pleasant experience because of a murder, a mysterious threat on Uncle Walt's life and a battle with an armed killer, we decided to bring the wives with us again on this brief trip.

Al and I took vacations from the paper. Martha Todd, the gorgeous Cape Verdean woman I'd married since my last trip to

Martha's Vineyard, took a leave from the St. Paul law firm where she works as an attorney. Al's high school teacher wife, Carol, took some accrued family leave time. And Dave's wife, Cindy, left her duties as an executive at a small private college in the hands of her assistant—all for "just a few days."

I would actually be doing some reporting about what occurred on this trip because Walt Jerome had once been the very popular editor of the *St. Paul Daily Dispatch*. He had been fired by the publisher under bizarre circumstances many years ago, and had later become the editor of a weekly called the *Martha's Vineyard Chronicle*, from which he'd retired at the age of 75.

"Uncle Walt always said that fall is the best time to be on the Vineyard," Dave had told us. "He said all the summer tourists are gone, the traffic is almost zero and the weather is still beautiful." We had found these claims to be partially true upon arrival on the first Friday of October. The number of tourists was reduced but not "gone," and the traffic was less than it had been during our summer visit but it was nowhere near "zero." The one fully accurate claim was the weather, which was "still beautiful" on this Saturday morning as we drove to Lucy Vincent Beach in a Dodge van we had rented for $129 a day (plus the tax) and were welcomed by a naked Dick Rylander. When Rylander approached us sans swim suit, Al, Dave and I were glad that the women had decided to walk the beach in the opposite direction and "leave all the legal chatter to the boys."

"I just couldn't bear to sit inside a stuffy old law office on a gorgeous day like this," Rylander said. "It's the perfect time to let it all hang out here on the beach. I brought Walt's will along, and some papers for Dave to sign, and I've got some blankets to sit on over here. Just follow me."

He turned his back, revealing a drooping, flabby and deeply tanned ass, and we followed the rolling and bobbing cheeks to the blankets. He let it all hang out as he lowered himself onto the corner of a blanket and sat facing us with his legs stretched straight out in front. After an awkward moment during which all three of us were looking everywhere but straight ahead, Rylander placed a red-and-white striped beach towel and a brown leather briefcase across his lap and we all relaxed.

Rylander withdrew a pack of folded papers from the briefcase. "Here's your uncle's will. He updated it last May. He had a mild heart attack early in May, you know."

"No, I don't know," Dave said. "He didn't communicate with me all that much."

"Well, he did have a scare, and it motivated him to update the will. He's left money to a couple of his pet charities, but the bulk of the estate goes to you, Dave. You now own a home on Martha's Vineyard that's assessed at a little over eight-hundred-thousand dollars. Fortunately, the mortgage has been paid in full and there's also more than enough cash in an investment account to keep up with the taxes and whatever you need to spend for maintenance and caretaking."

"Uff-da! Eight-hundred-thousand?" Dave said. He was accustomed to more modest Minnesota real estate prices.

"That's nothing. If you put a tower on it, so you could see the ocean over the top of the house in front of it, the place would be worth well over a million. Actually, you could probably get a million for it as it is."

"So what am I going to do with a high-priced house on Martha's Vineyard when I live fourteen-hundred miles away in Minnesota?" Dave said.

"That's where the cost of maintenance comes in," Rylander said. "I assume you'll want to hire someone to take care of the house and the yard, and also hire an agent to handle rentals to vacationers when you're not here. I can give you some advice along those lines."

"I hope you can also give me advice on finding a realtor to sell the place," Dave said.

Rylander looked surprised. "You mean you won't be spending your summers here?"

"I can't imagine that," Dave said. "A couple of weeks would be fun, but all summer just doesn't make sense to me. And I can't imagine years of dealing with upkeep and rentals long distance from Minnesota just to have a couple of weeks here every summer."

"You might want to talk with the missus before you make a snap decision to sell," Rylander said. "She's a teacher, isn't she? Spending all summer here might make sense to her. You're only a ten-minute walk from the Oak Bluffs town beach and you're close to all kinds of restaurants."

"And T-shirt shops," Al said. "Circuit Avenue is T-shirt shoppers' heaven."

"I need more T-shirts like that ocean out there needs more water," Dave said, waving a hand toward the waves breaking on the shore. "I'll sell the house to you, and you can take an early retirement and live here wearing Martha's Vineyard T-shirts all year 'round."

"Sorry, but you'll have to mark the price down about ninety percent before it's in my ball park," Al said.

Dave was silent for a moment while he did some mathematical computation. "Okay, give me eighty-thousand in cash today and it's a deal."

"Sorry again. I'm a few bucks short in my billfold and I didn't bring my check book. Do you take MasterCard?"

"Strictly cash in your case, Al. I guess I'll have to find a realtor after all. But that can wait. What else have you got for me, Mister Rylander?"

"Please call me Dick," Rylander said. "I was your uncle's friend as well as his attorney. I have some papers you'll have to sign in front of a notary public in order to transfer the house to your name and some paperwork to deal with taking custody of Walt's body after the autopsy is completed."

It was Dave's turn to look surprised. "Autopsy? You said Uncle Walt died of a heart attack. Why would they do an autopsy?"

"State law," Rylander said. "An autopsy is required for any unattended death. Walt's cleaning lady went into the house and found him passed away in a chair. It sure looked like a heart attack, but nobody was with him when he died, and the law is the law."

"So when will this needless autopsy be done?" Dave asked.

"It's scheduled for Monday. You can have a nice weekend on the Vineyard and make whatever arrangements you want on Monday. The stuff I'm giving you includes a document signed by your uncle, and witnessed by me, that says he definitely did not want any kind of funeral or memorial service to be held in his name, and that he wished to be cremated and have his ashes scattered in two places: his garden and a certain ferry landing in Oak Bluffs harbor."

"Is there anything else?"

"Oh, yes. There's the deed to a patch of woods that Walt owned on Chappaquiddick. That might be something else you'll want to sell."

"I remember that patch of woods," Dave said. Al and I said we did, too. Walt had hidden himself there while dodging the man who'd threatened to kill him. By following his housekeeper, who was surreptitiously supplying him with food and water, we rode across Edgartown harbor to Chappaquiddick on a very small ferry and found Walt living like a homeless vagabond in a tent among the trees.

"I'm not sure I could find that spot," Dave said. "It was almost ten years ago that we were out there."

"There's a map along with the deed," Rylander said. "That'll help you find it if you want to check it out." He passed the stack of papers to Dave and stood up. "That's all I have."

As Rylander stood facing us, it was obvious that he really didn't have much more. And the full frontal view reminded me that our beach-strolling wives might soon be turning around and heading our way.

"We should get back to the girls," I said in a tone that implied a need for speed. Both Al and Dave caught my implication.

"Ooh, you're right," Al said.

"Good thinking," Dave said. "Thanks, Dick. I'll give you a call on Monday. I'm sure I'll need your help with the cremation arrangements." He did not offer the nude attorney a parting handshake.

"Nice meeting you, gentlemen," Rylander said. "I'm going to hang out here as long as I can this morning."

"I assume he means hours and not inches," Al whispered as we walked away.

2

STILL A BEACH DAY

We barely intercepted our returning wives at an out-of-sight distance from our naked host. Without hesitation we turned them about and steered them toward the parking lot, where we all climbed into our six-passenger van.

"So how was the lawyer?" Cindy Jerome asked.

"He gave us the bare facts," Dave said.

"And he's not leaving with us?"

"Said he wants to hang out on the beach a little longer," Al said.

"Can't say I blame him," Carol Jeffrey said. "I wish we'd brought our swim suits."

"We were wishing the lawyer had brought his," I said.

"Why? Was he dressed up in a suit?" Martha Todd asked.

"He was dressed down, actually. In a tanned and wrinkled body suit," I said.

"Skin tight," Al said.

"Wait a minute; are you saying he was naked?" Martha asked.

"That part of the beach is clothing-optional, and the Honorable Mister Rylander chose the naturalist option," Dave said.

"Oh, my god," Cindy said. "I wish we'd gone with you."

"No you don't," I said. "On the Honorable Mister Rylander, *au naturel* was not an attractive option."

"He's not Superman," Al said. "In fact, he's not even Clark Kent."

"Santa Claus comes to mind," Dave said. "Without the beard."

It was lunch time when we got back to Oak Bluffs, so we parked the van at Dave's newly-acquired eight-hundred-grand cottage and walked the two blocks to Linda Jean's, a restaurant on Circuit Avenue where we had enjoyed good food and friendly service during our previous Vineyard sojourn. We found a line of would be diners that extended out the door and onto the sidewalk. Dave squeezed his way in, gave his name to a hostess and was given one of those electronic gadgets that flashes and buzzes when your table is ready.

We waited on the other side of the street in a little square with benches and small patches of flowers. When the lights flashed and the buzzer sounded we went back to the restaurant and presented ourselves to the hostess.

The interior had been redecorated since our last visit, but the seating, five rows of booths with a few free-standing wooden tables, had not changed. The hostess led us to a four-person booth along the right-hand wall and asked if we needed a chair at the end of the table. Luckily, none of us is wide bottomed, so we said no and all six of us sardined ourselves into the booth.

A middle-aged, dark-haired woman approached us with a smile and half a dozen menus. Her smiling face and the warmth of her greeting showed us that the service was still friendly, and fifteen minutes later, when she brought our orders, we all agreed that the food was still good, as well.

The sun was shining and the temperature was in the low seventies, a fabulous early October day, so after lunch we put on our swim suits and flip-flops and took a ten-minute walk to the town beach, leaving Sherlock Holmes, who had made the trip again, in the house as our watch cat. I am happy to say that we all looked better in our swim suits than Dick Rylander had in his birthday attire. The women were especially rewarding to view—blond Carol showing off her long-legs and slim waist, sandy-haired Cindy revealing a full curvaceous-figure, and dark-haired, brown-skinned Martha displaying the most exquisitely proportioned ass in the universe.

After a couple of hours of alternate toasting in the sun and splashing in the water of Nantucket Sound, which was already taking on an autumn chill, we went back to the house and took turns rinsing off in the outdoor shower. We then gathered on the front porch and had a little happy hour with some provisions we found in the kitchen—wine for everyone except Mitch the alcoholic, who drained a bottle of root beer, and some cheese with crackers that had been standing open on the pantry shelf a few days past their prime.

We ate dinner at a craft beer restaurant with the strange name City, Ale & Oyster, where the noise level was equal to an artillery barrage but the hamburgers were delicious. After dinner we three men inspected the living room while the women were in the kitchen washing the glasses from our happy hour, along with several clean-looking wine glasses that were sitting beside the sink.

The living room, which was at the front of the house, looked as Victorian as the cottage did on the outside, with voluminous white curtains on every window and a heavy multi-colored Oriental rug on the floor. Four white wicker chairs, a white wicker loveseat and an antique Queen Anne sofa with white cushions were arranged in an oval around the perimeter, each with an appropriate end table and elaborately-shaded lamp. The only off-Victorian note was the coffee table, which was almost four feet long and was topped with a two-foot-wide slab of rough-hewn oak. Al hauled out his camera and shot some pictures of the room, including a close-up of the coffee table. Dave asked him why he was doing that and Al said, "Because taking pictures is what I do. Forgive me, oh lord of the mansion, but I just can't help myself."

Soon our wives joined us in the living room, and the ever-industrious Carol set about straightening up some typewritten pages and some magazines that were scattered on the coffee table. Then she took a dust rag to that table and all of the wooden end tables. Just watching her in action made me feel tired enough to sit down.

Apparently Carol's cleaning frenzy had the same effect on Dave. "Wonder which chair the cleaning lady found Uncle Walt in," he said as he sat down on the white wicker chair with the thickest seat pad.

"You might be sitting in that very seat," I said.

Dave was on his feet in one swift motion. "You're right. I think I'll try the sofa."

Cindy and Carol dropped onto the sofa, one on each side of Dave, leaving Martha, Al and me looking at the four empty chairs. Not wishing to risk occupying any chair, or even the loveseat, in which Uncle Walt might have met his demise, all three of us went to the dining room, picked up wooden chairs from around the long oak dining table, and carried them back to living room.

We turned on the TV to watch the Red Sox and Indians in a play-off game and chatted about this and that as the game progressed. In the seventh inning, with Cleveland leading 7-2, Dave began telling the Jerome family story about how his Uncle Walt had been fired by *Daily Dispatch* publisher Herb Riley. It seems that Riley and his Minneapolis counterpart were getting snot-flying drunk together shortly after the family-owned *Daily Dispatch* had been purchased by a major corporation with a nationwide chain of newspapers. The Minneapolis publisher had been giving Riley a hard time about losing his autonomy and teasing him about "corporate now calling the shots."

Riley insisted he still had full authority to run the paper as he saw fit and the Minneapolis agitator, after downing his fifth Scotch on the rocks, said, "I'll bet you a case of Johnny Walker Black against whatever poison you name that you can't even fire Walt Jerome."

Riley took the bet, and the next morning, with his head still pounding from a hangover, he called Walt into his office, thanked him for his many years of service and told him he was being replaced by a younger man who would "take the paper in a new direction."

"That direction was down," Dave said. "People loved Walt for his no-nonsense editorials and his witty Sunday columns. The paper lost almost two thousand subscribers in protest of his firing, and Walt wound up taking over the *Martha's Vineyard Chronicle* from its founder, who happened to be Walt's grandfather."

"And your great-grandfather," I said.

"That's right."

"And you had no interest in taking over the Vineyard paper when Walt retired three years ago?" Martha asked.

"No interest in leaving Minnesota," Dave said.

"A man with a truly warm heart," I said.

"And a truly cold nose in the winter," Dave said.

"Here's looking at-choo," said Al, raising his glass in salutation.

"Bless you," Carol said. "And now it's time for bed."

It was about 11:30, Eastern Time, when we all went upstairs to take our pick of the four bedrooms. Dave pointed out Uncle Walt's room, noting that he had been alive and healthy the last time he'd used it, but none of us chose to spend the night there. Martha and I got a back bedroom, looking out over a narrow, moonlit lawn and a wide patch of flowers that were shriveling and bending their heads in surrender to the season. We drifted off to sleep with Sherlock Holmes curled up in a black-and-white furry ball at our feet.

All of us awoke around 7:30 on Minnesota time, which is an hour earlier than Massachusetts time. This meant we were running an hour behind the rest of the Vineyard visitors and we found a line of about a dozen people waiting outside Linda Jean's by the time we got there for Sunday breakfast. Dave gave his name to the woman inside, took the buzzer she handed him and returned to where the rest of us had gone to sit in the little open square across the street.

"Another beach day," Carol said, looking up at the sun and blue sky.

"I'd kind of like to go out to Chappaquiddick and find that wild patch of woods that I now own," Dave said. We all agreed that this would be a worthwhile trip. We also agreed to wear our swim clothes under our shorts and T-shirts so that we could go to a beach on Chappy after inspecting the woodland.

Back at the cottage, we made the clothing change, filled

Sherlock's food and water dishes, grabbed our water bottles and, with Dave at the wheel of the van, drove to Edgartown on the two-lane strip of road between the broad beach facing Nantucket Sound and the sliver of sand bordering Sengekontacket Pond. We wove our way through Edgartown, following the signs to the On-Time Ferry, and eventually arrived at the ferry landing, where we found three cars ahead of us in the waiting line.

The On-Time Ferry is so named because it has no published schedule and, therefore, is always on time. It carries a maximum of three vehicles and whatever number of hikers and bikers who want to get onboard. The trip to Chappy takes about three minutes across a channel with such a strong current that the ferry crabs into the flow and takes a curving route to the other side. During the summer the original On-Time boat is paired with a newer, identical craft named the On-Time II, and they pass each other as they crisscross the channel. On this off-season day only one was running, and it was just leaving the Edgartown slip with a full load.

We waited while the On-Time made the crossing, unloaded and reloaded on the far shore and returned. Then we waited some more while the On-Time unloaded and reloaded with the three vehicles—a van, a Jeep and a pickup truck—ahead of us. Now we were first in line, and we waited for a third time while the On-Time made the crossing, unloaded, reloaded, crossed the channel and unloaded on our side.

Being first in line, we were obliged to drive to the extreme forward, wide-open edge of the ferry, holding our breaths waiting for the attendant to tell us to stop and praying that the brakes would not suddenly fail in this crucial situation.

Once onboard, Dave proceeded at the speed of a snail on crutches, with his foot hovering over the brake pedal and his eyes focused on the young woman who was urging us to keep moving forward. I was certain that our front bumper was hanging over the edge, and Cindy expressed all of our feelings by saying, "Sheeze, that's scary," when we finally came to a stop. Dave set the handbrake with an extra hard tug and the attendant stuck a wooden chock in front of one front tire.

The crossing was circuitous but uneventful. When we landed, the attendant pulled away the chock, Dave started the engine and released the handbrake. We rolled off onto Chappy and drove onto a two-lane blacktop road. As we passed a row of tent-like beach cabanas with bright red-white-and-blue-striped roofs, Martha pointed and said, "Look, weren't those in the movie 'Jaws?'"

"Yes, but they were in a different place," Cindy said. "The film editors put them on the main beach in Amityville, which was the beach we drove along on our way to Edgartown."

Following Uncle Walt's map, we stayed on the blacktop when it took a sharp right at the intersection of the gravel road that Ted Kennedy took on a long-ago night when his car went off a bridge and sank to the bottom with a young woman named Mary Jo Kopechne trapped inside.

I remembered the next turn, a sharp left, because it was marked by a large rock bearing the carved message "Blow Your Bugle." Nobody we'd questioned on Martha's Vineyard had been able to explain the origin or the meaning of this command during our previous visit.

According to the map, the road into Uncle Walt's woodland retreat was less than a mile from the Bugle rock. I recalled that narrow sand and gravel road vividly because my first trip on it was aboard a bicycle, following Walt's housekeeper, a woman called Daffy Dolly. I had tracked her all the way from downtown Oak Bluffs on a hot August day and was exhausted by the time we reached this road.

"There it is," I yelled as I spotted it on the right. "That's the road."

Dave hit the brakes and made the turn. The road was only one-car wide and the sunken wheel tracks were so deep in places that Dave had to creep along in order to avoid a hard, bottom-scraping bounce. We wound our way through an assortment of oaks, evergreens and scrub oaks, and eventually the gravel disappeared and we were driving on soft sand.

"Whatever you do, don't stop in this sand," Al said. "We'll sink so deep we'll never get started again."

"We should have rented a four-wheel-drive," Dave said. "You might all have to push to get us out of here with this thing."

We came into a clearing about half a city block in size and the ground beneath our tires grew firmer. We were all relieved to have found a natural place where we could stop and turn around without sinking the van up to its hubcaps. We were not relieved by the sight of two unnatural accouterments standing before us in the clearing.

3

SQUATTER'S RIGHTS?

Dave stopped the van and turned off the engine. We sat for a minute looking at a rust-ravaged Landrover parked beside a small olive drab army surplus tent in the center of the clearing. As we all piled out of the van, a man crawled out of the tent and stood up to meet us.

The man was stooped slightly forward and would have been about six feet tall if he'd been standing up straight. His frame was as bony as a prison camp survivor, ringlets of yellowish white hair hung to his shoulders and his white beard covered his chest and belly with scraggly curls halfway down to his navel. The rest of his body was covered solely by a deep sun tan and a black speedo bikini that was only fifty percent less revealing than Dick Rylander's birthday suit. What really caught our attention was the foot-long double-edged knife he held beside his right hip, with the tip pointed in our direction.

All seven of us stood in silence waiting for somebody else to speak. The mop-topped man with the knife finally took the lead.

"This is private proppity," he said. "You folks are trespassin' and I'd advise you to git back into that van and git yourselves gone." He waved toward the road with the knife.

Dave took a baby step forward. "You're right, this is private property," he said. "And I happen to own it. So I suggest that you pack that tent into that bucket of rust and get *yourself* gone."

"Bullshit," the man said. "I know the man what owns this proppity and he give me the right to live here every summer for the last eight years."

"Do you have that in writing?" Dave asked.

"Course not. The man give me his word that I can stay here every summer till I take off for Florida in the winter."

"Do you have any witnesses to that promise?"

"I got witnesses that I been here every summer. I git visitors here. Lady visitors." He patted the front of his Speedo and I saw looks of horror on the faces of Cindy, Carol and Martha.

"Do you know the name of the man you say lets you stay here?"

"Course I do."

"Is it John Henry?"

He pretended to think for a moment. "Ay-yah, that could be it, but it don't sound quite right."

"That's because it's not right. For your information, the owner's name was Walter Jerome and he just died and left this land to me in his will."

"Ay-yah, that sounds more like it. Old Walt, folks calls him."

"Well, Old Walt is gone to heaven and I'm giving you notice to get yourself gone from here because I'm planning to sell this property."

"You can't sell this proppity without my say-so," the Speedo man said. "Old Walt lets me stay here and I got squatter's rights fer a good eight years. All you need is seven years. Ownership by occupation, they calls it."

"You don't have diddly squat," Dave said. "I'm selling this land and you need to leave."

"Bullshit you're sellin'. I'll fight you in court if I hafta. I got a right to stay here."

"I've got a deed that says you don't. If you aren't off by the next time I come, I'll have the police move you off."

"I'll sue yer ass if you try to sell this proppity. You can count on that. I know my rights under the law."

"Who the hell are you anyway? What's your name?

"My name is Teddy. Teddy Kennedy."

"Did you say Teddy *Kennedy*?"

"Ay-yah. That's me. Who might you be?"

"I might be David Jerome and I might be the sole owner of this property."

"Well, we'll see about that if'n you try to sell it without my say-so. Now I'm done talkin' to ya, so git." Speedo man waved the knife in a circle and Dave took an adult step back.

"Let's do what he says and git," Al said. "He's nuts enough to stab somebody."

"You're right," Dave said. "Everybody get on board. We'll check on this screwball when we get back to Edgartown. See what the cops know about him."

We all got into the van, Dave turned it around, and as we started down the sandy part of the road Cindy said, "If that guy gets lady visitors they must come with gas masks and strait-jackets to take him away."

"You never know," Al said. "For enough money, some quote, ladies, unquote, will do just about anything."

"Oh, please, I can't imagine there being enough money in the world, much less Martha's Vineyard, to persuade any quote, lady, unquote, to visit that filthy old creep," Cindy said.

"Maybe he has pictures," I said.

"Yuck. You're making me sick," said Cindy.

"I just fwowed up," Martha said.

"So you met old Teddy, did you?" said Edgartown Police Chief Morris Agnew. "Well, he's a harmless old man who just wants to be left alone." We'd caught the chief exiting through the front door of the Edgartown police station just as we were about to enter.

"The knife he was pointing at us didn't look all that harmless," I said.

"He says he's Teddy Kennedy," Dave said.

"Not always," Agnew said. "Some days he says he's Teddy Roosevelt."

"Looks like he's always Teddy Bare," Al said. "That Speedo he wears is nothing but a thong."

"Well, old Teddy doesn't dress up for company," the chief said. "Especially if he's not expecting you."

"Who is he really?" Dave asked.

"His real name is Teddy Brewster," Agnew said.

"Teddy Brewster?" Dave said. "That's right out of the play 'Arsenic and Old Lace.' That Teddy thought he was Teddy Roosevelt, too."

"Claims to be a descendent of the Brewster that came over on the Mayflower."

"He sure doesn't dress like a Pilgrim," Martha said.

"I don't care if his ancestors came here with Columbus, he's on my property and he needs to get off," Dave said. "I can't believe Uncle Walt let that screwball camp there every summer."

"Your Uncle Walt was a kind and generous man," Agnew said. "And Teddy is an old disabled fisherman who's never hurt anything that didn't have gills. It's not at all surprising that Walt let him camp there."

"How does he survive?" I asked.

"He has a post office box here in town and he gets a check from somewhere, probably Social Security, once a month, which he cashes at the bank," Agnew said. "Then he drives that old Landrover to the Stop 'n Shop and loads up on canned goods and dried food and hauls it back to Chappy."

"I hope he wears more than that Speedo when does all this," Cindy said.

The chief laughed. "He's got a pair of coveralls that he puts on for social occasions."

"Does he really go to Florida in the winter?" Al asked.

"Claims he does," Agnew said.

"Not in that Landrover," I said.

"Oh, god, no. He takes the bus."

"Any idea how he lives in Florida?" Dave asked. "Has he got another squatter spot down there?"

"I don't think anybody around here knows that," Agnew said. "Not any of our business, actually."

"The old Yankee 'let well enough alone' thing?" Al said.

"I guess you could call it that," the chief said. "That and the fact that nobody really gives a damn where the old coot goes in the winter. We're just happy that he's gone and we don't have to worry about him freezing to death out there."

"Well, I plan to sell that property so I need to get him off," Dave said. "He claims he'll sue me if I try to sell. If he won't go willingly I'll have to call on you for help."

"If I was you, I'd hold off on selling until Teddy is off to Florida, and then put up a fence to discourage him next spring," Agnew said.

"Putting up a fence will cost a lot of money."

"Might save you the cost of a lawsuit to do it that way. He's got a cousin who's a lawyer and they actually have sued one guy over ownership of a boat."

"He's got a cousin who's a lawyer? Why in the hell doesn't the cousin take care of him? Give him a place to live?"

"Teddy's got all he wants right there in the woods," Agnew said. "As you may have noticed, he's a little off center in the head. Now if you folks will excuse me, I have to go talk to a lady who claims she's being followed by the Russians."

"Good luck with that," I said. "We've got a guy in St. Paul who claims the Russians are watching him on radar."

"Damn Russians are everywhere," Agnew said. "Nice meeting you folks. Have a good day."

We got in the van and, by mutual agreement, drove back to Oak Bluffs without stopping at any beach. It was past lunch time and we were all feeling hungry and letdown from the encounter with Teddy Kennedy Roosevelt Brewster. At the cottage we were welcomed by a black and white cat, whose joyful greeting raised our spirits, and we hauled out some sandwich makings purchased the day before that assuaged our hunger.

After lunch I tapped out a story about this strange twist in the saga of the late Walt Jerome on my laptop and emailed it to the *St. Paul Daily Dispatch* along with a couple of photos of Teddy and his camp that Al had shot surreptitiously during our confrontation with the squatter. Sunday Editor Gordon Holmberg sent back an email saying this package would be good reading for all the old-timers who remembered Walt from his years as editor.

We spent the rest of the day reading, talking and dozing on the porch and tried a restaurant overlooking Oak Bluffs harbor for dinner. After that we did our best to walk off the fried clams and French fries we'd consumed with a stroll along the town beach, and relaxed in the living room for a while before bedtime.

The last thing Dave said before going upstairs was, "Tomorrow everything gets back to normal. We have Uncle Walt's body moved from wherever they're doing the autopsy to the closest crematorium. Then on Tuesday we get his ashes and scatter them before we leave as scheduled on Wednesday. I'll have plenty of time to worry about all the red tape involved in this whole cottage and woodland thing later."

What an optimist.

4

RED TAPE TURNS YELLOW

We all got up on Eastern Daylight Saving Time the next morning. I put down bowls of food and water for Sherlock Holmes and we again left him in charge of the cottage while we walked to Circuit Avenue for breakfast. It being Monday, we expected to find the crowd much smaller at Linda Jean's than it had been on the weekend.

We were wrong. The line again was out the door and Dave again gave the hostess his name, took the electronic buzzer from her and joined us in the little park, which we had learned from a plaque was named David M. Healey Square.

"Why so many people on the Vineyard on a Monday in October?" Al asked.

Martha pointed to a sign at the entrance of a clothing shop that faced us across the square. "That's why," she said.

The sign read: "Columbus Day Special."

"Oh, my god, we're here on a three-day holiday weekend," Dave said. "Talk about timing."

Eventually we were buzzed to the restaurant, where we broke our fast and made our plans for the day. This was Martha Todd's first visit to Martha's Vineyard. At the time of our previous trip we weren't yet married, and she had been filling a scholarship obligation as a law clerk in her native Cape Verde, so she hoped to see more of the island after the business of Walter Jerome's autopsy and cremation was taken care of. We decided to drive up-island, toward the town of Aquinnah and the Gayhead lighthouse, after Dave and Cindy finished meeting with Dick Rylander in the lawyer's Circuit Avenue office.

We left the restaurant at about ten o'clock, an hour before the scheduled meeting with Rylander, so Dave and Cindy decided to walk back to the cottage with the rest of us. "Don't want to be early for the meeting with Dick," Dave said. "Got to give him time to put some clothes on."

"Better hope his office isn't clothing-optional," Al said.

"I just hope he won't be billing me double for working on a holiday."

The women stopped to check out the Columbus Day Special at the dress shop, but we three men continued on, walking past Ocean Park where some kids were playing on the bandstand gazebo and turning a corner toward Dave's newly-acquired cottage. When the cottage came into view, we stopped walking and stared with amazement at what we saw.

The cottage was surrounded by yellow plastic tape with the words OAK BLUFFS POLICE DEPT. printed in black letters.

Two Oak Bluffs police cruisers with blue lights flashing and an unmarked black sedan were parked in front of the yellow tape and two uniformed police officers were standing on the front porch, one on each side of the front door. A man in a dark gray suit with a white shirt and a plain blue tie was emerging through that door with Sherlock Holmes' brown plastic pet carrier in his right hand.

Ever a man of action, Dave went into sprint mode toward the yellow tape. Al and I followed at full speed, and we reached the outside of the tape at the same time as the man with the cat carrier arrived at the inside. The two uniformed cops, seeing us storming the barricade, ran down the porch steps to join the man in the suit.

We all stopped and stood facing each other across the yellow tape, and I recognized the man bearing the cat carrier as Detective Manny Gouveia of the Oak Bluffs PD. We three had encountered Gouveia in our last island visit, and Al and I had also dealt with him in an earlier trip in which we were covering the murder of a vacationing St. Paul businessman. Gouveia had not been appreciative of our investigative skills either time.

Gouveia broke the silence. "Where do you gentlemen think you're goin'?"

"Into my cottage," Dave said. "I'm the owner of this cottage. What do you think you're doing in it?"

"I don't think, I know for a fact, that I'm investigatin' a crime scene," Gouveia said.

"Crime scene? What kind of crime do you think happened here?"

"A homicide."

Dave was turning purple in the face as he yelled, "What homicide?"

"The owner of this house was murdered here," Gouveia said.

"You're crazy. I told you, I'm the owner of this house."

"Maybe you are and maybe you ain't. The fact is that the officially listed owner was murdered in this house and we're investigatin' the crime."

"The listed owner is dead from a heart attack," Dave said. "He was my uncle and he left the house to me in his will. I'm due to sign all the legal mumbo-jumbo this morning to take over the house and my uncle's body, which was held for a stupid autopsy."

Gouveia's dark eyes roamed across the three of us before he spoke again. "It so happens that the results of what you call a stupid autopsy were given to us this mornin' because it showed that the man you claim was your uncle died from arsenic poisonin'. His body was found in this house, which makes it a crime scene, which we are here to process. And haven't I met the three of you somewhere before?"

"Right here in this house you met us," Dave said. "Almost ten years ago we were here to visit Uncle Walt. The place had been ransacked and there was all kinds of crap going on about a sunken treasure ship, and a couple of people got killed while we were here that time."

"And I was almost murder victim number three," I said. The

killer had forced me onto a catamaran, planning to shoot me and dump my body into Nantucket Sound, but I was saved by another man who'd been hiding on the boat.

"Oh, yeah, now I remember," Gouveia said. "You guys work for a newspaper out west somewhere, and you were royal pains the ass while I was workin' on those homicides."

"We might have been royal pains in your ass but we solved the case before you did," Al said. "That's how Mitch almost got to be the third victim."

Gouveia's face turned as red as a glass of burgundy. "Like hell you solved it before me. And you better not get in my way while I'm solvin' this one."

"We just want to get into my cottage," Dave said. "We'll stay out of your way."

"You'll stay out of the cottage till we're done with it," Gouveia said.

"We're staying here. All our stuff is here—clothes, luggage, laptops, tablets, everything."

"Everything including my cat, who travels in the carrier you've got in your hand," I said.

"As a matter of fact, there's a cat in this box right now," Gouveia said. "It's on its way to the animal shelter in Edgartown."

"Like hell it is," I said. I reached under the tape, snatched the carrier out of his hand and was immediately grabbed by the two uniforms who ripped down the yellow tape as they came after me. One of them cranked my left arm up behind me in a very painful position and the other yanked the cat carrier from my right hand. The rough transfer shook the carrier and brought an angry sounding "meow" from inside.

I knew enough not to struggle because I'd seen too many times how police handle resistors. But I could still talk. "That's my cat, detective, and he isn't going to any animal shelter. He certainly wasn't a witness to whoever poisoned Walt, and he sure as hell isn't going to be interrogated or put on the stand at a trial. Just let me have him and there won't be any problem."

Gouveia stared at me the way a school principal looks at a kid who has sprayed-painted four-letter words on the classroom windows.

Dave chimed in. “Come on, detective, the cat’s not evidence. And he was in St. Paul, Minnesota, when Uncle Walt died.”

The cop on my left was still locking my arm up behind me and my shoulder was feeling like it was about to pop out of its socket. Gouveia finally shook his head and said, “Okay, give the man his cat and let him go.” My arm was set free and the carrier was pushed back into my right hand.

“Thank you,” I said. I’m always polite to cops, no matter how angry I am. I set the carrier on the ground so I could rub my aching left shoulder with my right hand and my massage was interrupted by a female scream. We all turned to see Cindy, Carol and Martha running toward us.

“What’s going on?” said Cindy, who won the race to join us.

“This is a crime scene, ma’am,” Gouveia said. “Nobody can go in till we’re done.”

“Is he serious?” Cindy said to Dave.

“He claims Uncle Walt was poisoned and that they have to, quote, *process* the cottage. He won’t let us in.”

“That’s crazy.” She turned to Gouveia. “What do you think you’re going to find?”

“We’re lookin’ for anything that will help us determine who poisoned the victim,” he said. “Fingerprints, glasses with traces of arsenic, stray hairs, dirt off shoes, you name it. Any kind of sign of who was here when the victim died.”

“Well, good luck with that,” Cindy said. “We’ve been here since Friday and we’ve cleaned the house completely and washed all the dishes, including some wine glasses that were standing on the counter by the sink.”

Gouveia’s face went scarlet again. “You washed glasses that might have had arsenic on them? I could charge you with interferin’ with a crime scene.”

“Who knew it was a crime scene?” I said. “You’ve got everything ass backwards. Nobody bothered to check out the scene for a homicide when Walt's body was found. You just assumed it was a heart attack and trucked him off for an autopsy because the law required it."

"I had nothin' to do with the original call," Gouveia said. "So don't point the finger at me. You people have f ... I mean *screwed* up the scene, and now I have to do the best I can to find anything you might have missed while you were cleanin' up the place."

"So you might as well let us in, right?" Dave said.

"Wrong. There ain't nobody comin' into this cottage until me and my team have checked out every inch of the place, includin' every glass in the cupboard."

"If you'd let me in I could show you which glasses were on the counter," Cindy said.

"Not necessary. Our lab will test every glass in the house."

"So how long will it take for you to do all this processing?" Dave asked.

"Couple of days, probably."

"So where do we go? We're here until Wednesday. How do we get our clothes and all that stuff?"

"Not my problem," Gouveia said. "Now if you'll excuse me, I got work to do inside." He turned and walked back to the cottage and went inside. The two uniforms picked up the fallen yellow tape and strung it back in place while we stood and watched with mixed feelings of anger, frustration and despair.

After the cops went back to their posts on the porch, Martha spoke first. "So, Dave, where *will* we go?"

"I'm starting with the lawyer's office," Dave said. "You're all welcome to join me."

We turned and started back toward Circuit Avenue, with me lugging a carrier containing a complaining cat. "Sorry, Sherlock," I said. "Look at it this way—right now you're the only one of us with a roof over your head."

5

HOMELESS

Attorney Richard, call-me-Dick, Rylander was fully clothed in sharply-creased khaki pants, a sky blue shirt and a navy blue blazer when he opened the door of his walkup third-floor office above one of the many T-shirt shops on Circuit Avenue. His eyebrows rose in surprise when he saw all six of us standing in front of his door.

His gaze shifted from our unsmiling faces to the jeweled watch on his wrist. "You're a little early, and I was only expecting Dave and Mrs. Jerome," he said.

"We're all here and we're a little early because none of us can get into my newly-acquired eight-hundred-thousand-dollar cottage," Dave said.

"Why not?" Rylander said with a smile. "You lose your key?"

"We lost possession. The place is swarming with cops who have declared it a crime scene. Homicide, no less."

Rylander's eyebrows rose again. "Homicide? Are they saying that Walter Jerome was murdered?"

"They are. With arsenic. And they're telling us we can't go inside until they're finished processing, whatever the hell that entails. They say it will take them two days to do it."

"Are you serious?" the lawyer asked.

"As serious as we're standing here without a place to sleep," Dave said. "And without such amenities as razors, toothbrushes and clean underwear for the morrow."

An unhappy thought hit me. "I'm without my laptop, and I have to write a story about the murder for the *Daily Dispatch*, of which the victim was a longtime editor. I really, really, really need that computer—even more than my toothbrush."

"Don't be so sure of that," Martha said softly. "Unless your computer will kiss you goodnight." I jabbed my elbow softly into her ribs.

Rylander stepped out and closed his office door behind him. "Okay, let's go talk to the police," he said. "Keeping you out of your house for two days is ridiculous."

We voiced unanimous agreement with that legal opinion. "I hope you can either get us back in or find us three double beds for the night," Dave said. "Your park benches don't look all that comfortable."

Accompanied by Rylander, we traipsed back to the cottage, reiterating our conversation with Detective Manny Gouveia along the way. Rylander replied that Detective Gouveia was not the easiest person to bargain with, which we already knew, but the lawyer was optimistic about our chances of getting back into the cottage before the current day's sunset.

We saw a plainclothes officer we didn't recognize carry a large cardboard box out of the cottage as we approached. Moving quickly for a short, fat man, Rylander hustled ahead to intercept the man. They met behind an additional unmarked car that had joined the police entourage since our last visit.

"I'm Richard Rylander, the attorney representing the owner of this home," Rylander said. "Please tell me what's in that box."

"Evidence," said the man. He popped the car's trunk and put the box inside.

"What kind of evidence?" Rylander asked.

"Glassware that may have been used to poison the owner of this home. We're taking every vessel that might have been contaminated with arsenic to the crime lab for testing."

Rylander pointed to two other boxes in the trunk and asked what those contained.

"More evidence," the man said. "Mainly telephones and computers that might tell us who the victim was communicating with around the time of the murder."

This jolted me. "Not my computer?" I said. "Don't tell me that my laptop is in there."

"Every computer—desktop and laptop—that was in the house is in these boxes."

"My laptop wasn't in the house until last Friday, two days after the body was found. It's absolutely no use to you as evidence and I need that laptop for my job."

"Our technical people will have to determine whether it's of any use to us. We'll return it immediately if they find it has no relevance."

I stepped up to within six inches of the man's face. "Relevance, shmelevance! That laptop was in Minnesota until three days ago. You're wasting the tech's time examining that computer."

"The technical experts will have to determine that, sir. If you're correct, we should have it back to you by next week."

Next week! Rylander grabbed my arm, pulled me back before I could explode and spoke with much more calm than I could have mustered. "Officer, the gentleman's laptop was, as he said, first introduced to this house on Friday, several days after the alleged poisoning of Mister Jerome. It would be a waste of your technician's valuable time, not to mention an unwarranted invasion of the laptop owner's constitutionally guaranteed privacy, to examine this machine. As representative of the home's owner, I formally request that you return the laptop to its owner, who is a guest at this house."

"Can't do that without my boss's consent."

"And your boss is?"

"Detective Gouveia."

"Then I need to speak directly with Detective Gouveia."

Rylander went to the yellow tape and was lifting it to crawl under when the officer caught him by the shoulder. "You can't go in there."

Brushing away the officer's hand, Rylander said, "Then kindly go in yourself and ask Detective Gouveia to come out here."

"I don't think he'll do that."

"Tell him that if he declines I'll be back with a judge's order within an hour." For all his lack of clothing on the beach, Rylander was now looking like a knight in shining armor.

The officer stared at the lawyer for a moment, let out an exasperated sigh, turned and walked to the cottage. We waited by the yellow tape for several minutes before Manny Gouveia appeared in the doorway. He looked us over from the top step before walking out to face us across the tape. "Jeez, Dick, Tommy didn't tell me you had a whole army with you," he said.

"This whole army, as you call it, needs to get into the residence that you are currently occupying," Rylander said. "I do hope you have a warrant for this surprising visit."

Gouveia reached into a pocket inside his coat, withdrew a sheaf of papers and handed them to Rylander. "All typed out in legalese and signed by a judge this mornin'," he said. "We're tryin' to process the scene as fast as we can, but it's takin' us a long time because the scene was disturbed before we got here and we ain't findin' nothin'. We also might be chargin' somebody with tamperin' with the evidence." He looked hard at Dave, then Al and then me."

"Like we said before, nobody knew it was a crime scene," Dave said.

"My client is correct, detective," Rylander said. "Your designation of this home as a crime scene comes after they've been living here for three days without knowledge of a crime being committed on the premises. You have zero case against them for tampering, disturbing or whatever you're thinking about charging them with."

"That's why we need to go over everything very careful more than once. These people ain't comin' in until we're done."

"Then you need to step up your pace. Under the circumstances, it's unreasonable to keep the occupants out of their home for more than a few hours. You said yourself that you aren't finding anything."

"At least let me have my laptop," I said. "It's worthless as evidence; it wasn't in the house until several days after the crime was committed."

"That's up to our technical experts to decide," Gouveia said. "How do I know you didn't set up the murder with an email to somebody on-island before you and your buddies came to claim the house?"

"That's total nonsense and you know it," I said. "I'm not even the one who got the house in Walter's will. Dave would have been the one setting up a long-range murder on email."

That didn't come out the way I meant it to sound, and Gouveia quickly jumped on my screw-up. "I've thought of that and I'm plannin' to question Mister Dave. We might need to see his computer, too."

"Oh, come on, detective," Dave said. "You're only holding the laptop because you have a personal gripe against us from nine years ago."

"That's bullshit," Gouveia said. His face turned scarlet and his tone turned buttery. "Oops. Sorry about the language, ladies."

"The ladies have heard the word before, detective," Martha said. "But in this case the ladies very strongly disagree with you."

The detective looked at Martha and puffed out his chest. "You can disagree all you want, ladies, but I'm in charge of this investigation."

"This place was locked," Martha said. "How did you get in, anyway?"

"We have our ways of gettin' into locked houses, ma'am. Now if you'll excuse me, I need to get back to work. And all I've got to say about you gettin' into this house is that you'll get in when I say so, and not one minute before."

"We'll see about that," Rylander said. "Within the hour I'll be talking to a judge about an order to return the laptop and the house to their rightful owners. Have a good day, detective." He turned to us and said, "Come on, folks. We're off to see a judge."

We all turned and walked away, leaving a red-faced and angry detective standing behind the yellow tape.

"Where will we find a judge?" Dave asked.

"In Edgartown," Rylander said. "We can take my car if not everybody goes."

Nobody volunteered to stay in Oak Bluffs, but after some discussion it was decided that only Dave and Cindy, who owned the house, and me, who was stranded without my confiscated computer, would make the trip to Edgartown. Al, Carol and Martha said they would sun themselves on a bench in Ocean Park until we returned with an order from the judge.

As we were walking toward Rylander's car, which was parked near Circuit Avenue, I was getting antsy about sending a story to the *Daily Dispatch*. I had visions of some local Vineyard reporter checking the police log, discovering that Walt had been murdered and putting a story online where my editor would see it before hearing from me. I hauled out my cellphone, called City Editor Don O'Rourke and explained my lack of laptop dilemma.

"You got enough to dictate a story on the phone?" Don asked.

"I could try," I said.

"I'll transfer you to Corinne Ramey. Give her the facts and let her smooth it out into a story."

Corinne Ramey was a young, aggressive reporter who sat at the desk closest to mine in the newsroom. She answered her phone with a cheery greeting and was amazed when I identified myself. "I thought you were basking on a beach on a tropical island somewhere," she said.

"My basking has been interrupted by the murder of a former editor of the *St. Paul Daily Dispatch*," I said. "The island in question is Martha's Vineyard, which is a long way from tropical, and Don wants me to give you the facts for a story because I am unable to use my laptop at this particular moment."

"Murder? My god, everywhere you go somebody gets killed. How do you do that?"

"Just lucky, I guess. You ready to copy?"

"Shoot."

"No, in this case it's poison." I gave her everything I knew about

Walt, the discovery of arsenic during the autopsy and the search of the cottage. I suggested that she check the library for additional background on Walt and asked her to switch me back to Don. When he picked up, I told him that Al and I would be on Martha's Vineyard until Wednesday and that I would update the story if I learned anything new.

"Will they arrest somebody by Wednesday?" Don asked.

"I have no clue. We're dealing with a detective who remembers that he didn't like us nearly ten years ago when Walt was a missing person and people were getting killed over a sunken treasure ship."

"Well, stay in touch. Be sure to call me before you leave the island, whether you have anything new or not."

I told him I would do that and ended the call. As I put my phone away, it occurred to me that some of us might be stuck on Martha's Vineyard longer than Wednesday.

6

GOOD NEWS AND BAD

District Judge Benjamin Newton was not in the courthouse on this particular Monday because it was a holiday. However, Dick Rylander knew the judge's home address from previous excursions to obtain warrants at non-business hours. "Let's hope his honor isn't out fishing," Rylander said as he parked in front of a very large white colonial with black shutters on a hill above Edgartown harbor. "He has a boat big enough to land a whale."

"Is it called Moby, Dick?" I asked.

"Very good," he said with a laugh. "Actually, it is called the Pequod."

The door of the house was opened by a short, stout woman wearing a crisp black-and-white maid's uniform—black skirt with a white fringe, white blouse with puff sleeves, little white cap. She gave us some bad news; the judge was playing golf.

"Which course?" Rylander asked.

"Don't know, sir," she said.

"Would Mrs. Newton know?"

The maid nodded briskly. "She might, sir."

Rylander sighed. "Could you please ask her?"

Her eyes widened and she smiled. "Oh, I guess I could, sir. Would you like to come in and wait a moment while I run and find her?"

We said we would, and she stepped back to allow us into a foyer the size of a tennis court facing a 12-foot-wide staircase with dark wood banisters polished to a soft glow.

"Must be from Maine," Rylander said when the maid was out of sight. "Down there they only answer the question you've asked, never anything more."

Something seemed cockeyed in that statement. I knew Maine was north of Massachusetts, so I asked, "Don't you mean *up* there in Maine?"

"Oh, no. Maine is down east, same as Edgartown is down island. It's because of the longitude, I think."

"Okay, up is down if you're going east," I said. "But where I live, we say that Maine is *out* east."

"Guess that makes Maine down and out," Al said.

Rylander laughed. "There are parts of Maine that fit that description."

The maid returned with the information that the judge was playing on the Farm Neck course, the one favored by presidents and other political mucky-mucks. We thanked her and went back to the car.

"Where's Farm Neck?" Dave asked.

"Back in Oak Bluffs," Rylander said. "Part of it runs along the road we came out on. That's the part where people try to gawk at whichever president or ex-president is playing golf on-island. The entrance is around on the other side of the downtown area. I guess our best bet is to go to the clubhouse and try to intercept him when he comes off the last hole."

"Could we maybe try to hunt him down on the course?" I asked. The missing laptop was weighing heavy on my mind.

"Too dangerous," Rylander said. "Might get a golf ball stuck in your ear. They don't always yell 'fore' before they hit it like you see on TV."

Our route to the Farm Neck entrance took us past Ocean Park. As we zipped by, I was hoping that Al and his harem didn't see us. We drove past the Steamship Authority terminal, turned left onto Dukes County Road, made a right at the end of that street, turned left at a four-way stop sign by the fire barn and soon saw the entrance to Farm Neck on the left, almost directly across from a sign for the town landfill.

"Hey, neat," Al said. "If you have a bad day on the course, the town dump is right there handy for you to get rid of your clubs."

"Wouldn't be surprised to hear that somebody's done that," Rylander said. He turned onto the Farm Neck entrance road, drove through a grove of trees that hid the clubhouse from the riff-raff passing on the main road and parked as close to the front door as he could get. We traipsed into the clubhouse, with Rylander leading the way. I thought back to the morning when we'd followed him at the beach and decided that the rear view was a lot better with pants on. At the reception desk, he asked about the whereabouts of Judge Newton.

The young man behind the desk flipped through a pile of papers, picked one out and said, "Should be coming in soon. They've been out long enough to have played fifteen or sixteen holes by now."

Rylander thanked him and suggested that we sit on the broad, white-pillared veranda and wait for the judge. We found comfy chairs near the entrance and our patience was rewarded about thirty minutes later when Rylander rose and approached four men coming off the course. "Judge Newton, may I have a quick word with you?" he said. Cindy, Dave and I got up and joined the group, and Rylander introduced us to the honorable Benjamin Newton.

Judge Newton was a thin, angular man with stony dark eyes, a substantial nose and flecks of gray showing at the temples beneath a flat beige golfing cap. He was dressed impeccably for the links in a lemon yellow polo shirt, open at the throat; creased white trousers, and well-polished tan leather shoes.

The judge's golfing companions departed and we stood before him like a chorus line waiting for the downbeat while Rylander explained the situation. He finished by asking for an order admitting us to the house before nightfall and, nodding toward me, an order allowing a member of the working press to reclaim his laptop immediately.

The judge looked at me with all the relish of a vegetarian staring at a bacon burger with cheese. "You're a reporter?" he asked.

"Yes, your honor," I said. "I work for the paper that the murder victim was editor of for something like twenty years. There's a lot of interest in this story in St. Paul and I need my laptop to do a proper job of writing it." I wanted to correct my first sentence to say "of which the murder victim was the editor," but this was not the time for verbal editing.

"Well, we wouldn't want you to do an improper job, would we?" Newton said without changing his facial expression.

I was stuck for an answer. Was he joking, being sarcastic or belittling my work? Apparently he was not a fan of the free press. I decided on a minimal response: a smile and a nod in agreement.

Newton turned his eyes back to Rylander. "Is it your position, Mister Rylander, that the police can do a proper job of investigating a crime scene with these people occupying the house?"

"I am sure, your honor, that these people will do their utmost to stay out of the investigators' way. Mister Mitchell and the other gentleman, Mister Jeffrey, have covered many crime scenes for their newspaper and are aware of the needs of the investigators."

Newton looked back at me. "That true, Mister ... uh ...?"

"Mitchell. Yes, your honor. Both Mister Jeffrey and I have worked at many crime scenes, including several homicides. We would make certain that nobody got in the way."

Newton put down his golf bag, folded his arms across his chest and stared at something above our heads while he pondered our requests. We stood silent, like a rank of wooden soldiers, waiting for his decision. When it finally came, it was a mixed blessing.

The bad news was that he would issue an order requiring the investigators to vacate the premises and allow the residents to return by 8:00 p.m. on Tuesday, October 10. The good news was that he would order my laptop returned by 3:00 p.m. today, Monday, October 9.

Rylander thanked Judge Newton, I thanked Judge Newton and Dave thanked Judge Newton. However, Cindy broke protocol by asking, "So where do we spend the night?"

The judge's mouth smiled but his eyes did not as he said, "There are numerous tourist facilities on this island, and, as it is the off-season, I suspect that many of these facilities will have space available, Mrs. ... uh ..."

"*Ms.* Jerome. And is there any way for us to retrieve some stuff we need, like toothbrushes, hair dryers and other personal items, to use while we're staying at one of those tourist facilities this evening?"

"Mmm," said the judge. "I will attach a writ requesting that the investigators allow one member of each couple to enter the house for fifteen minutes to acquire such items, under the supervision of a police officer."

I wanted to say, "You're all heart, your honor," but I suppressed the urge to be a smart-ass out of fear that he might take back some or all of the crumbs he had tossed to us.

The judge pulled a cellphone out of his back pocket and made a call. When he was finished, he told Rylander that the clerk would email the paperwork to his office from the Edgartown courthouse in about half an hour. "The clerk can sign everything under my authority," he said. "You might want to thank him for interrupting his holiday." I interpreted this as meaning a monetary gratuity. We all, including Cindy, again thanked the judge for interrupting *his* holiday, and started back to Rylander's car.

Halfway to the car, Rylander's cellphone rang. He talked for a minute, shook his head and ended the call. "More bad news," he said. "Because your uncle is now a murder victim, the morgue is holding the body for another day for further examination before sending it to the crematory. You won't be able to get Walter's ashes until Wednesday morning."

"Oh, wonderful," Dave said. "We'll have all of half an hour to scatter them on our way to catching a ferry to the mainland. What else can go wrong today?"

"Well, the police could call you in for questioning. You are deriving considerable benefit from Walt's unnatural passing."

"Are you saying that I could be a suspect?"

"I'm saying that Detective Gouveia will probably want to talk to you. And I'm saying that you can call on me if you need the advice of an attorney."

"I sure hope that won't be necessary," Dave said.

Back on the road, we discussed the question of overnight quarters. Rylander said he could give us a list of several hotels within walking distance of the occupied cottage. I thought about the boxed-up cat I'd left in Oak Bluffs with Martha and said we'd need a place that allowed pets.

"That narrows the list a little," Rylander said. "But I'm sure we can find you something."

"This ups the cost of the trip a bit," Dave said. "Sorry about that, Mitch."

"Because I'm sending stories to the paper about Walt's murder, I'll see if I can put tonight's quarters on my expense account," I said. "Al sent back some pictures so he can give that a shot also."

"Hey, if the paper would buy a drawing of the late editor, Walter Jerome, for the editorial page maybe I could write it off, too," Dave said.

"Or you could sit on a street corner with a paper cup in your hands asking for quarters," Cindy said. "You two sound like homeless old men who can't afford a room."

"Wait'll you see the prices for a room on Martha's Vineyard," Rylander said. "You might want to sit on a corner with a paper cup in your hand."

"Begging your pardon," Cindy said.

Back on Circuit Avenue, we rounded up Al, Carol and Martha and followed Rylander to his office to use his computer to print out the emailed documents from the judge's clerk. Next we began to look for a hotel. I remembered a three-story Victorian-style hotel overlooking the Oak Bluffs harbor that Al and I had seen on our first visit to Martha's Vineyard. It was at the fringe of a circular cluster of gingerbread cottages known as the Martha's Vineyard Campground, a National Historic Landmark that had been formed as a Methodist summer religious retreat in the 1840s.

I remembered that the hotel was named after John Wesley, founder of the Methodist Church, and suggested this hotel to Rylander. He said the Camp Meeting Association had sold the hotel to a corporation that renamed it Summercamp, and he looked it up on the computer.

"They have rooms available," Rylander said.

"Check whether they allow cats," I said.

He scrolled down and clicked on policies. "Oops, no pets allowed."

"Well, they're out," I said. "We need to find a place that takes pets."

Rylander resumed the search, clicking on Oak Bluffs hotels and checking their policies. Down the line he went: Samoset, Pequot, Nashua House, Serenity, Narragansett House, Oak Bluffs Inn, Walker House—all said no pets allowed.

"Oh, here's one," Rylander said. "The Island Inn will let you bring in a pet for an additional twenty-two dollars a night."

"Is that the only one left?" I asked.

"There's one more, the Surfside down by the harbor." He opened its website and clicked the policies button. "Hey, they take pets for free."

"The winner," said Dave. "Do they have any rooms available for tonight?"

More clicks on the computer. "Uh, oh," said Rylander. "No vacancies. The end of a three-day holiday weekend. I guess a lot of people aren't going to go off island until tomorrow morning."

"How about the twenty-two-dollar deal?" I said.

More clicks. "You're in luck; they have two rooms available."

"Some luck," Al said. "We need three."

"Looks like you'll have to split up," Rylander said. "One of the couples without a pet will have to find another hotel."

"I could never take you to a no-pet hotel," Carol said to Al.

"Why not? I'm housebroken," Al said. "Maybe they'll make an exception if I sit up and beg."

"We'll go somewhere else," Dave said. "I'm the one who got

you into this mess so we'll leave you guys together and give you a chance to talk about me."

"Oh, that'll be fun," Al said. "The man with an eight-hundred-thousand-dollar home who has to sleep in a hotel."

Dave and Cindy settled on Summercamp and Dave made a reservation online. Al and I did likewise for the Surfside. We thanked Rylander for his help and said we would see him the next morning to finish any unfinished paperwork. He reminded Dave that his uncle's ashes would be available Wednesday morning at a funeral home in Vineyard Haven and wished us a good remainder of the day. What a joke!

Nobody laughed. Rylander waited for the Edgartown clerk to email the judge's orders, and the six displaced persons started the trek to the Jerome cottage to wait for the orders and present them to Manny Gouveia so we could collect our personal items and changes of clothing—and my laptop. It was agreed that the women would represent all three couples because of their superior instincts for determining which necessities were actually necessary.

We turned the corner and the cottage came into view. We stopped and stared.

The yellow tape and all of the police vehicles were gone.

7

DOUBLING UP

"Well, ain't that a kick in the crotch," Al said.

"Nuts," I said. "We've paid for hotel rooms we don't have to use."

"Can we get refunds?" Cindy asked.

"Not likely," Dave said. "We can try to cancel our reservations but I don't expect any sympathy from hotel management."

"I don't expect any sympathy from Manny Gouveia, either, if he ever finds out that we made reservations before we checked the house," I said.

"He must never know about this," Al said. "We'd be the laughingstock of the Oak Bluffs Police Department."

Once inside, we found a number of things missing, including all the glassware and cups from the kitchen, all the wine and booze bottles from the liquor cabinet and all the cushions from the living room chairs and sofa. Also among the missing were Walt Jerome's desktop computer and my laptop. This meant that a trip to the police station would be necessary for me to present the judge's order and retrieve the laptop.

"See you later," I said, and started off to get the order from Rylander and make my claim. "Call the hotels while I'm gone and see if you can get refunds."

Martha volunteered to walk part of the way with me. "We need sandwich stuff and some wine and some paper cups to drink it from," she said. "And I'll get you some ginger ale."

"Did they leave us any ice for the ginger ale?" I asked.

"Oh, god, I never thought about that. They might have taken the ice cube trays."

"It's cool that they left the refrigerator. Better buy a bag of ice."

She pulled her cellphone out of her purse. "I'll call Cindy and have her check the freezer." With that, we split and went our separate ways.

When I returned to the cottage bearing my laptop, I learned that both refund requests had been denied and that the cops had indeed taken the ice cube trays from our freezer. We gathered on the porch to sip wine and ginger ale and eat chicken salad, with cranberries and walnuts, sandwiches on whole wheat, all of which Martha had purchased.

"It's only one-thirty. That's awfully early for wine," I said.

"It's five o'clock somewhere," Al said.

"More like five-thirty," Dave said.

"That means we're half an hour behind the folks who are drinking wine in somewhere," Carol said.

"Better late than never," Martha said. "Here's to a better day tomorrow, both here and in somewhere." We all raised our drinks in hope that everything would go right for a change. Of course we should have known better.

Tuesday dawned cloudy and considerably cooler, definitely not a beach day. The cops had taken both the coffee pot and the teapot, so we had no choice other than to go out for breakfast. This time there was no waiting line at Linda Jean's. We were greeted by a handwritten sign that instructed us to seat ourselves at a <u>clean</u> table. We pulled two of the free-standing tables together (they were both clean) and seated ourselves in comfort around them.

After a stroll around the harbor to settle our breakfasts, all six of us went to Richard Rylander's law office to keep Dave's and Cindy's morning appointment. "You guys sure stick together," Rylander said when he again found our little sextet grouped outside his office door.

"One for all and all for one," Dave said.

"Like the Three Musketeers?" Rylander said.

"More like the three musty steers," Dave said. "And our three trusty dears," he added quickly, gesturing toward the women.

"That just saved you guys three busted ears," Cindy said.

"Well, come on in," Rylander said. "I have a surprise for you, whatever you're calling yourselves today." He stood aside and we filed in.

The surprise was seated in the two visitors' chairs. They were both women. They were both red-haired, both about thirty years old, and both about thirty-six inches around the bust line. Both had heart-shaped faces with cute snub noses and the kind of lips that any man would yearn to kiss. In other words, both were gorgeous, and except for their clothing, they were identical.

They rose in unison and stepped forward to greet us with identical dazzling white smiles. The one on the left was wearing a dark blue pantsuit with a pale blue blouse and a short string of pearls around her neck. The one on the right was wearing a white blouse with a frilly collar, a burgundy skirt and a silver charm necklace. Both wore gleaming black leather shoes with at least four-inch heels, which brought them up to within an inch of six feet in height.

Rylander introduced them. "Folks, meet Walter Jerome's financial advisers, the co-CEOs of Double Your Money, the island's most glamorous advisory firm."

"Ima Jewell," said the twin on the left, reaching out to shake hands with Dave Jerome.

"Ura Jewell," said the twin on the right, reaching out to shake hands with Cindy Jerome.

"Are you serious?" said Dave.

"That's what our parents named us," said Ima Jewell. "Our daddy got the idea from a Texas billionaire named Hogg, who called his daughters Ima and Ura."

"I've heard of Ima Hogg and Ura Hogg," I said. "I'm glad you're not Hoggs, but it's still a really weird way to name your daughters."

"They stuck us with that and we've stuck with it," said Ura Jewell. "One thing about it, nobody ever forgets our names even if they can't always tell us apart."

"How *do* we tell you apart?" Cindy asked.

"I usually wear the pants in the family," Ima said. "But sometimes I don't."

"I'm usually the frilly one," Ura said. "But sometimes I'm not."

"And we're both still Jewells 'cause we're both still single," they said in sing-song unison.

"We started our financial adviser business right after getting our MBAs six years ago," Ima said. "Walter Jerome was one of our first clients. Called us because we advertised in his paper, the *Martha's Vineyard Chronicle*."

"Now you know all about us," said Ura.

"Not quite," I said. "Who's older?"

"Me," said Ima. "I got called Ima because I was there first."

"Mom's always liked her best," said Ura.

We were all smiling as we milled about, shaking hands and introducing ourselves. Then Rylander guided Dave and Cindy and the Jewell twins to the desk where there were more papers to be signed and notarized. Ima Jewell was a notary public and performed that service.

The notarized papers transferred Walt's financial holdings—stocks, bonds and cash in an IRA—to Dave and Cindy. "I guess we'll be able to pay for this trip okay," Dave said. "If I read this right, there's slightly over half a million dollars in this retirement fund."

"Not bad for a small island newspaper editor," I said.

"Wonder if the guy who replaced him at the big city newspaper made out as well," Al said.

"How about the guy who fired him at the big city newspaper?" I said.

"The old boy did Walt a favor," said Dave. "Did us a favor, too. After all, money is one of my favorite things."

"Please don't try to withdraw any of it immediately," Ima Jewell said. "It usually takes five business days to complete the transfer process from one owner to another. And after that, any withdrawal will also take five business days to move the money from the fund to your personal bank account."

"So what you're saying is I can't buy myself a yacht for ten days?"

"At least. No need to rush unless you really need that yacht in an awful hurry. Remember, the longer you leave the fund alone the more it grows. Also remember that in order to make a withdrawal you have to request it through Double Your Money."

"I have to go through your office to withdraw money from my account?"

"The firm that holds your investments provides you with security by only dealing with licensed financial advisers. It's to guard against someone stealing your identity and draining your account. If you want to withdraw money, you just give us a call or send us an email. Here's our card. Both our phone number and our email address are on there." Ima handed Dave a business card. "Here, have two. You can keep one in your mainland home and one in your island cottage." She handed him a second card.

"So I have no direct way to withdraw from this account?"

"That's right. You need to work through Double Your Money. Don't worry. We'll process your request so fast you won't be delayed a single minute," Ima Jewell said.

"Jewells on the spot, that's us," Ura Jewell said.

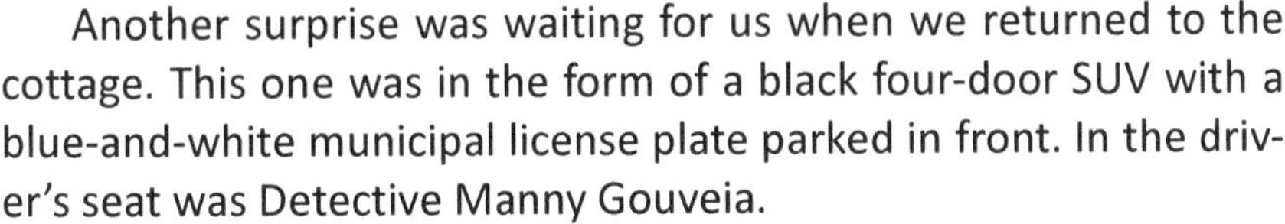

Another surprise was waiting for us when we returned to the cottage. This one was in the form of a black four-door SUV with a blue-and-white municipal license plate parked in front. In the driver's seat was Detective Manny Gouveia.

We approached the car like Sherman's troops marching through Georgia, and Gouveia slid out to meet us. "I was hopin' youse hadn't gone to the beach for the day," he said.

"What can we do for you, detective?" Dave said.

"You—and just you, I don't need the whole mob—can come with me to the station to answer some questions about your whereabouts last week and any recent correspondence you may have had with anybody here on Martha's Vineyard."

"Oh, god, Rylander was right. Do you actually think I had something to do with my uncle's murder?"

"As the heir to his house and all his money, you had a very strong motive, Mister Jerome. Standard police procedure says that we need to talk to anyone who has a motive. We also need to check your phone records and your email traffic to see if you also had a means."

"Good luck with the email traffic. My computer is back in St. Paul."

"No portable device with you here?"

"Only my cellphone. My computer is a desktop model that I use in my work. I draw my cartoons on it and send them to my subscribers with it. There's no way it's coming out here for you to look at."

"Then we'll have to ask your local police in St. Paul to pay you a visit when you get home. When will that be, Mister Jerome?"

"Tomorrow night sometime. Might be midnight. We've got a flight from Boston late tomorrow afternoon."

"You'll be havin' official visitors the next day, and I'd advise you not to delete anything before they come. They'll know how to find what's deleted and how to retrieve it. Now please get into my car and come with me to the station."

"Can't we talk here in the house?" Dave said.

"Standard police procedure says we interview you at the station," Gouveia said. "Now please get in the car." He opened the rear door on the passenger side and waved toward the back seat.

Dave got in, Gouveia closed the door, walked around the front of the vehicle and slid in behind the wheel. They drove away, leaving the rest of "the whole mob" standing silent and subdued.

Finally Cindy broke the silence with a suggestion that we sit on the porch and wait for Dave to be returned to us. "At least I hope returning him is part of standard police procedure," she said.

As we walked toward the front steps, I noticed the man next door was sitting on his porch watching us.

I touched Al's arm. "Let's go talk to Walt's neighbor."

"Neighborly thing to do," Al said.

"Let's hope he sees it that way. I've heard that traditional New Englanders can be very standoffish."

"How old is that tradition? Was Miles Standish standoffish?"

"Could be. He couldn't propose to Priscilla himselfish."

Al and I strolled over to the foot of the neighbor's front steps, with him watching us all the way. We stopped, waved and said, "Good morning."

The man nodded and said, "Mornin'," without pronouncing the "R."

"Could we come up and chat?" I said.

"S'pose you could. Steps ain't very steep."

"Thanks, we'll only be a minute," Al said.

"A minute don't give us much time for a chat."

"How about five minutes," I said as we climbed the steps.

"Whatever it takes," the man said. "I ain't goin' nowhere till lunch."

The man looked a lot like Colonel Sanders, with free-flowing white hair, a white mustache and a white goatee framing a tanned, weathered face. Barely visible transparent wires on his ears suggested the presence of hearing aids. He was wearing a white short-sleeved shirt and khaki shorts, revealing tanned and bony arms and legs, and a pair of flip-flops that were well along in years. As for his own years, I was guessing them to be at least eighty in number.

We introduced ourselves and said we were longtime friends of Walt Jerome's nephew, Dave. He said his name was Raymond Oswald and that folks called him Ozzie.

"I figured one of you gentlemen must be Walt's kin," Ozzie said. "Wasn't sure which one. Weren't you all here a few years back?"

"Almost ten," I said. "I'm surprised you remember us."

"Walt didn't get much company. Mostly that lawyer guy and them two cuties that run the financial service."

"See anybody visiting Walt the week that he died?"

"Can't say as I did. But from what the cop said when he talked to me, somebody must have dropped in some time or other. Might have been in the evenin' after I turned in. I turn in about eight-thirty, nine o'clock now days. Nothin' to stay up for."

"The police talked to you?"

"A-yah. Chubby little detective. Manny somethin', I think his name was."

"That would be Manny Gouveia," I said. "Actually, when was the last time you saw anybody visit Walt?"

"Don't recall the exact day," he said. "I think it was at least a week afore they found him settin' in the parlor dead." I marveled that he could say "parlor" without pronouncing either "R."

"Do you remember who the visitor was?"

"Don't know who the fella was. But I'd seen him afore. Skinny fella wearin' coveralls that looked like the stuff they make blue jeans outta."

"Sounds like that nut cake Teddy," Al said. "Didn't the Edgartown chief say he wore coveralls when he went to the store?"

I nodded in agreement and asked, "We heard that it was the cleaning lady who found Walt's body. Is that correct?"

"A-yah. Nobody answered her knock, but the door was unlocked so she let herself in, thinkin' maybe old Walt was takin' a nap. She walked in and found him settin' right there in the livin' room. Thought he was asleep, but when she couldn't wake him up she called the cops."

"Would this housekeeper be the woman known as Daffy Dolly?" Daffy Dolly had been Walt's cleaning lady and errand runner during our previous visit. She'd been in her early seventies then, so I thought it unlikely that she'd still be cleaning Walt's house.

I was right. "Oh, no, poor old Dolly's in the nuthouse," Ozzie said. "She never was too stable and she went over the edge when she turned eighty-two last year. Family had to put her away she was carryin' on so."

"What do you mean by carrying on?"

"Walkin' off in the middle of the night. Gettin' lost on her way to the store. Cussin' at people on the sidewalk when she thought they was too close. Stuff like that. Now her niece cleans Walt's place. Or did."

"So Dolly's niece was the first one on the scene and she called the police?"

"A-yah. Told me she like to pee her britches when she couldn't wake him up and couldn't find no pulse."

"She knew how to look for a pulse?"

"A-yah. She does housekeepin' at the island hospital so she sees how the nurses do it. They don't do it with dead folks, though."

Here was somebody we needed to talk to. "Do you know this woman's name?"

"First name's Dorie, but I ain't sure of her last name. Might be Brewster, but then again maybe not. You could ask at the hospital. Tell'em you're lookin' for Daffy Dolly's niece and they'll know who you're talkin' about."

Might be Brewster? Where had we heard that name before?

8

FAMILY TREE

Standard police procedure did include returning the suspect, or person of interest, or whatever Dave Jerome was classified as, to his place of residence. The rest of us had been schmoozing and snoozing on the porch for nearly three hours when Gouveia's black SUV pulled up out front and Dave emerged, this time from the front passenger seat.

"I see you got promoted from the suspect seat to riding shotgun," I said as Dave climbed the porch steps.

"That's because I didn't shoot off my mouth at the police station," he said.

"You exercised your right to remain silent all afternoon?"

"Not silent, but patient and cooperative. Manny and another guy questioned me, and they asked me the same questions so many times in so many different ways that I was ready to bang their heads together. But I kept my cool, and finally Manny said I was free to go home and not worry about anybody checking my computer."

"What a good boy," Al said. "So, you're off the hook for having hired the killer?"

"Seems that way," Dave said. "After checking my cellphone log, they wrote down the number in case they have further questions, but I think they decided I was too dumb about things on Martha's Vineyard to be able to hire a killer long-distance."

"Sometimes it pays to be ignorant," I said. "While you were

chatting with the cops we learned some interesting things from the old guy next door."

Cindy handed Dave a paper cup of wine and he took a hearty gulp before he asked, "So what interesting things did you learn?"

"We learned that Walt had a recent visit from a man who looked very much like a guy who thinks he's Teddy Kennedy or Teddy Roosevelt but whose name is really Teddy Brewster," I said.

"And we learned that Walt's body was found by a cleaning lady whose last name might also be Brewster," Al said.

"Did they both come over on the Mayflower?" Dave asked.

"No, but their family might have," I said. "Seems that the cleaning lady's aunt is the woman we knew as Daffy Dolly when last we visited this crazy island."

"I remember her. Is she named Brewster, too?"

"We need to find out. Our source told us that Dolly went so daffy that they put her in, quote, the nuthouse, unquote, and that the niece works at the island hospital."

"So we should visit the island hospital," Dave said. "Try to catch the cleaning lady."

"We should," Al said. "We could do that tomorrow morning when we go to Vineyard Haven to pick up your uncle's ashes. We go right past the hospital on the way to the funeral home."

"Won't give us much time to talk to her. It'll take us some time to scatter Uncle Walt's ashes, and we need to get on the 1:15 ferry in order to catch a bus to Boston in time to make our flight."

"Want to try the hospital now?" I said. "I haven't been slugging down wine so I could drive. The cleaning lady, whose name is Dorie, by the way, should still be working, assuming she's on the day shift."

"Let's do it," Dave said. He stood up, raised his wine cup to his lips and emptied it. "Lead on, designated driver." With that, the three musty steers bid their three trusty dears farewell and went off to the hospital, seeking clear answers to muddy questions from the woman whose job it was to keep things clean.

The Martha's Vineyard Hospital is a sprawling brick structure located about halfway between the Oak Bluffs harbor and the

Vineyard Haven harbor. We went in the front entrance and approached a desk that said INFORMATION. Behind the desk was a middle-aged, dark-haired woman wearing too bright a shade of red lipstick and a name tag that identified her as Virginia. She smiled an automatic smile and asked if she could help us.

"I hope so," Dave said. "We're looking for a housekeeper here named Dorie. We think her last name is Brewster and her mother's name is Daf ... uh ... her mother's name is Dolly."

Virginia's smile faded. "May I ask why you are looking for this person?"

"She worked for my uncle. Cleaned his cottage in Oak Bluffs. Uh, maybe I should start from the beginning."

Virginia nodded. "Yes, maybe you should."

Dave explained that he was Dave Jerome, the nephew of Walter Jerome, whose dead body had been found by Dorie when she came to clean the cottage. "I'm leaving the Vineyard tomorrow and I'd really like to talk to her before I go. Ask her about what she found and what happened when the EMTs and police came. Things like that."

Virginia nodded again. "Do you have identification, Mister Jerome?"

Dave pulled out his billfold, extracted his driver's license and handed it across the desk to Virginia. She glanced up and down three times, comparing the mug shot to his face. "Stick out your tongue and cross your eyes," she said.

Dave complied, and Virginia grinned, nodded and handed back the license.

"You did that on your driver's license?" I said.

"After waiting in line for forty minutes I was bored," he said. "The clerk either didn't notice my pose or didn't give a damn."

"Finding your uncle's body was a very traumatic experience for Dorie," Virginia said. "I'm not sure that she'd be willing to discuss it with you. It's the sort of thing that one doesn't care to keep fresh in one's memory."

"I can see that," Dave said. "So, could you, or someone, find her and ask her if she would be kind enough to talk to me? I'm not going to grill her like a cop; I just would like to get a first-hand report on what the scene was like when she found him."

Virginia's eyebrows rose like the mercury in a thermometer. "The scene?"

"I mean where he was and what was around him. What she saw around the living room and the kitchen."

"Can't you ascertain that from the police report?"

"I asked about that but they wouldn't show it to me. The police in Oak Bluffs are not very friendly to strangers."

Again Virginia nodded. "The police on this island often see strangers under very unpleasant circumstances, Mister Jerome. I wouldn't judge them too harshly if I were you."

"I'm not judging them. I'm just saying they're not releasing any details about my uncle's death, not even to me."

"What is it that concerns you so much? I understand Mister Jerome died of a heart attack."

"We understood that, too, until yesterday, when the police informed us that the autopsy showed a lethal level of arsenic in my uncle's body."

Virginia sat up straight as a yardstick and this time her rising eyebrows almost collided with her hairline. "Excuse me, Mister Jerome, did you say arsenic?"

"I did. That's why I'm so interested in what Dorie might have seen before the EMTs and police responded to her 911 call."

Another nod. "I understand." She steepled her hands on the desk top and thought for a moment before she said, "Please have a seat, gentlemen, while I have someone locate Dorie and ask her if she'll talk to you. She may not, but if she will, I suggest that you talk to her alone, without your companions, Mister Jerome. Dorie is rather on the shy side, and I suspect she would find the three of you quite intimidating."

Dave agreed to do a solo interview and we all sat down to wait. We saw Virginia pick up her desk phone and make a call that lasted a couple of minutes. After she put the phone down, another visitor approached the desk and was greeted with the automatic smile. We continued to wait.

As a reporter, I always carry a pocket-size recorder wherever I go, even when I'm supposedly on vacation on an island far from the *Daily Dispatch*. I'd slipped it into my shirt pocket before leaving the cottage and now I handed it to Dave. "Just casually reach into your pocket and press this button when she starts talking," I said. "It'll hold about 30 minutes of sound."

"Don't you have to inform a person when you're recording them?"

"Not unless you're planning to publish it or use it in court."

"You don't trust me to give you an accurate report of our conversation?"

"The human mind is not a perfect machine when it comes to remembering every nuance of a conversation. I'd like to hear what she says straight from the horse's mouth."

"But you're not going to put any of it in your story?"

"Not directly. It's for background, Dave. Just for background."

We waited some more. After about fifteen minutes, a stiff-backed, sturdy-looking man wearing a dark gray suit and a light gray crewcut came out of the hallway behind Virginia's desk. He looked around the room, saw us and came directly toward us. He stopped a few feet in front of where we sat and asked if one of us was Mister David Jerome.

Dave stood up and announced himself. The man nodded and said that he was Donald Anderson, the head of hospital security. He requested Dave's ID, and again Dave presented his Minnesota driver's license for scrutiny. Anderson studied the license intensely and stared quizzically at Dave. I was expecting Anderson to ask Dave to strike a pose with protruding tongue and crossed eyes, but the security chief just frowned and handed the license back.

"And who are these gentlemen?" he asked.

"Friends," Dave said.

"Moral support," I said. "Not that Dave's morals need supporting."

Anderson did not smile at my little attempt at light-heartedness. "Ms. Brewster has agreed to speak with you, Mister Jerome," he said. "I'll have to ask your friends to wait here."

"No problem," I said.

Anderson gave me a look that said of course there's no problem, you numbskull; then he nodded toward Dave. "Come with me, please, Mister Jerome." He did a smart about-face and started marching toward the hallway behind Virginia. Dave said, "See ya later," and followed at a gallop.

"Good thing he didn't say 'walk this way,'" Al said. "I don't think Dave could have matched that Marine Corps strut."

Al and I waited. We had our choice of magazines—sports, medical, gossip or women's. Al decided on gossip and chose a copy of *People.* I went for sports and picked up a two-month-old *Sports Illustrated*.

I had exhausted the stale news in *Sports Illustrated* and was about to exchange it for a magazine with a cover story that promised to answer all my questions about multiple sclerosis (which wouldn't take very long) when Dave reappeared, still under the escort of Donald Anderson. They stopped beside Virginia's desk, and Dave thanked both Virginia and Anderson for their help before joining Al and me.

"I got the whole Brewster family tree," Dave said as we walked toward the van in the parking lot.

"Complete with all the nuts?" Al asked.

"Enough to fill a bowl. But it took a lot of shaking."

"Are they what they're cracked up to be?"

"I don't think she was playing a shell game."

"Did you start the recorder to get every kernel of truth?" I asked.

"Got every morsel, along with some of the branches that will surprise you. Let's get back to the cottage and you can listen to it while I have another very badly needed glass of wine."

9

SHAKING THE TREE

When the wine had been poured into paper cups for everyone else and a can of refrigerator-chilled ginger ale with no ice had been placed in my hand, Dave set the recorder on a small table on the porch and the six of us circled our chairs around it. Although Dave had promised not to grill Dorie like the cops, the conversation took that tone as he asked question after question and Dorie, in a thin, wavering voice, gave her minimal answers.

"I warn you, getting answers out of her was like pulling teeth, one at a time, from a shark," Dave said. The questioning started with him asking Dorie her name.

"It's Doris," she said. "But people have called me Dorie since I was a little girl."

"And what's your last name?"

"Brewster."

"And you have an aunt named Dolly?"

"Yes, my aunt's name is Dolly."

"How about your mother? What is her name?"

My mother's name was Debbie."

"Was? Does that mean your mother's not living?"

"She passed away when I was a baby. My Aunt Dolly raised me."

"What about your father? Why didn't he raise you?"

"He left the island before I was born."

"Do you know why he left?"

"Aunt Dolly said he was scared of having a baby."

"So he deserted your mother?"

"I guess you could say that."

"So Dolly is your aunt. Do you know a man named Teddy Brewster?"

"Yes."

"Is he related to you?"

"My cousin."

"Your cousin. Are you saying that Dolly is his mother?"

"Yes."

"And Dolly's last name is Brewster?"

"Yes."

"Was she married to a man named Brewster?"

"Yes."

"And he was related to your father?"

"Yes."

"How related?"

"Brothers."

"Brothers. I see. Is your uncle—Dolly's husband—still on the island?"

"No."

"Did he run away, too?"

"No."

"So where is he?"

"He got drownded when his boat sank."

"So he's dead?"

"Yes."

"How old were you when he drowned?"

"Five."

"So Dolly was left to raise both you and Teddy?"

"Yes."

"Do you ever see Teddy now that you're both adults?"

"Sometimes."

"Does he come to visit Dolly?"

"He comes to visit Mister Jerome."

"That's where you see him?"

"Yes."

"Does he visit very often?"

"No."

"When was the last time you saw Teddy at Mister Jerome's house?"

"Fireworks night."

"The Oak Bluffs fireworks?"

"Yes."

"That was the Fourth of July?"

"No. It was August."

"The fireworks were in August?"

"Yes."

"Not in July?"

"Always in August."

"Mister Jerome's next-door neighbor saw a man who looked like Teddy visiting a couple of weeks ago. Didn't you see him then?"

"No."

"I'm told you were the person who discovered that Mister Jerome had passed away. Is that correct?"

"Yes."

"When did you last see Mister Jerome alive?"

"Two weeks before."

"Was that your regular cleaning schedule? Every two weeks?"

"Yes."

"What time did you arrive the day you found him passed away?"

"About five thirty."

"So you went there after your shift here at the hospital?"

"Yes."

"What was your routine? Did you knock and he let you in? Or what?"

"I always knocked. If he didn't open the door I used my key."

"So you used a key that night?"

"The door wasn't locked."

"It was unlocked, but Mister Jerome didn't answer your knock?"

"Yes."

"Was that kind of strange?"

"Yes."

"So what did you think?"

"That he didn't hear me."

"Had that ever happened before?"

"One time when he was asleep."

"So did you think he was asleep this time?"

"I thought maybe he was."

"What did you do when you went in?"

"I called his name and said I was here."

"From the doorway?"

"Yes."

"And he didn't answer?"

"No."

"What did you do then?"

"Went into the living room." (The obvious answer since the front door opened directly into the living room.)

"What did you see in the living room?"

"Mister Jerome in his chair, slumped over sideways like when he was asleep that time."

"So you thought he was asleep?"

"Yes. But he didn't say anything when I said hello again. And then I went closer and I saw his eyes were open."

"His eyes were open?"

"Yes."

"Then what?"

"I was kind of scared. I said hello again real loud and he still didn't answer. Then I did what the nurses do when they check for a pulse."

"You checked for a pulse?"

"Yes. It was scary. And I couldn't feel any pulse on his throat."

"Was his skin cold?"

"Yes." (We heard a shiver in her voice when she said this.)

"So what did you do?"

"I ran to the phone in the kitchen and called 911."

"Did you tell the operator that Mister Jerome had passed away?"

"I told her I thought he had."

"What did you do while you waited for the EMTs and police?"

"I sat out in the kitchen. I didn't want to look at Mister Jerome no more."

"You sat in the kitchen."

"Yes."

"What did you see there? Were there dishes in the sink or anything like that?"

"There were some dirty dishes and some wine glasses beside the sink."

"The wine glasses weren't dirty?"

"Some were, but some looked clean and they were wet. Like they'd just been washed."

"But not dried?"

"No."

"How many wet ones were there?"

"A couple. Maybe there might have been more. I don't remember for sure."

"What happened next?"

"I heard a noise from the laundry room behind the kitchen so I went there to see if the police were at the back door."

"And were the police there?"

"No. Nobody was there."

"Do you think the noise you heard might have been somebody going out the back door?"

"Maybe."

"Did you hear anything more while you were waiting?"

"No."

"No car leaving or going past?"

"No. I wasn't really listening or thinking about anything."

"Who got there first, the police or the ambulance?"

"The police."

"Did they look at Mister Jerome?"

"Yes."

"Did they check for a pulse?"

"One did."

"What did he say to you?"

"He said that the poor dude must have had a heart attack."

"Do you know if he'd ever had a heart attack or any heart problems?"

"He was in the hospital once because of his heart."

"How long ago was that?"

"Last spring. April or May, I think."

"So he had a heart problem of some sort. Did he ever tell you exactly what it was?"

"He said it was a minor heart attack and they put something in some of his arteries so it wouldn't happen again."

"A stent?"

"Maybe. It was something I'd never heard of."

"When the EMTs came that night, did they check for a pulse?"

"One of them did."

"And what did he say?"

"It was a she."

"Sorry. What did she say?"

"That Mister Jerome must have had a heart attack."

"Did the police ask you any questions?"

"Yes."

"What kind of questions?"

"Like you've been asking. When did I come in? What did I see? What did I do?"

"Did you tell them about the sound you heard?"

"I don't remember. I don't think I did."

"Did the police look through the house beyond the living room?"

"No."

"So they just watched the EMTs work on Mister Jerome?"

"They didn't really work on him. They just put him on a gurney and covered him up and took him out."

"Did the police leave as soon as Mister Jerome's body was in the ambulance?"

"Yes."

"What did you do then?"

"I locked the door and went home."

"You didn't do any cleaning or picking up? Didn't touch anything on the coffee table?"

"No. I was so bummed out that I was shaking. I went home and drank a glass of wine."

"Have the police questioned you since that night?"

"No."

"So they haven't told you that Mister Jerome didn't have a heart attack?"

"No. Mister Anderson told me just now when he asked if I would talk to you."

"He told you that Mister Jerome was poisoned?"

"Yes. Poor Mister Jerome."

"Can you think of anyone who would want to harm Mister Jerome?"

"Oh, no. He was the nicest man. Everyone liked him."

"Even your cousin Teddy?"

"Teddy liked him best of all. He let Teddy camp in his woods all summer."

"So you have no idea who might have poisoned Mister Jerome?"

"None in the world."

"Where is your Aunt Dolly now?"

"In a hospital for old people with mental problems."

"On the Vineyard?"

"No. Somewhere on the Cape, I think."

"Cape Cod?"

"Yes."

"Well, thank you, Dorie. Here is my card with my phone number. If you think of anything you saw or heard that might help find the person who poisoned Mister Jerome, please call me."

"Oh, I will. I can't imagine what I'd think of, but if I do I will."

"Is there a number where I can reach you? Other than this hospital I mean."

Dorie recited her home phone number, Dave turned off the machine and we all let loose a collective sigh.

"You weren't kidding about pulling teeth," Al said.

"I feel like I wore out six pairs of pliers," Dave said.

"The wet glasses and the noise in the back," I said. "The killer must have been washing the wine glasses when Dorie opened the front door and yelled, and just had time to run out the back door."

"She was actually in the house with the killer. Lucky for her he decided to run."

"I wonder if Dorie has made that connection."

"Maybe that's why she was shaking so bad that she needed a glass of wine."

10

NEW SCHEDULE

We arose early on Eastern Daylight Time Wednesday morning, knowing that it was going to be a busy day, picking up Uncle Walt's ashes in Vineyard Haven, scattering them in Oak Bluffs and packing up to leave, all while facing a tight deadline—the 1:15 p.m. ferry departure at the Oak Bluffs terminal.

Because we still had no means of making coffee at the cottage, we hustled off to Linda Jean's where we were lucky enough to be seated immediately. We ordered our eggs, French toast, omelets and what have you before the server set the menus on the table. When the food arrived, we gobbled it with a minimum of conversation. At the end, we dispensed with our normal after-breakfast chatter over a third round of coffee and asked immediately for our checks. Thus Dave and Cindy were on their way to the Vineyard Haven funeral home on a quest for ashes by eight o'clock while the rest of us were back in the cottage, stripping beds, washing sheets and pillow cases in the tiny laundry room just inside the back door, and packing our bags and backpacks for the trip home.

My packing task was interrupted by two calls on my cellphone. The first was from Dave, complaining that the funeral home was locked and wouldn't be opened until nine. The second was from City Editor Don O'Rourke at the *Daily Dispatch*.

"Anything new on Walt's murder?" Don asked.

"Not really," I said. "I sent you a piece last night summarizing what we got from the cleaning lady who found him."

"We're running that but we could use more. Is the cleaning lady a suspect?"

"No way she could ever kill a man. She's the meekest, mildest little mouse you'd ever want to meet, and she had no motive. No big bucks in the will for her. On the other hand, her cousin, the guy in the woods on Chappy, would have a motive. He could possibly become the owner of that piece of very valuable property through what he calls squatter's rights in the event of Walt's death. Plus he's nuts enough to plan something like a poisoning if he thought it would benefit either of the delusionary Teddies, Kennedy or Roosevelt."

"Your story said the guy visited Walt sometimes."

"And the next door neighbor saw a guy who fits his description visit Walt a couple of weeks before the killing."

"Have you checked with the cops this morning?"

"No," I said. "We're trying to clean up the house and pack our duds in time to catch the 1:15 ferry after we scatter Walt's ashes."

"You're leaving that early?" Don said.

"We need to catch a bus that gets us to Boston in time for our flight home."

There was such a long silence that I was about to ask Don if he was still there before he said, "Would you consider staying a couple more days to cover the story? We're getting phone calls, texts, emails, tweets, everything under the sun, from old-timers interested in Walt's murder. He was sort of a god around here before the old man fired him and everybody wants to know what happened out there."

"But we've all got no-refund flight reservations."

"Let us deal with the airlines on this end. You and Al stay for at least a couple more days to give us first-hand reports."

"What about our wives?"

"It's up to you whether they stay at your expense."

"They won't be happy."

"Are wives ever happy?"

"Mine is usually ecstatic in my presence."

"Really? What have you got her smoking?"

"That's a hot one. Okay, I'll give everybody the word about the change. Will you pay the rent if Dave Jerome charges us to stay in his cottage?"

"I thought Dave just inherited so much money that he won't even have to charge us for his cartoons anymore."

"There isn't that much money in the world," I said.

"Too bad," Don said. "Now get on the phone to the local cops and get us a fresh story for this afternoon."

"When can we go home?"

"I'll let you know when the time comes," said my city editor.

I shut off the phone and turned around to face Martha, who was behind me when she asked, "Who's not going to be happy?"

"You and Carol," I said. "Don wants Al and me to miss our flight and stay here for a couple of days but won't pay for you and Carol to rebook your flight."

"You're right; we won't be happy. On the other hand, I am due at the office tomorrow morning and I assume Carol is scheduled to resume facing her classes. You and Al are going to have to cover the story without the sage advice of your brilliant wives."

We decided to wait until Dave and Cindy returned before breaking the news to Al and Carol. Might as well give the speech one time for all. Consequently I was still stuffing some wet sheets into the dryer when I heard the front door open and Dave Jerome yell, "You won't believe this shit!"

11

PLENTY OF NOTHIN'

We gathered in the living room to hear Dave's supposedly unbelievable complaint. "Would you believe the damn coroner or medical examiner or whatever they have on this screwed up island didn't get Uncle Walt to the funeral home until five o'clock yesterday? They're not cremating him until this afternoon because somebody is ahead of him this morning, and the ashes won't be ready for pickup until tomorrow, after we've gone home."

"Some *body* is ahead of him?" Al said.

"No problem, Dave," I said. "Al and I will be here to pick up the ashes." This, of course, brought a startled response and demands for an explanation from everyone except Martha Todd.

When the room was quiet and all eyes were focused on me, I told them about my phone conversation with Don O'Rourke. I finished by saying that I assumed Dave would be okay with Al and me staying in his cottage for a couple more days. "We'll wash the sheets again," I said.

"What the hell; I'll stay with you," Dave said. "The world can survive without my cartooning genius for a few more days. You guys can hold my hand while I scatter the ashes."

"What about us?" said Carol and Cindy in unison.

This led to a discussion of time, job priorities and (mostly) the cost of rebooking the women's flights. It was decided that all three wives would depart as scheduled, leaving all three men to fend for ourselves. "Just promise to keep your swim suits on when you go to the beach," Carol said.

"We'll barely have time for the beach," I said. "We'll be busy scattering Uncle Walt's ashes and searching for the naked truth about Uncle Walt's murder."

"Oh, I'm sure you guys will be working your heads to the bone from dawn to dusk," Carol said. "Tell us another."

"Speaking of work, I need to get started on checking with dear Detective Gouveia. Don is expecting some kind of story before lunch time today."

I set up my laptop on the dining room table and grabbed a note-pad and a Martha's Vineyard telephone directory from beside the phone in the kitchen. I found a non-emergency number for the Oak Bluffs Police Department, called it and pressed a string of numbers through the menu until I reached Manny Gouveia's extension. Naturally, I got his voice mail. This is the life of a reporter: leaving messages and hoping for return calls. I had developed a working rapport over the years with the chief of homicide in St. Paul, but my relationship with Gouveia was far from cordial and although I left a message I didn't really expect him to call back.

My expectation proved to be accurate. After fifteen minutes without a return call, I began repeating the procedure every fifteen minutes. After an hour, I finally heard Manny Gouveia's growling voice saying, "Homicide, Gouveia."

"This is *St. Paul Daily Dispatch,* Mitchell," I said. "My city editor has asked me to check with you on the progress of the Walter Jerome murder investigation."

"Why is the St. Paul ... uh, whatever you said, so interested in a homicide on Martha's Vineyard?" Gouveia asked.

"Because the victim was a native Minnesotan who worked for many years as a very popular editor of said newspaper. He still has many friends and fans there, even though his family is all gone, with the exception of his nephew, David Jerome, who you interviewed at some length yesterday."

"And you're askin' me about progress, Mister Mitchell?"

"I am, in fact, asking about progress and hoping there is some to report."

"Well, you can hope until the whales come home but there ain't been any progress worth reportin'. As I'm sure you well know, we got nothin' worth reportin' from our at some length interview with the victim's nephew." Did I detect a note of sarcasm there?

Whatever. I kept pushing. "How about progress that isn't worth reporting?"

"What good would that do you?"

"It would give me something to discuss with my city editor."

"Well, you can tell him we are interviewin' island people who knew the victim but have not learned anything that would help us identify the person who committed this crime."

"Any suspects? Persons of interest?"

"None. Apparently Mister Jerome was a very popular editor on Martha's Vineyard like he was in St. Paul because we have not been able to establish a motive for the crime."

"Nobody with a strong dislike of the victim, or an argument with anybody or threats from anybody?"

"Not that we've discovered at this time. Will that be all, Mister Mitchell?"

"I guess it will be for now."

"You ain't gonna be stickin' your nose into this case as some kind of amateur detective, are you?"

"I'm going be following this investigation as some kind of professional journalist. Are you, as chief of homicide, planning to hold any press conferences about this case?"

"Not until we know something to tell the press about. How long are you gonna be hangin' around the island?"

"Until my city editor tells me to leave," I said. "Could be days, could be weeks. The sooner you make an arrest the sooner I can leave." I was really, really hoping it wouldn't be weeks.

"Well, that's an extra incentive for me to make a quick collar, ain't it?" said Gouveia. "Have a nice day, Mister Mitchell." The receiver did not go down gently.

"So, what did you get from Manny?" said Al from behind me.

I held up the blank notepad and said, "A ration of crap and this."

"Don will not be happy."

"True. And when Don's not happy, nobody's happy."

"I'm happy that I'm not the one who has to call him and tell him we haven't got squat."

"Then I'm happy that you're happy."

"And I'm happy that you're happy that I'm happy."

"And I'm ... oh, forget it. I'd better call Don and take my earful of abuse." This was an exaggeration. Don never abuses anyone, but he has a provocative way of encouraging one to do a better job.

When I called Don, he was, in fact, provoked. "I've just got one question for you: What the hell is the matter with that homicide detective that he can't come up with anything at all on the murder of a prominent citizen? And why in hell can't you squeeze some kind of quote out of him that's worth putting in the paper?"

"That's two questions," I said. "Answer number one is that it's a small police department and he doesn't have much investigative help. Answer number two is that he is a close-mouthed kind of guy who hates the news media in general and me in particular."

"Looks like you and your twin are going have to go out and do some more digging on your own." Because we work together so often—and, I might add, so well—Don refers to Al and me as the paper's Siamese twins, saying that we are joined at the funny bone, which, in our case, is the skull. I keep telling him that the modern, politically correct term is conjoined twins, but he insists he won't change until he gets an official complaint from the king of Siam.

"We're planning to do some digging," I said. "I think we should start by visiting the guy in the woods again—the screwball with an actual motive."

"Do it right away."

"As soon as we put our wives on the ferry."

"Don't take too long kissing them goodbye."

When I put down the phone, Martha was standing beside me. "The sun is shining, the temperature is seventy degrees and the beach is calling our names," she said. "My Smartphone says it's raining in the Twin Cities so this will be the last chance to get some rays for us girls. Care to join us?"

I did care, and I did join the "girls," as did Al and Dave. After an hour in the sun on the sand, we went back to the cottage, where we changed into street clothes. The "girls" had their last bowl of Linda Jean's delectable clam chowder with us before joining the line of ticket-holders waiting for the ferry. After a round of kissing and hugging, Dave, Al and I watched our wives walk down the gangway and wave goodbye as they reached the ferry entrance. We were all hoping our island bachelorhood would be brief.

At 1:18 p.m., the ferry pulled away with a blast of its horn, and the three bachelors turned away and walked across the street to Ocean Park, where we settled on a bench to plan the rest of the day. Our first move was to renew the van.

"You want to take it for a week?" the agent, whose name tag identified him as Marty, asked. "Like I told you when you first come in, it's cheaper if you do it that way. Only $750, plus the tax, for seven days."

"We're only staying for two more days," Dave said. "That's $258, plus the tax, right?"

"You're the boss."

Our second move was to hit the road to Edgartown and the On-Time Ferry. Don had given me an order and Al and I had no choice but to obey it. As for Dave, he was eager to have another conversation with Teddy Kennedy Roosevelt Brewster. "That old bastard had better be packing up and getting ready to leave," Dave said as we turned off the Chappy blacktop onto the deep-rutted woodland road. "His days as a squatter on my *proppity* are over."

12

COLD FEET

We bounced along through the humps and ruts and emerged into the campsite clearing. The olive drab tent was still there and the decrepit Landrover was still parked beside it. Dave stopped the van on a firm patch of ground and we all got out.

The sound of doors slamming did not bring our man out of the tent. Dave called his name. "Come out right now, Teddy; we want to talk to you." Still no movement from the tent.

"Maybe sleeping off a drunk," Dave said. He yelled Teddy's name two more times, then stepped up to the tent, grabbed a corner of the canvas and shook it.

Still no response.

"Maybe out fishing?" I said.

"It's a long walk to the water," Dave said. "You'd think he'd take the Landrover for that." He shook the tent and yelled again. Nothing.

"I'm going to drag him out if he's in there," Dave said. He knelt in front of the opening, pulled the flap aside and looked in. "The old coot's sleeping all right," he said. "All he's wearing is that damn bikini and his bare feet are sticking out this way. This'll wake him up."

Dave stuck his head and shoulders into the tent. He grabbed both of the prone man's feet and gave them a yank. The movement brought no response from the owner of the feet.

Dave stopped pulling, dropped the feet like the proverbial hot potato and backed out. “Jesus,” he said. “His feet are ice cold, and he didn’t wake up when I pulled on them. I think maybe he’s … more than just sleeping.”

“You mean he’s …” Al said.

“Not alive,” Dave said.

“Oh, shit!” Al said.

“Exactly,” Dave said.

“Aren’t dead bodies supposed to smell?” Al said.

“That body smelled when it was alive,” Dave said.

“Should we check for a pulse?” I asked.

“Not me,” Dave said. “I’m not crawling in there with a guy who looks like he’s dead.”

“I’m calling 911,” Al said. “Let them look for a pulse.”

Al made the call and we sat like a row of vultures on a log, facing a circle of stones that enclosed ashes from an open fire, waiting for the first responder to arrive. It was a long wait, with little conversation and frequent time checks on a wristwatch (mine) and two cellphones (Al’s and Dave’s).

Police Chief Morris Agnew was the first to arrive, driven by a sergeant in an Edgartown cruiser. The sergeant parked beside our van and they both got out. “Sorry it took us so long to get here,” the chief said. “We had to wait for the On-Time to load up on this side and unload on our side before we could get on. Pissed off some people waiting in line when we took off and left them sitting there.”

We waved them toward the tent and they walked over, knelt down, pulled open the flap and peered in.

“Jeez, he’s damn near naked,” the sergeant said.

“Gross. Never seen him without his coveralls,” the chief said.

They closed the flap and stood up.

“Looks like old Teddy is a goner,” Agnew said. “Can’t have been dead very long or you wouldn’t have been able to stick your nose in there to look for him. You guys touch anything?”

“I pulled on his feet,” Dave said. “I thought he was sleeping.”

“So you moved the body?”

"Not very far. His feet were like ice and he didn't wake up when I pulled on them so I let go in a hurry."

"Nobody went into the tent?"

"You kidding? You couldn't pay any of us to do that."

All eyes were diverted toward the road at the sound of a vehicle banging and clanking over the pits and humps. An Edgartown Fire Department ambulance emerged from the trees and stopped on the other side of our van. Two EMTs in crisp white uniforms got out and walked toward us.

"Your customer is in the tent, but there's no need to check him for a pulse," the chief said. "He's been dead long enough to turn stone cold."

"So we wait for the photographer and the M.E. before we load him up?" said the older of the EMTs, whose name tag read MIKE.

"I'm just about to call them," Agnew said. "You guys might as well find a log or a rock and sit down until they get here. Sergeant Bennett and I will take a quick look inside the tent."

Dave, Al and I resumed our vulture-like position on the log, where Al showed me a photo of the two cops on their knees with their butts in the air peering into the tent. "Don's going to love this one," he said. "It can go with your breath-stopping, on-the-scene piece about finding a dead body in the late Walter Jerome's woods."

A half hour went by before two men dressed in civilian clothing—short-sleeve shirts and khaki trousers—came into the clearing on foot. One was carrying a brown leather camera bag and the other was lugging a black leather medical bag.

"We're stuck in the goddamn road," said the man with the medical bag. "You have to give us a push or none of you will get out of here. You should have told us to bring the four-wheeler to drive in that goddamn sand."

"I told your girl that we were in the woods on Chappy," Agnew said. "That should have been a clue. Anyway, your client is in the tent. Doc, you won't need your stethoscope, and good luck getting pictures, Jimmy. It's pretty tight quarters in there."

"Anybody touch the body?" asked Doc.

"One of those gentlemen tried to wake him up by grabbing his feet and pulling him forward a little bit."

"Gave his toes a tow," Al whispered.

"Not funny," Dave said. "I'll be having nightmares for a week about wrapping my hands around those cold bare feet."

"Playing footsie in the woodsie."

"Shut up. You're being a heel."

"You gentlemen got something to say?" Chief Agnew said.

"Nothing for the record," Al said. "Just discussing some footnotes."

"Wondering when we can step away," Dave said.

"Well, obviously nobody is leaving until we push the Doc's car loose. And after that we'll be wanting to take statements from all three of you at the station."

"Does that have to be today?"

"My mother always told me, never put off until tomorrow what you can do today," the chief said. "Yes, it has to be today, while your memories are fresh."

"There's not all that much to remember, except the feeling of those cold feet," Dave said. "That'll stay fresh for a long time."

"Be sure you include that in your statement," Agnew said. "Now it looks like Doc and Jimmy are done with the body, so let's all go push them out of their hole."

Actually their car, a black Ford sedan, wasn't in a hole. It was hung up between two holes on a large mound of sand. The man called Doc put the car in reverse and we all pushed like football linemen on a blocking sled until the vehicle slid off the mound and all the tires touched terra firma.

"Hey, Doc, have fun backing out," Agnew said as Jimmy the photographer got into the passenger seat. They'd have to make the outward trip in reverse gear because there was no place to turn around between this spot and the blacktop road.

Out the driver side window, Doc said, "Can't be any worse than forwarding in." Slowly the car backed away and disappeared in the trees around a curve.

"Hope he makes it all the way out," Agnew said. "Now let's go get old Teddy loaded into his chariot so Sergeant Bennett and I can go over the inside of the tent a bit. Then you gentlemen can join me in the station for tea and statements while the forensic crew that I've called for sweeps the scene and gathers up anything that might tell us what sent old Teddy on his way to the happy fishing grounds."

"What's the medical examiner's name, other than Doc?" I asked.

"Edward. Doctor Edward Newman. But everybody calls him Doc."

"Did Doc say anything about the cause of death?" I asked.

"No word on that, other than it didn't look like a homicide."

"Neither did Walt Jerome's death at first."

"Sure hope what killed Walt isn't catching."

We waited for another twenty-some minutes before a four-wheel-drive Jeep carrying the forensic crew banged and rattled its way into the clearing. A man and a woman wearing loose, light blue jumpsuits got out and joined us by the fire pit. After a brief consultation with the chief, they put masks over their faces, baggies on their shoes and latex gloves on their hands and crawled single file into the tent. The woman's baggy-covered feet didn't make it all the way in. Another good photo-op for Al.

"Pretty tight quarters," said Sergeant Bennett.

"Hope those two get along with each other," Chief Agnew said. "Anyhow, I guess we don't have to chaperone them. We're going back to the station; you gentlemen will kindly follow us there."

"When you put it that way, who could refuse?" I said.

"Your hospitality is overwhelming," Al said.

"Look at the bright side," said the chief. "You'll have a police escort to let you jump the line for the On-Time Ferry."

We did get priority, plus some dirty looks from the occupants of six vehicles waiting to board the ferry, when we bypassed the line and were waved onboard behind the chief's cruiser, which had all lights flashing. I couldn't tell whether the people in those vehicles thought we were privileged dignitaries or arrested scalawags. It really didn't matter.

On the other side of the harbor, we continued to follow the chief's flashers through the streets of Edgartown to the police station, where we were confronted by our second surprise of the afternoon. This surprise was much more pleasant than the one we'd found in the tent. It was in the form of a tall, auburn-haired woman who was waiting at the front door with a reporter's notebook in her left hand. Her gray slacks and plain white blouse clung to a figure that was slender but outwardly curvaceous in all the right places. I estimated her age at something a bit under thirty.

She greeted the chief with a smile worthy of a toothpaste commercial and said, "We heard on the police radio that you've got a body out on Chappy."

"We did have a body out on Chappy," Agnew said. "It's now resting in peace on the medical examiner's table."

"Do we know who this body belonged to?"

"We do, but we're not identifying it until we've notified the next of kin. All I can say at this time is that it's the remains of an adult male. You know the rules, Alison."

"Okay. Do we know the cause of the unidentified adult male's death?"

"Not until the M.E. has done an autopsy. It looks like natural causes, but again you know the rules. We have to do the autopsy on an unattended death."

"So many rules," she said with a sigh. "And who might these three gentlemen be?"

"These three gentlemen found the body, but they aren't going to tell you anything about its identity." He looked hard at us. "Are you?"

"Not a word," I said. "We know the rules."

Alison stepped past the chief and offered me her right hand.

"Alison Riggs. Staff writer. *Martha's Vineyard Chronicle*." Bright blue eyes looked through thin-rimmed glasses into mine.

I took the hand and shook it. The hand was smooth, but not soft, and the grip was strong. "Warren Mitchell. Better known as Mitch. Staff writer. *St. Paul Daily Dispatch*."

She withdrew her hand and presented it to Al, who shook it and said, "Alan Jeffrey. Staff photographer. Better known as the Incomparable Al. Same paper as him."

Next it was Dave's turn to shake her hand. "David Jerome. Newspaper cartoonist. Better known as freelance Dave. Nobody's staff anymore."

"Wow," said Riggs. "A trio of journalistic body finders. What brings you to Martha's Vineyard?"

Dave looked at Chief Agnew, whose mouth was turned down in a scowl. "Actually, it was another body," Dave said. "We came here because of my uncle's death. You might have known him, depending on how long you've been with the *Chronicle*. He was the editor until three years ago."

"You don't mean Walter Jerome?"

"I do mean Walter Jerome."

"Oh, god, he was a great guy. He gave me my first reporting job. I heard he passed away from a heart attack. That's what the obit that's running in tomorrow's paper says."

The chief stepped in quickly, like a referee stopping a boxing match because one fighter was too woozy to continue. "Okay, that's enough chatter, Alison. I need to get statements from these three men. You can call me later, in an hour or so, if you want a comment from me."

"I do and I will," she said. "And I'd like to talk to these gentlemen when you're finished with them."

"I strongly advise them not to talk to you," Agnew said. "Come on, gentlemen, let's go in and get this over with." We followed him into the station, leaving Alison Riggs alone.

The interviews and the writing of statements did take a full hour because each of us was interviewed individually by the chief and an athletic-looking, fortyish detective named Aaron McGee. When it was my turn, I said to the chief, "You're treating this like a homicide."

"Can't be too careful, even with no signs of foul play," he replied. "Especially after the way Oak Bluffs fucked up on your buddy's uncle."

"What did they do wrong?"

"That house should have been sealed until the cause of death had been determined by the autopsy. I hear you guys came in and cleaned up everything that might have helped them get a lead on whoever poisoned the victim."

"You can blame that on our wives."

When the grilling was over, the three of us walked out into the late afternoon sunshine to get into our van. We found Alison Riggs, staff writer, leaning against a front fender.

13

MINDING YOUR Q'S AND A'S

Alison stood up straight and stepped forward to greet us. "Are you going to follow the chief's strong advice?" she asked.

"Of course not," I said. "We're in the same business you are. We'll tell you everything we can, short of naming the dead man."

"Thanks for that. I guess my first question is: where was the dead man found?"

"In a patch of woods owned by my uncle," Dave said.

"He was living in a tent out there," I said.

"We found him in the tent," Al said.

"We thought he was sleeping and I tried to wake him by yanking on his bare feet," Dave said. "I'll be having nightmares about that."

Alison was scribbling in her notebook as fast as she could. "Did you say he lived out there in the tent?"

"He stayed there every summer for years," Dave said.

"Oh, my god," Alison said. "Did he have a rusty old wreck of a Landrover?"

"He did," Dave said. Alison's eyes lit up and her lovely lips curved upward slightly in a satisfied smile.

"We just told who it is, didn't we?" I said.

"You did, in fact, narrow it down to one person," she said. "But my story won't be published until Friday, and by then I should have the official word from the chief. I mean, they don't have to go very far to notify his next of kin. The lucid one, anyway."

"When you put out only one issue a week, you're lucky you don't have any competition on the island," I said.

"Oh, but we do. There's another, newer weekly, a tabloid. And they started publishing on Thursday, just to get the jump on us I think."

"Maybe we'd better get out of here then before somebody from your competition shows up and finds us talking to you."

"You're probably right. But first tell me why on earth you guys went out there to see ... uh ... that man?"

"To get him out of there," Dave said. "I'm Uncle Walt's only survivor and that property was willed to me. I intend to sell it and I didn't want ... uh ... anybody ... squatting on it."

"Well, I guess nature took care of that problem for you," Alison said.

"At least we hope it's nature," I said.

She cocked her head and looked at me. "That's a funny thing to say. What else could it be?"

"I'm just being cynical. I'm sure it is nature in this case. But here's a tip about something the other weekly might not have yet, Alison. Call Detective Manny Gouveia at the Oak Bluffs PD and ask him about the cause of death for the late Walter Jerome."

"Are you saying it wasn't a heart attack?"

"I'm saying call Manny Gouveia and ask him that question."

"Are you playing games with me?"

"Not at all. I know something you don't, but I'm not an official news source. Manny Gouveia is."

Alison said she would definitely call him. She asked us a few more questions about the body in the tent and checked to be sure she had our names spelled correctly. She had us all properly identified, which impressed me because I have a problem remembering who is who if I'm introduced to more than one person of the same gender at a time. We described the campsite for her, and Dave gave her directions and permission to go there with a camera. We did not give her a description of what apparel the body in the tent was wearing.

Our session with Alison Riggs reminded me that I had a news story to write for the *Daily Dispatch*. I thought that a dead body found on property newly acquired by a popular Minnesota cartoonist who was on the staff of the paper for many years would certainly be of interest to our readers in St. Paul. Night City Editor Fred Donlin, who had taken over the desk at 3:00 St. Paul time, agreed when I phoned him and told him what Al and I had for a story and pix.

"I can't believe all the weird stuff you guys are running into out there," Fred said. "How do you and Al always manage to dig up a body wherever you go?"

I laughed and said, "I'm not sure. They say that some people have a nose for the news; maybe we have a head for the dead."

When the call ended, Al asked, "What'd Fred say that made you laugh?"

"He wondered how we always dig up a body wherever we go."

"You should have said skullduggery."

A couple of hours later, after we had emailed my story and three of Al's photos to Fred, he replied with an email that said the shot of the two uniformed cops on their knees with their butts in the air was running on page one, in color, with a headline that said "Vineyard Blues."

Still later, after we'd dined at the hamburger and ale emporium, I got a call from Martha Todd, saying that the flight home had gone smoothly—arriving almost on time, even—and that everybody was safely back in St. Paul (she and Sherlock Holmes and Carol) and suburbia (Cindy). "This part of the world could not be quieter or duller," she said.

"This part of the world is somewhat less mundane," I said. Then I told her all about our afternoon visit to Teddy's campsite and the Edgartown police station, including our interview with Alison Riggs, staff writer, *Martha's Vineyard Chronicle*.

"So what are the cops saying? Did the old weirdo have a heart attack?" Martha asked.

"That's what it looks like. But they're not saying anything until the autopsy is complete, having learned caution from Oak Bluffs's blunder with Walt Jerome."

"Speaking of Walt Jerome, anything new there?"

"No, Walt is still dead."

"I'm rolling with laughter. You know what I mean; have the cops made any progress?"

"As you will learn from reading the *Daily Dispatch*, they have nothing to report. Frankly, I don't see how they'll ever come up with anything."

"You don't think Manny Gouveia is a master detective?"

"I don't think even a master detective, which Manny Gouveia certainly is not, could crack that case. If there was any evidence left in the cottage, we managed to wipe it away. And nobody can think of anyone who had any reason to kill Walt except for Dave, who inherits everything but obviously did not hire a hit man while sitting at his drawing board back in Minnesota."

"So when are you coming home?"

"Depends on Don O'Rourke. I suspect it will be soon if nothing happens for another day or two. I don't think there's any money in the budget to pay for a long watch by two staffers on Martha's Vineyard."

"I hope you're right. Sherlock Holmes misses you."

"I miss him, too. Also I miss you."

"Yeah, I've got that problem, too." We said goodbye, made kissy sounds into our phones and ended the call.

I was sure Martha and I wouldn't be apart for more than two more days. Tomorrow we would pick up Walt Jerome's ashes and scatter them. After that, neither an unsolved murder nor the natural death of a man who happened to know the murder victim could keep us on Martha's Vineyard any longer. Could it?

14

ASHES TO ASHES

Naturally it rained on Thursday. I can't imagine anything messier than scattering an old man's ashes with a cold autumn rain drizzling down and a gusty wind changing direction every couple of minutes.

Dick Rylander had told us that Walt Jerome's instructions were to scatter his remains in two places, his backyard garden and the Oak Bluffs harbor, as close to the Island Queen ferry landing as possible. The Island Queen is a passenger ferry that shuttles people between Oak Bluffs and Falmouth on the south shore of Cape Cod. It is much smaller than the vehicle-carrying Steamship Authority ferry, which we had taken because that was where the bus from Boston's Logan Airport dropped us.

Walt had preferred to ride the Island Queen to the mainland because it landed just a short walk from stores and restaurants that he patronized in downtown Falmouth. The Steamship Authority boats go into Woods Hole, which has the world famous Oceanographic Institution but nothing much that beckoned to Walt. He only rode that boat on the rare occasions when he wanted to take a car across Nantucket Sound. There are also fast passenger ferries that run from Oak Bluffs to Hyannis, on Cape Cod, and Providence, Rhode Island, but Walt had no use for either of those.

We had breakfast in the usual place, and lingered over third cups of coffee in hopes that the rain would quit. The rain did not quit. Finally, we slogged back to the cottage, got into the van and drove slowly to the funeral home in Vineyard Haven that held Walt's ashes, hoping that the rain would quit. Again, the rain did not quit, so we drove back to Oak Bluffs at the slowest possible speed, hoping that the rain would quit.

The rain did not quit. In fact, it was raining harder by the time we got back to the cottage and walked to the garden with Dave carrying one of the two square blue boxes the funeral director had given us. We stood in the center of a patch of drooping, dying plants as Dave said a few words about what a great guy his Uncle Walt was and how he hoped the man was resting in peace before he opened the box. "Ashes to ashes," Dave said as he began to wave the box around in wide circles in front of his chest. A white powder spewed out and rode away from us on the wind, which we had been careful to put at our backs.

With the box about half empty, the wind shifted about ninety degrees and we dodged quickly to starboard to escape a white cloud that was suddenly blowing back toward us. As we dodged, Al tripped on the fallen stalk of a dead sunflower and landed on his hands and knees in a patch of mud. What he said as he hit the ground was not the sort of blessing one normally hears at a funeral.

When the garden scattering was finished, we went inside and Al washed his hands and rubbed the mud off the knees of his jeans with paper towels. He held up two scratched palms and said, "Glad I wasn't wearing shorts or my beautiful legs would be marred like this."

"Looks like you won the ash dodging contest hands down," I said.

We debated whether to make sandwiches and eat them, hoping for the rain to stop, or to take the other box of ashes to the harbor while our clothes were still soggy. The Island Queen is a seasonal boat and makes its final run on Columbus Day, so we didn't have to work around the ferry schedule at the landing.

We went out onto the porch and scanned the sky. The clouds were still heavy overhead with no sign of a break, and the rain was still falling. We decided to get the job done, come hell or high water. The one concession we made to the weather was taking the van to the harbor instead of walking through the relentless rain.

Dave had been worried about someone like the harbor master objecting to the scattering of ashes in the harbor water. We had considered waiting until dark, but because of the rain and the wind there wasn't a living soul on the walkway that ran the length of the Island Queen landing area. We three fools with a box full of ashes were the only people brave enough—I refuse to say dumb enough—to battle the elements at that particular moment.

We lined up at the edge of the pier, beside a sign showing the Island Queen summer schedule, and Dave opened the box. The wind was coming from behind us on our right quarter when he shook the box and a huge cloud of white powdery ashes floated into the air. When the first shower hit the water, Dave shook loose another white cloud. And the wind changed direction.

When the wind went round to our front side, it blew that cloud of white back into our faces and chests and arms and legs. Remember, we were soaking wet. We were not simply covered with dust that we could brush off. The dust stuck to our wet bodies and melted onto our clothing, faces and bare arms, forming a pasty white dough that resisted our frantic efforts to remove it.

Al and I retreated and ducked behind the sign, brushing and scraping at our arms and faces. Dave shouted, "Oh, the hell with it," and dumped the rest of the box's contents straight down into the water. Then he joined us behind the sign and did his best to remove some of the gooey jetsam that clung all over his body.

"Let's get back to the cottage, peel off our clothes and take turns getting into the shower," I said.

"There's two showers," Dave said. "I've got dibs on the one by Uncle Walt's bedroom."

We actually ran to the van. On the way back to the cottage, Dave said, "Do you guys notice anything different?"

Neither of us did.

"Okay, what is it?" I said.

"I don't need the windshield wipers."

"You mean *now* it's quit raining?" Al yelled.

"Timing is everything," Dave said.

We spoke not another word until the van was parked and we were walking up the steps onto the front porch. Seated in a rocking chair on that porch was Alison Riggs, staff writer.

"My god," she said, jumping out of the chair. "Did you guys get hit with a big bowl of oatmeal?"

"Actually it was bone meal," I said.

"What's that?" she asked."

Her eyes opened wider with each chapter as we told her the story of scattering Walt Jerome's ashes in the garden and having them blow back all over us at the harbor.

"Why didn't you wait until the rain stopped?" she asked when we'd finished the soggy tale.

"Looked like it was going to rain all day," Dave said.

"What about waiting until tomorrow?"

"We're hoping to get the word from our editor that we have plane tickets for home tomorrow," Al said. "Anyway, what brings you here at this most inopportune time?"

"I'm sorry to interrupt your ... um ... ritual. I just came by to thank Mitch for sending me to Detective Gouveia. I tried the phone in the cottage but you must have been outside doing your ... uh ... ritual. And I didn't have your cellphone number so I just decided to drop by."

"You're welcome for the tip," I said. "And I'm sorry we're not in a more presentable condition for welcoming visitors."

"I must say I've never seen anything quite like your condition." She hauled her cellphone out of the small leather handbag hanging from her shoulder and aimed the camera eye toward us. "How'd you like to see your picture in Friday's *Chronicle*?"

"No way," I said.

"Don't you dare," Dave said.

"Put that thing away," Al yelled.

"You sure?" Alison said, slowly lowering the phone.

"I'll stomp your phone into little bitty pieces if you take our picture in this condition," Dave said. "I'm not even sure scattering ashes in the harbor is legal, much less looking like an idiot with them plastered all over me."

"Okay, okay. You don't need to get violent." She put the phone back into her handbag. "But you're depriving my readers of seeing a unique slice of Vineyard life."

"Anyway you cut it, your readers aren't going to see this slice," I said.

"You, as a reporter, should be ashamed. Stifling the news."

"This news is not fit to print. Which reminds me, I have to write a sanitized version of our, as you call it, ritual, for the paper in St. Paul."

"You're going to omit the most interesting part?"

"It's called self-editing," I said. "And we're not sending a selfie of us covered with the remains of Walter Jerome."

"I guess I can't blame you for that," Alison said. "Now I've got to get back and write an unedited version of the poisoning of Walter Jerome. There was nothing in today's *Vineyard Voice* and we will have it on page one tomorrow, thanks to you, Mitch. The only other thing I need is a comment from Dave. Would you care to say how you feel about your uncle's murder?"

"I don't really have any comment," he said. "I just hope the Oak Bluffs police are successful in their investigation and that the dirty bastard who did it is quickly brought to justice. Okay?"

"Very good; we certainly know how you feel. Are there any other family members surviving?"

"I'm the sole survivor. Walt's wife and his brother—my dad—both died years ago, and he never had any children."

"Okay. Thank you, Mister Sole Survivor. Does that mean you inherited this lovely cottage?"

"It does. Along with the patch of woods out on Chappy where the other dead guy was found."

"Wow. Didn't getting all that make you a suspect?"

"No comment."

"Oh, oh. I'll bet Detective Gouveia questioned you."

"You can ask Detective Gouveia about that."

"He said he had no suspects or persons of interest, which I assume eliminates you. Anyway, I'm off to write a story. Ta-ta, guys." She walked briskly off the porch and got into a well-worn gray Chevrolet parked in front of the cottage.

As the Chevy pulled away, Dave said, "Ta-ta?"

"Must be short for 'bye-bye,'" Al said. "Probably an islander thing."

After we had all stripped, showered, put on fresh clothing and dumped our ashes-imbedded duds into the washing machine, I tapped out a story about our adventure with Uncle Walt. I wrote about the steadiness of the rain and the unpredictability of the wind, but I did not identify the second, watery scattering point or go into detail about our condition after the wind shift. I felt it was better to let the readers use their imagination about the convergence of ashes, wind and wet bodies. And, as I had sworn to Alison Riggs, we did not send a selfie.

Don O'Rourke was still on the city desk, and he responded to that story with a question about my progress on the search for Walt's killer. I said I would be checking with Detective Gouveia immediately but I wasn't expecting much, if anything. "This murder case is at a dead end," I wrote, hoping this little pun would get us a live ticket to the Twin Cities.

"Speaking of dead, how about the old guy who died in Walt's woods?" was the reply.

"Waiting on the autopsy report for cause of death. Could be several days."

"Go talk to Gouveia and see what he's got. Tomorrow find some people who knew Walt and get their take on who might have wanted him dead. Talk to the publisher of the paper. He might think of something Walt wrote that would turn into a longtime grudge."

"Tomorrow? You want us to stay another full day?"

"Just one more. I'll get airline reservations for you and Al for Saturday afternoon."

"What about Dave?"

"Dave doesn't work for us."

"Can you book him on the same flight and have him reimburse the paper?"

"I'll think about it. Get to work on Gouveia."

I closed and said, "We're here until Saturday, guys."

"Things must be really dull in St. Paul," Dave said.

"No, Don just likes having us away from the office," Al said.

I picked up my cellphone and called Manny Gouveia. His voice mail answered and I left a message without much hope of getting a return. How in the world was I going to find people who knew Walt Jerome?

15

FRIDAY THE 13TH

We pondered the problem of locating Walt Jerome's friends and acquaintances the next morning over French toast with blueberry syrup, sausage patties and coffee in a back corner booth at Linda Jean's.

"I'm not sure where to start," I said. "It's too late to put a personal ad in this week's island newspapers."

"Hey, speaking of, we should pick up a copy of today's *Chronicle* and see what our friend Alison wrote about Uncle Walt's murder," Dave said.

"Good idea, but it won't help us find any of his friends," I said.

"It's too bad that Walt nixed a funeral," Al said. "If you'd had a service for him, you'd have a guest book listing everyone who came."

"I know. But Uncle Walt was fanatical about funerals. He once wrote a long piece that said funerals are a gruesome, medieval exhibition where your cold, stiff body is put on display as a work of the mortician's art. I'll never forget that line."

"What did he not like about memorial services, the kind without the dearly beloved's cold, stiff body on display," I asked.

"He said a memorial service is just a ritual where family and friends say nice things about the dearly beloved that they don't really mean or maybe aren't true."

"Well, a list of mourners certainly would be helpful to me now, whether they meant what they said or not."

"You know who might have some suggestions?" Dave said. "Dick Rylander."

"You mean the only lawyer I've ever met who was happy to be without a suit?" Al said.

"That's the possible bearer of information I'm thinking of," Dave said.

"You're right," I said. "He might have a barebones list of people close to Walt."

"Let's go rattle his cage," Dave said.

"Let's hope he's clothed and in his cage and not hanging out at the beach," I said. The weather had improved immensely overnight, and it was not improbable that a dedicated beachophile would be taking advantage of an unseasonably warm and cloudless October day.

On the way to Rylander's office we stopped at the car rental office to extend our lease for another two days at another $129 per day, plus the tax.

"That's $258, plus the tax. You sure you don't want to take it for a week?" Marty said. "It's twenty bucks a day cheaper that way."

"We're only staying two more days," Dave said. "I'd be crazy to pay for a week."

"You're the boss," said Marty.

We climbed the stairs to Dick Rylander's office and rapped on the door. It was opened by the man himself, fully clothed in a white shirt, striped tie and crisply creased khakis. His face registered surprise and a touch of disappointment. We smiled and said, "Good morning, Dick," in unison.

He took a step back and said, "Oh, yes, good morning, gentlemen. You surprised me. I was expecting it to be my nine o'clock appointment."

We promised not to keep him long and he invited us in. When we told him what we were looking for, he said he could give us a couple of names and asked if we had looked at the call log in Walt's cellphone.

"The cops have the cellphone," Dave said. "I guess they think he might have made a date for drinks with whoever spiked the wine."

"What about a written list? Some people keep a notebook of names and numbers by their landline phones."

"Now there's a real possibility," Dave said. He turned toward me and said, "Why wouldn't a reporter think of that?"

"Must be the salt air," I said."

"Or the sea breeze blowing through your ears," Al said. With friends like that ... et cetera?

Rylander went to his desk, picked up a ballpoint pen and wrote the names of three men and the towns they lived in on a notepad. He tore off the sheet and handed it to Dave. "I don't have house addresses or phone numbers but I'm sure you can find them in the Island phone book in Walt's cottage. Sorry, I mean *your* cottage."

We thanked Rylander and were about to leave when he said, "That was quite a write-up about Walt's being poisoned in today's *Martha's Vineyard Chronicle*, wasn't it?"

"Haven't seen it yet," Dave said.

"Oh, then you haven't seen the story about you guys finding poor old Teddy Brewster's body out on Chappy, either."

"You're right, we haven't."

"You should get a copy. Great picture of the three of you right on the front page."

"Our picture?" I said. All I could think of was Alison Riggs pointing her cellphone camera at us, covered with Walt Jerome's ashes, standing in a row on the steps of the cottage front porch.

"Yeah. You better go buy a paper."

We agreed, and I opened the door to reveal a woman with red hair and an open-mouthed look of surprise standing with her fist raised ready to knock. It was one of the Jewell twins.

I said, "Hello there. Are you Ima or Ura?"

"Yes," she said.

I laughed. "You know what I mean. Which one are you?"

"I'm Ima. Don't you remember? I'm the one who doesn't wear skirts." She was, in fact, clad in a combination of T-shirt and shorts that was much more interesting to the male eye. Her tautly-stretched T-shirt ended well above her belly button and the skin-hugging shorts that started well below it barely reached the bottom of two enticingly rounded buns.

Behind me, Rylander said, “I see my nine o’clock has arrived.”

“Sorry I’m a little late,” Ima said.

“Nice seeing you, Ima Little Late,” I said. “We were just leaving.”

I went out the door past her, followed by Al and Dave, and we went down the stairs and headed at almost a trot toward the Corner Store, which sold newspapers from Martha’s Vineyard, Cape Cod and Boston.

“I’ll bust that little sneak’s phone into smithereens if she took the picture I’m thinking of,” I said.

“I’d rather bust her arm,” Al said.

“I think she’s counting on us being the sort of gentlemen who would not physically attack a woman,” Dave said.

“She might have miscounted,” I said.

We reached the Corner Store, found the shelf filled with newspapers in the third aisle and Dave snatched a copy of the *Martha’s Vineyard Chronicle* off the top of the pile.

There was our picture on the upper left corner of the front page.

We were standing in a row on the front steps.

Of the Edgartown police station.

“Good looking trio,” Dave said.

“We should compliment the photographer,” Al said.

“We should tell her how lucky she is to be alive,” I said.

I gave the clerk a dollar for the paper and we walked back to the cottage, where I read aloud Alison’s story about three visitors to Chappy finding a dead man’s body in a tent. She had the basic facts in order, had spelled our names correctly and had managed to acquire the name of the deceased. She mentioned Dorie and Dolly and a cousin named Toby Pilgrim as the surviving next of kin but had no comments from any of them (not that I expected one from Dolly).

Next I read aloud Alison’s report on the murder of former *Chronicle* editor Walter Jerome. She had done a good job of quizzing Detective Gouveia, but hadn’t managed to squeeze anything out of him that we didn't already know. She included Dave's comment, substituting the word "expletive" for bastards, and described him as the sole survivor who had inherited an eight-hundred-and-thirty-thousand-dollar cottage in Oak Bluffs and a strip of undeveloped woodland on Chappaquiddick. She also mentioned that Gouveia had no suspects or persons of interest at this time.

"How'd she know what the cottage is worth?" Dave asked.

"You can get that from the town clerk," I said. "It's public information."

"If you ask me, that shouldn't be anybody's business but mine."

"That's probably why she didn't ask you."

After finishing our critique of Ms. Riggs' journalistic endeavors, we initiated a search for a written list of telephone contacts. After opening every door and cupboard on the ground floor, we decided that, if such a list existed, the police must have scooped it up along with almost everything else that wasn't nailed down.

The one helpful item that hadn't been scooped was the island phone book. I used that to find numbers for the three men on the list that Dick Rylander had given me. One was in Oak Bluffs, another was in Edgartown and the third was in Aquinnah.

"Let's try the closest one first," I said, and punched in the number for Daniel Webb. After four rings, a woman's voice advised me that I had reached the Webb residence, said that no one could come to the phone just now and invited me to leave a message after the beep. I left my name and number and explained that I was looking for friends of Walter Jerome.

I tried the next closest name, Everett Gibson in Edgartown, with similar results except the voice mail message was delivered by a male. I was batting oh-for-two.

The third name on the list was Claude Rousseau, a resident of Aquinnah, which is the Native-American name of the town formerly known as Gayhead, located at the western tip of the island. When a woman answered the phone, I asked for Mister Rousseau and she asked who was calling. I said who and why, and she advised me to hold on for a moment. Next came a male voice that could have been heard without the phone. "This is Claude. What can I do for you?"

"My name is Mitch Mitchell and I'm a newspaper reporter doing a story about the late Walter Jerome, and I'm looking for people who knew him as a friend," I said. "His attorney mentioned your name as someone who fits that description. Would you say that's correct, Mister Rousseau?"

"Yah, I guess you could say we were friends. We saw things pretty much eye-to-eye over the years."

"What kind of things would that be?"

"Political things. That's what we mostly talked about."

"Are you a politician?"

"I'm the chief of the Wampanoag tribal council here on the island. We've had a lot of political issues, especially the last couple of years, and Mister Jerome was very good to us, both in reporting the news and taking an editorial position in our favor on some differences of opinion."

"So you got along with Mister Jerome very well?"

"Definitely. I was very sorry when he retired and even more sorry to hear that he died. And now I see in the paper that somebody poisoned him. That's just awful."

"Do you know of anybody who would have a reason to poison Mister Jerome? Maybe someone who differed with his political views or his editorial position on something?"

"Oh, god, no," said Claude Rousseau. "I can't imagine anybody on this island getting that riled up over an editorial or the man's politics."

"Nobody who opposed the issues that he supported you on would be that angry?" I said.

"Oh, I sure hope not. They might be coming after me next if that's the case."

"For your sake, I hope that's not the case. Did Mister Jerome ever mention anybody who was strongly opposed to any of his editorial positions?"

"Well, we both knew who was on what side in the tribal issues, but the folks that was against us don't go around poisoning people."

"What kind of issues were involved?"

"Well, one was the case of a recreation building being used as a gaming hall, and another was the mainland tribe's wanting to build a gambling casino in Aquinnah. And there were a couple of questions about tribal land—who controlled it and how it could be developed. Stuff like that."

The words "gaming" and "gambling" raised red flags in my mind. These were issues that always involved a lot of money and sometimes involved people who would do anything—even murder—to acquire that money. "Can you give me the names of a couple of people who opposed your positions on the gaming and casino issues?" I asked.

"I don't think any of them had anything to do with Mister Jerome's murder."

"I don't really, either," I lied. "But I'd like to talk to some of them just to get a perspective on his editorial stands."

"Oh, god, Mister, I can't do that. I just don't want to get involved in anything like that. Tell you what. There were stories in the paper that quoted those people, and some of them wrote letters to the editor. I bet you that you can find them in the files at the newspaper office if you go there and look."

"How far back would I have to look?"

"Not too far. The casino was in the news this past summer and the gaming question was hot the summer before that."

"And there were letters to the editor opposing Mister Jerome's editorials?"

"There were letters both ways—for and against. You can't miss'em."

"Well, thank you, Mister Rousseau. You've been very helpful."

"Oh, you're welcome, Mister Mitchell. I sure hope the cops find out who killed poor Mister Jerome. And is that nephew that was mentioned in the story still on the island?"

"Yes, he is. He's right here with me, in fact."

"You give him my sympathy, please, would you Mister Mitchell."

"I'll do that."

"And tell him to be careful as long as he's here."

Claude Rousseau ended the call before I could ask him why he'd said that.

16

SPREADING THE WORD

"I should be careful while I'm here?" Dave said.

"That's what the man said," I replied.

"Why?"

"That's what the man didn't say."

"Weird."

"There's a lot of that going around."

"Must be the salt air," Al said.

"I did get something that might be useful from Rousseau," I said. "He told me that Walt wrote some controversial stuff about gaming and gambling casino issues in Aquinnah. Either of those could involve people who might be inclined to eliminate their opposition. Rousseau wouldn't name anybody who disagreed with Walt, but he suggested looking at editorials and letters to the editor from the last two summers. I'm going to email a short story to Don, and then I think it will be time for a trip to the *Martha's Vineyard Chronicle*."

I sent my brief story to Don, who replied that he'd be looking for more and better stuff to follow. So what's new, I thought, but did not respond.

We were munching sandwiches on the front porch a few minutes later when my cellphone rang. I grabbed it quickly, hoping it would be either Daniel Webb or Everett Gibson returning my call. I saw that it was even better: Martha Todd.

Her greeting was not as good as I expected. "You won't believe what's happening," she said. "ICE has arrested my dad."

"ICE?" I said. "The immigration people?"

"That's right. Immigration and Customs Enforcement."

"They've arrested your dad?"

"You heard me. It's bizarre."

"I guess it is. What the hell is going on?"

"Dad had a heart attack and the ambulance took him to Regions Hospital. It seems that ICE has an agent stationed there checking on people with African or Muslim-sounding names. He ran Dad's name through the system and found some glitch in his annual reporting process so he arrested Dad while he was in the ICU recovering from surgery. Have you ever heard of anything so crazy?"

The man Martha calls Dad is actually her step-father, a Cape Verdean whose name is Carlos Mascarenhas. Her birth father, a Brit named Charles Todd, was killed in a plane crash when she was two years old and her Cape Verdean mother, Rita Mendes Todd, married Mascarenhas two years later. Martha came to the United States as a college student and settled down here, graduating from the University of Minnesota, getting married, working, getting divorced, attending night law school and eventually earning her citizenship. Her mother, her step-father, and her grandmother, Gramma Mendes, joined Martha in the United States sixteen years ago, a reversal of the usual parents-first immigration pattern. The parents have been living in this country (Gramma Mendes died about a year ago) under one of the programs that requires an annual review. Don't ask me what number or what acronym it is, they all sound alike to me.

"It's politics, pure and simple," I said. "ICE is doing crap like this because of the immigration uproar in Washington. What about your mom? Are they arresting her, too?"

"Not yet, but we're expecting a visit from ICE any time now."

"So what can you do about your father?"

"Linda has taken charge of his defense," Martha said. Linda is Linda L. Lansing, the super lawyer who heads the firm where Martha works.

"He couldn't be in better hands," I said. Sometimes known as Triple-L, Linda L. Lansing is unquestionably the best defense lawyer in the Twin Cities.

"That's the one thing we've got going for us."

"You said he had surgery. What kind and how did it go?"

"He had some blocked arteries and they put in a couple of stents. He's doing okay. Still groggy from the anesthesia; doesn't comprehend that he's under arrest yet."

"They haven't cuffed him to the bed?"

"They'd have to knock me out cold and take me away in chains before that happened."

"I can believe that."

"So what's happening out there with the murder story? When are you coming home?"

"Nothing much is happening with the murder story, unfortunately. Talked to a friend of Walt's who said Walt had written some unpopular editorials about gaming and gambling casinos in Aquinnah, which might have made him some dangerous enemies. Last I heard from Don, he's going to get us tickets for home tomorrow."

"God, I hope so. I need your shoulder to cry on."

"You're welcome to use my pillow until my shoulder gets there."

"That's a very poor substitute. Too squishy."

"Well, hang in there and give your dad my best. I'll call as soon as I know my arrival time."

"I'll keep the phone in my hand until you call. Bye, sweetie." We made kissy sounds into the phone and ended the call.

"Martha got a problem?" Al asked.

"Big time," I said, and went on to describe her dad's health condition and immigration status dilemma.

"Well, if anybody can keep her daddy in the U.S. of A., it's Triple-L," Al said.

"That was my initial response," I said.

"She'll melt ICE with the letter of the law."

We drove to Edgartown, found the *Chronicle* office on a side street, parked the car two blocks away after a five-minute search for a spot and marched in the front door single file. Facing the door was a wooden desk, behind which sat a heavy-set, middle-aged woman with curly brown hair surrounding an impassive face. A small copper plaque in front of her said "Ms. Brody."

I introduced the three of us and informed her of our mission. She smiled briefly, advised us to have a seat, motioned us toward a row of chairs to our left, and picked up her desk phone. Like good little boys in a school room, we moved to the row of chairs and sat down.

After a minute or so on the phone, Ms. Brody hung up, looked over at us and said, "Someone will be with you gentlemen shortly."

We muttered a chorus of thank you and rose from our chairs. A moment later a thin, gray-haired woman who stood barely five feet tall emerged through a door to Ms. Brody's left.

"Shortly is right," Al whispered.

The woman approached us, introduced herself as Alice Goodenough and said she was in charge of the paper's archives. She led us through the door and a maze of office spaces to a small room with a desk, a chair, a computer and a printer. She clicked a few keys on the computer and said, "It's all set up to search. Just enter the date you're looking for and click on the 'go' button. That week's issue will pop up and you can page through it by clicking on the arrows. If you need help with something, I'm in the next room." And out she went, closing the door behind her.

"Do we flip a coin to see who gets the chair?" Dave asked.

"I'm doing the computer search, so I get the chair," I said.

"Unless we flip you," said Al.

"Sit on the corners of the desk; there's room if you don't get too cheeky," I said.

"You don't mind if we butt in?" Al said.

"Just don't bum up the computer," I said.

Following Alice Goodenough's instructions, I clicked my way into a late August issue of the *Chronicle*, but found no mention of plans for an Aquinnah gambling casino. I decided to work my way backward from there, and finally hit the jackpot in a mid-July issue. There were two letters to the editor attacking editor emeritus Walter Jerome for a previously published guest column in opposition to the casino proposal. One was from a Massachusetts mainland Wampanoag tribe official in New Bedford and the other was from a casino developer in Las Vegas. Both were nasty in tone, said the frivolous concerns expressed in the column could easily be dealt with and strongly suggested that the editor emeritus had no business poking his nose into tribal affairs.

I wrote down their names, Edward New-Moon and Lysander Kraft, closed that issue of the paper and opened the previous week's editorial page. The column in question pulled no punches in listing the problems that a casino located in the most inaccessible corner of the Vineyard would create. Walt saw these as changing the nature of the tiny rural town, creating unmanageable traffic jams on narrow, twisting up-island roads and introducing potential criminal elements to the island.

"I can see why those two casino backers were pissed off about this column," I said. "He lists everything that could go wrong and at the end suggests that the supporters of the casino plan are money-grubbers who have absolutely no regard for the people and the environment of Martha's Vineyard."

"Those two letter writers could be the type of money-grubbers he's writing about," Dave said. "The mainland branch of the tribe, and maybe some individuals, would make a mint by abusing the island tribe's land, and the developer will hit the jackpot if he wins the contract to build it."

"Think either of them would be pissed enough to kill the editor emeritus?" I asked.

"My money would be on the guy in Las Vegas," Al said. "He's in a really cutthroat business and doesn't have any local ties."

"I wonder if our buddy Gouveia is checking either of these guys out," Dave said.

"That's a question I will ask him first thing tomorrow," I said.

"Tomorrow?" Al said. "I thought we were supposed to get out of here tomorrow."

"Knowing Don, he'll want a story before we leave," I said. "But you did just remind me that we haven't heard about airplane tickets from our lord and master."

"Call him quick, before he goes home," Al said.

I hauled out my cellphone and made the call. Don answered with, "What have you got?"

"What I haven't got is an airplane seat," I said.

"I was just going to call you about that. The story of Walt's murder has gone national on TV. You need to stay there a little while longer to keep us up to date."

"How did it all of a sudden go national? Did a Twin Cities station send it to a network?"

"No, actually the stations here haven't shown much interest in the murder of a retired small-town newspaper editor way out in Massachusetts, even though he did work in St. Paul for many years before he went east. But apparently a Boston TV station picked it up from a story in a local paper out there and shot it to CBS with the hype that the victim had been a popular and outspoken newspaper editor and the murder was committed on glamorous Martha's Vineyard, where millionaires and presidents live and play."

"Did you say they picked it up from an island newspaper?"

"That's the story I got."

"Shit! That island newspaper reporter got the tip from me. It's really my fault that Boston TV got the word."

"Well, lucky you. You've just bought yourself a couple of more days on the millionaires' playground."

"I don't want them. I need to be back in good old flyover land. Martha has a family problem that I should be helping her with."

"Martha will have to wait a couple more days. What's the problem?"

"Oh, just that her father's had a heart attack and has been arrested in the hospital by the troops from ICE."

"That is nasty, but it sounds like a good doctor and that ace lawyer Martha works for will be a lot more help than you could be."

"My help is emotional, not practical."

"I feel for you—and for Martha—but we really need you to be practical on Martha's Vineyard at least over the weekend. Now, what have you got for today?"

I ran quickly over the printed dispute between Walt Jerome and the casino backers and said I would search back a few more weeks for news stories about the proposal. "I'm also going to check with Oak Bluffs police to see if they are pursuing the casino connection," I said.

"Give me as much as you can," Don said. "Our readers are interested, even if the schmucks who run the TV stations here are not. Talk to you later."

I stared at the "call ended" message on my cellphone for a moment, then passed the news about the unexpected extension of our unwanted vacation time to Al and Dave.

"Oh, god, I'm sorry I got you guys into this," Dave said.

"Not your fault that we're stuck here," Al said.

"If I hadn't dragged you out here with me, you wouldn't be stuck here. They'd have never spent the money to send you to Martha's Vineyard just to cover Uncle Walt's death."

"No use crying over spilled arsenic," I said. "Let's look at a few more issues for casino stories and opinions and then get back to Oak Bluffs. I've also got to call Manny Gouveia and get his daily no comment on the case."

I clicked back through all the July and June editions of the *Chronicle* and found three news stories about the casino proposal, an editorial that didn't really take a stand either way, and letters to the editor from Edward New-Moon and another mainland Wampanoag named Chester Lonetree supporting the plan, and a letter from Claude Rousseau opposing it. I ran everything, including Walt's column and the responses, through the printer and shut down the computer. We walked out and I knocked on the door that Alice Goodenough said she would be behind and we heard her say, "Come in." I opened the door, and we all stuck our heads in and recited our gratitude in unison. From behind a pile of papers on her desk, she asked if we'd found what we were looking for and I said that we had. After another round of "thank you," we withdrew.

"I almost told Ms. G. that her instructions were good enough," Al said.

"Good that you didn't," I said. "She's probably heard enough of that tired joke."

Back in Oak Bluffs, we went to the car rental agency to extend the lease through Sunday. "You could still take it for the seven-fifty weekly rate," Marty said. "You already been here for one week, payin' the daily rate."

"We won't be here for another week," Dave said. "Just give us two more days at the daily rate."

"That'll be $258, plus the tax."

"That's what we'll do."

"You're the boss," Marty said.

I put in a call to Manny Gouveia. This time he actually picked up the phone. I asked if there was anything new to report.

"Only thing new is we've now got Boston papers and TV stations on our ass in addition to you and that little girl from the *Chronicle*," he said. "I spent more time answerin' phone calls from reporters than I did workin' on the case today."

"Have you questioned anybody who might know why Walt would be murdered?"

"I ain't commenting on who I've questioned."

"How about people who didn't like his stand against the Aquinnah casino plan?"

"What about'em?"

"Could the murder be connected to what Walt wrote?"

"You suggestin' that the Wampanoags killed him?"

"Maybe. Or maybe the developer from Las Vegas who wrote a nasty letter to the editor. There's millions and millions of dollars involved. A very strong motive for removing any serious opposition."

"That's a really big stretch, Mister Mitchell. I don't think I can call in the guy from Vegas on anything as thin as a letter to the paper."

"Just a thought," I said.

"Yeah, well let me do the thinkin' and you stick to the reportin', okay?"

"Hard to turn off my overactive brain," I said. "Especially when there's so little provided for me to report."

"Well, just make sure that overactive brain doesn't over-report something that hasn't really happened. Have a good day, Mister Mitchell."

I put down the phone and Al asked, "Anything new?"

"He's pissed about being called by the media from Boston and he called Alison Riggs a little girl, which I'm sure she'd love to hear. Oh, and he said for me to have a good day, which he's only done once before."

"That's progress. Maybe he likes you better after dealing with all those hard-asses in Boston."

"He still doesn't want me to do any thinking on my own. Had no interest in my casino theory."

"I guess you'll have to go it on your own with that one, whether Manny likes it or not."

"Just call me Lonesome Polecat."

I wrote a story that I wasn't very proud of because it didn't contain any concrete news and emailed it to St. Paul. Don O'Rourke had gone home and Fred Donlin responded that he'd received the story. He didn't comment on its quality, for which I was grateful.

At five o'clock we turned on the Boston TV news to see what, if anything, they were saying about the murder of Walt Jerome. About five minutes into the newscast the scene switched from the talking heads on the news desk to a young woman holding a microphone in front of a camera and talking about the mysterious poisoning of a former Martha's Vineyard newspaper editor.

"Hey, look at what's behind her," Dave said. "Those restaurants."

"She's here in the harbor," Al said.

"Won't Manny be thrilled to have her reporting live from Oak Bluffs?" I said.

My cellphone rang and I saw that the call was coming from a Martha's Vineyard number.

"Hello," I said.

"Mister Mitchell?" a man's voice replied.

"Yes, this is Mitch Mitchell."

"This is Daniel Webb. You left a message on my phone saying you want to talk to me about Walt Jerome."

17

A FISHY DEAL

Daniel Webb described himself as one of Walt Jerome's poker playing buddies.

"There were five of us who'd get together on the third Friday of every month for a night of poker and booze and bullshit," Webb said. "In fact, we called it PBS Night. It was low stakes poker. I don't think anybody ever lost more than twenty bucks and nobody ever won more than thirty. But the booze was always top shelf stuff."

"It sounds to me like you'd quit playing before Walt died," I said.

"We had. One of the other guys passed away in June and another went off-island to live with his son and daughter-in-law in August. None of us were getting any younger."

"That seems to be a common problem. How long did you know Walt?"

"From the time he came to the island. I was circulation manager at the *Chronicle* when he became the editor. I retired about two years before he did."

"So no more poker after August?"

"That's right. The three of us that were still ambulatory got together a couple of times for the booze and bullshitting, but a three-handed poker game isn't all that much fun."

"So when was the last time you actually saw Walt?"

"It was a couple of weeks before he died—must have been the

third Friday of September. He and Andy Goff, the other poker survivor, came to my house that night and we did major damage to a fifth of Johnny Walker Black. Luckily they both live close enough that neither one of them had to drive home."

"How was Walt acting?" I asked. "Did you see any signs that he was worried about anything or having problems with anybody?"

"Not really," Webb said. "He seemed the same as always, full of stories and laughs."

"Did he ever talk about anybody who didn't like him or disagreed with him?"

"Oh, he mentioned people who didn't like his editorials or his columns off and on, but there wasn't anybody that he seemed to be worried about. Certainly nobody who might take a notion to kill him."

"What about the most recent debate over the casino plan for Aquinnah? Did he ever talk about the people who wrote letters to the editor in response to his anti-casino column?"

"Oh, he commented on them when we got together right after the letters ran in the paper, but he didn't take them any more serious than the usual letter writers. He wasn't too complimentary about the guy he called 'the asshole developer from Las Vegas.'"

"Walt called him that?"

"He did. That was pretty strong talk for Walt. He didn't usually use that kind of language but this guy really pissed him off."

"Do you remember what Walt said about him?"

"Just that the guy was known for running over people and ignoring things like environmental rules when it came to selling his services. Oh, he also said he'd had a real nasty personal email message from the guy."

"How nasty? Was it threatening?"

"Umm, I don't remember that he said anything about a threat. It was mostly just nasty name calling, I think."

"Sounds like his description of the guy was accurate," I said. "But you can't think of anybody local, on the island, who might have put poison in Walt's wine?"

"No, I sure can't. I just can't picture anybody local doing a thing like that," Webb said.

"Did Walt ever talk about Teddy Brewster?"

"You mean Daffy Dolly's nutty son? Oh, yeah, he talked about Teddy every now and then."

"Did he have a problem with Teddy?"

"Well, a few years back he did. When he first caught Teddy squatting on his land out on Chappy. But they worked out a deal where Walt gave Teddy permission to stay for the summer in exchange for an occasional striper or blue fish as long as Teddy left the place clean when he bailed out for Florida in the fall. I think Walt went easy on Teddy because he didn't want to hurt Dolly in any way."

"Walt had no plans to use the land himself?"

"Not really. It came to him through his daddy's will, but he had no use for it. What was he going to do, build a second home on Chappy? He mentioned more than once that he was thinking about selling it."

"Did Teddy know that?"

"I have no idea what he might have said to Teddy."

"Did Teddy bring the fish to Walt or did Walt have to go out and get it?"

"Teddy delivered it in that beat-up Landrover he drove. He'd just show up with a fresh striper or bluefish in an ice chest every once in a while."

"Just showed up without advance notice?"

Webb laughed. "I don't think Teddy had a telephone if that's what you mean?"

"I guess you're right. Well, thank you, Mister Webb, and if you think of anything or hear anything please give me a call. I'm trying to piece things together for my readers in St. Paul."

"Okay," he said. "And you can call me Dan."

"Oh, one more thing. Can you give me Andy Goff's phone number?"

He did, and we said goodbye.

I summarized the conversation with Dan Webb for Al and Dave, and Al said wouldn't it be ironic if Teddy knew that Walt was thinking of selling the woodland and put arsenic in one of those stripers or bluefish. "The medical examiner didn't say that wine and arsenic were the only things in Walt's stomach."

"It would be ironic," I said. "Teddy poisoning Walt and then dying of a heart attack or a stroke or whatever. I wonder if the good doctor in Edgartown would give us a complete list of what all was in Walt's stomach."

"Can't hurt to ask," Al said.

"Too late to call him now," I said. "I'll try to catch him in the morning."

"Tomorrow is Saturday, you know. A lot of doctors don't open their office on Saturday."

"If not, I'll look for his home number in the phone book."

"A lot of doctors don't list their home numbers in the phone book."

As bedtime approached that night, I called Martha in St. Paul. "How's your dad?" I asked.

"Better," she said. "Looks like he'll be okay with the stents unless the ICE men drag him out of bed and haul him off to jail."

"They can't do that, can they?"

"God knows what they can do. Linda's researching that. Meanwhile she's got a doctor's written statement that Dad can't be moved. What's happening there?"

"Not much." I told her about Teddy trading fish for squatter's rights and Walt's expressing a desire to sell the land on Chappy.

"My god, you don't think Teddy poisoned Walt so he could stay in the woods, do you?"

"I've heard of crazier things. I'm going to call the M.E. tomorrow and ask what the total contents of Walt's stomach were."

"Oh, yuck. What a great way to spend a Saturday."

"We all have our own little ways of having fun."

"Yes, we do. Mine will be sitting beside my sick father, making sure nobody takes him away from the hospital."

We talked about more pleasant topics for a few minutes, made kissy sounds and hung up. I went to sleep thinking about poisonous fish swimming in Walt's stomach. At least I didn't dream about them.

After downing one of Linda Jean's ham, cheese and mushroom omelets at breakfast the next morning, I learned that Dr. Edward Newman was one of those doctors who do not keep office hours on Saturday. The message on his voice mail instructed me to call 911 if I had an emergency or otherwise call back after 9 a.m. on Monday.

Next I learned that Dr. Edward Newman was also one of those doctors who do not list their home numbers in the phone book.

Because Edgartown Police Chief Morris Agnew seemed to very chummy with Dr. Newman, I decided to ask him for help. I called the Edgartown PD's non-emergency number and asked to speak to him. "Chief's not in today," said Officer Smithson, who'd answered the phone. "It's Saturday, you know."

"I'm becoming more and more aware of that," I said. "Can you or somebody there give me a number where I might find Dr. Newman on Saturday?"

"If he ain't cuttin' up a body, you can usually find him on his sailboat on Saturday this time of year. Actually, speakin' of that, I think he *is* cuttin' up a body today. Poor old Teddy Brewster went to that big fishin' hole in the sky yesterday and Doc's doin' the autopsy."

"On Saturday?"

"I heard the chief tell Doc that he wants to get the book closed on Teddy by Monday afternoon. No reason to drag it out over next week."

"I'm fine with that. Is there a phone where he's doing the autopsy?"

"Don't know the number. But I think we got Doc's cellphone. Hang on a sec."

I hung for about a minute before Officer Smithson came back. He gave me the number, and I thanked him and said goodbye.

My call to Doc went to voice mail. So what else is new? I left a message. What else can a roving reporter do? I certainly wouldn't want him to reach into his pocket for a phone if he's cutting up a body.

The doctor returned my call in mid-afternoon, just minutes before the time I had set as my deadline for calling him again. After all, how long can it take to cut up a body as skinny as Teddy Brewster's? I asked him for a list of Walt Jerome's stomach contents.

"Why on earth do you want that?" he asked.

"I'm a reporter, remember?" I said. "Reporters are curious beasts."

"I agree with that, and you can take the curious part any way you want to. I don't happen to have the list in front of me."

"Do you recall if one of the items was fish?"

"Fish?"

"Fish."

"You are a curious beast all right. I do remember that it looked like his last meal included fish. I couldn't say for sure what kind, if that's your next question."

"Actually, I was going to ask if it was striped bass or bluefish."

"I didn't test it for species, but I don't think it was bluefish."

"But it might have been striped bass?"

"Might have been. Or it might have been cod or haddock or flounder or any kind of white-fleshed fish you can think of."

"Thank you, doctor, that's what I wanted to know."

"If you want the complete list, I can get it for you Monday."

"No need for the whole thing if you're sure there was fish. While we're talking, what did you find out about Teddy Brewster's cause of death?" I said.

"I can't release that information until the police chief gives me the okay," he said.

"So that will be Monday sometime?"

"Should be."

"I'll probably be back in St. Paul by then."

"Oh? That's too bad. If you're really a reporter you might want to stick around until Monday."

"Why is that?"

"Like I told you, I can't say anything until the police chief gives me the okay."

"But you're telling me that the cause of Teddy's death is newsworthy?"

"Wouldn't be surprised. Now I'm going to say goodbye before I say something I shouldn't say before Monday. So, goodbye, Mister Mitchell. Have a nice day."

18

DÉJÀ VU

After I told Al and Dave about Dr. Newman's advice, we decided that we needed to stay on Martha's Vineyard through Monday. This would entail me calling Don O'Rourke with a request for a later flight and all of us calling wives who would not be pleased to hear about another change in schedule.

"Do you think the doctor found something to link Teddy to Walt's murder?" Dave said.

"All I know is that there was fish in Walt's stomach and Teddy was known to have provided him with fish," I said. "Whether there's a connection between Teddy's fish and Walt's murder, who knows?"

"It all sounds fishy to me," Al said.

"Did Teddy have fish in his stomach?" Dave asked. "Maybe there's a strain of poison fish swimming around the island."

"That's too bizarre even for this case," I said. "And I don't know what Teddy had in his stomach. That's what we'll find out Monday if we ask."

My first call went to Don O'Rourke at his home number. "What have you got, Mitch?" he said when he picked up the phone. The joys of caller ID.

"A recommendation that we stay until Monday," I said. "I hope you haven't booked us a flight for tomorrow yet."

"I was just thinking about that. Why Monday?"

"It involves the autopsy on Teddy, the guy who was squatting on Walt's land. The M.E. says that it might be newsworthy but he won't tell me any more until the chief gives permission."

"Could it be suicide? Did he leave a note?"

"Not that we've heard of. It strikes me as strange that the chief was in such a hurry for the autopsy, but he's not available to ask."

"Well, then you'd better hang around until Monday. I won't book a flight before Tuesday."

"I hope we can get the Teddy thing settled and get out of here by then."

"Have you got a statement from Teddy's family or a friend or anybody? Something about his relationship or whatever it was with Walt would be good."

"I've got some quotes from a friend of Walt's I can use. Teddy has a couple of cousins here—one of them was Walt's cleaning lady—she found the body. I wrote about her, remember? And I was told the other cousin is a lawyer but I haven't met him. I'll try to talk to both of them."

"Speaking of Walt, do you know anything new?"

"I know there was fish in his stomach and that Teddy was giving him fish for letting him squat on his land in the woods."

"So, Teddy might have—"

"He did have a motive. That's the main reason his death is so interesting to us."

"Okay. Put everything together for Sunday morning's paper and stay in touch."

My next call was to Martha.

"Tuesday!" she said so loud that I pulled the phone away from my ear. "Why Tuesday?"

"Boss's orders, and he's buying the plane tickets," I said. I gave her a rundown of everything that was happening and got no response when I finished. "You still there?"

"I'm still here. And I'm still all alone with a mopey Sherlock Holmes, a sick father and a mother who's worried out of her mind. I need you here, sweetie."

"I want to be there and I'm sure Don will let us come home

after Monday's autopsy report. With so little to write about, I can't imagine staying beyond that."

Always the optimist, I.

The next person I needed to talk to was Dorie Brewster, to get both her reaction to her cousin's death and to learn the whereabouts of Teddy's other cousin, Toby Pilgrim, who must be the one Chief Agnew had said was a lawyer.

I didn't know if Dorie worked on Saturday, but the hospital phone number was at my fingertips so I called and asked for her. "Dorie's never here on Saturday," said the woman who answered the hospital phone after I pressed through the recorded choices and reached a live human being.

"Do you have a number where I could reach her?" I asked. I knew what the answer probably would be, but it was worth a shot.

As expected, she said, "We do not give out the home numbers of our associates."

That meant going back to the tape of Dave's conversation with Dorie and fast-forwarding all the way to the very end when she gave him her home number. This time I wrote it in my reporter's notebook.

Would she be home? Of course not. After ten rings I gave up. No voice mail; no way to leave a message.

"Guess you'll have to keep calling until Dorie comes home," Dave said.

"There might be another way to find the other cousin," I said. I picked up our copy of the *Martha's Vineyard Chronicle*, found a phone number in the masthead and punched it in, hoping there'd be somebody keeping watch in the newsroom on Saturday. I was rewarded with a male voice that said, "*Chronicle*, Williams."

"Hello, *Chronicl*e, Williams," I said. "This is Mitch Mitchell. I'm a reporter for the *St. Paul Daily Dispatch*, and I'm on Martha's Vineyard covering the death of our former editor, Walter Jerome, which has led me to covering the death of his friend, Teddy Brewster, and I have a question about Teddy's cousin, who I'm told is a lawyer."

"Whoa," Williams said. "You want to run that by me again? How is it you're chasing Teddy's relative?"

I went through the rigmarole again, slower and with the added explanation that I was with Walt Jerome's nephew, who was Walt's only surviving family member, and that Teddy had expired on Walt's property, which was now Dave's.

"O-o-okay," Williams said. "And just what do you want from me?"

"I'm looking for the whereabouts of Teddy's cousin, Toby Pilgrim, who was listed as a survivor in your paper yesterday. I'm thinking that he must be the lawyer the police chief told me about."

"Yes, that would be Toby, but he's not a cousin. Toby is actually Teddy's step-brother by his mother's first marriage."

"Dolly was married twice?"

"That's right. Both times to a fisherman and both times they drowned. She really knew how to pick'em."

"She should have taught them to swim better. Anyhow, I hope they both had good life insurance."

"Not likely. The premiums for a small-boat fisherman would be more than he'd make selling his catch."

"I didn't think about that. Anyhow, I'm hoping that you or somebody there can steer me to Toby so I can get a comment on Teddy's death."

"One of our reporters has actually talked to Toby already. He has an office here in Edgartown but he's never in there on Saturday. She might have his home phone number, which ain't in the book. Problem is, she's not working on Saturday either."

"It figures. Do you have a home number for the reporter?"

"We've got her cell number, but she might not answer. Knowing her, she's probably out paddling a kayak somewhere with the weather this good. Hang on a sec while I look."

I hung, he looked, found the number and recited it. "Her name's Alison, by the way. Alison Riggs."

"Great," I said. "I've met Alison."

"You know her?"

"She took my picture. It was on your front page yesterday."

"Oh, you're one of the three stooges ... uh ... one of three guys who found Teddy's body?"

"Is that what she called us? The three stooges?"

"Oh, god, I shouldn't have said that. But, well ... yeah. But she was just kidding around while she was writing the cutline. Please don't tell her I told you about that."

"I may have trouble withholding that information when I talk to her."

"She'll kill me for blabbing that."

"May you rest in peace, Mister Williams. And thanks for the information."

With that I ended the call, leaving poor Williams to wonder what retribution would be wrought when I revealed his blunder to Alison Riggs.

I punched in the number that Williams had given me, wondering whether she was sitting in a kayak or standing where she could answer. After three rings, I heard, "Hi, this is Alison."

"Hi, this is Curly," I said. "Or maybe it's Larry or Moe."

"I'm sorry?" she said. "Who did you say this is?"

"This is one of the three stooges you photographed at the police station the other day."

"Oh, god, who told you I said that?"

"A guy named Williams at the *Chronicle*. He said you'd kill him for telling."

"I will. Slowly and painfully. So which one ... I mean who ... are you really?"

"I'm the good-looking one."

"You're all good-looking."

"Flattery will get you nowhere after calling us three stooges. But I'm Mitch, the reporter, and I'm willing to forgive you in return for Toby Pilgrim's home phone number."

"Won't do you any good. He's not talking to the media."

"He didn't give you any kind of a statement?"

"He gave me a statement all right. He said, and I quote: It's none of your goddamn business how I feel about my brother's death. Now fuck off and leave my family alone."

"That's a very clear statement," I said. "Hard to print in an obit, though."

"I don't know how we'll even run an obit," Alison said. "We normally get some information from the family to go with what the funeral home tells us."

"What about Dorie?"

"I haven't been able to talk to her either."

"I ran into a dead end there, too. Nobody home when I called."

"My guess is she's over in Hyannis visiting her aunt Dolly in the mental ward. Maybe she'll be home tomorrow."

"I'll keep trying to reach her. And right now I'm going to call Mister Toby Pilgrim and see if he's as friendly to me as he was to you. Maybe I should identify myself as Curly."

"Oh, please don't take that crap seriously. I was just joking about a possible cutline."

"That's what your tattletale buddy Williams said. Glad you have your stories straight."

"It's the truth, damn it!"

"As I said, I'll forgive you in exchange for the number."

"I saved it on this phone. Wait'll I find it."

She found it and I copied it.

"Okay, Curly forgives you," I said. "I can't speak for Moe and Larry, though. You'll have to deal with them separately. Anyhow thanks for the number and so long for now, Glinda."

"Glinda?"

"The good witch of Oz. Be glad you're not green."

Next I took a deep breath and punched in Toby Pilgrim's number. After four rings his voice mail instructed me to leave a message after the tone. Considering his comment to Alison Riggs, I decided that leaving a message would be a waste of words. Manned space ships would be landing on Mars before Toby Pilgrim would return a reporter's call.

I tried Dorie Brewster's number again, listened to ten rings and hung up. What next? I spotted another name and number on my pad—Andy Goff, the other surviving poker player. I called the number, a woman answered and I asked for Andy. "He's out fishing," she said.

"Do you know when he might be back?" I asked.

"Depends on how they're biting."

"If they're biting good he'll stay out a long time?"

"No. If he catches a couple of quick blues he'll come right home and cook them up for supper."

I told her who I was, why I wanted to talk to Andy and my cellphone number. She said to give her sympathy to Walt's nephew and that she was sure Andy would want to say a few words about him. "Hope the bluefish are biting like mad," I said.

I sat down with my laptop and put together as much of a story as I could with what I had, stopping to call both Toby and Dorie again without success. It was almost time for the five o'clock news when my phone rang. A cheerful voice said, "Hi, this is Andy Goff. My wife said you wanted to talk to me about Walt Jerome."

"I do," I said. "I understand you were one of his closest friends."

He chuckled. "You could say that if you count losing a couple bucks to him every third Friday as friendship."

"I'd count anybody who gave me money as a friend," I said.

"Well, I'm going to miss old Walt, money or no money. How come his nephew ain't holding any kind of a memorial service?"

"Walt's living will said he didn't want a service."

"The kid could have had one for his friends anyway. How would Walt know about it?"

"Good point. What would you have said about him if there'd been a service?"

"That he was a good man, a great writer, a wonderful friend and a nasty cutthroat poker player."

"Do you have any thoughts on who might have poisoned him?"

"Not for publication, I don't."

"How about off the record?"

"Promise you won't print it?"

"I swear it on a stack of newspaper style books."

"Good enough. That was Walt's bible. If I was the cops, I'd be looking at somebody connected to the Aquinnah casino project. There's a ton of money at stake there, and Walt was a very prominent leader of the opposition."

"I've thought of that, too. Anybody else you can think of? How about Teddy Brewster?"

"The old screwball that was squatting on Walt's land? I don't know. He didn't seem like the kind of screwball who'd kill somebody."

"Can you think of anybody else who might have hated Walt, or had a grudge or anything like that?"

"There was generally somebody or other who didn't like what Walt wrote, but I can't point to anybody who might kill him for that. He'd always print both sides of an issue no matter which side he took himself."

"Did you know Walt a long time?"

"Almost from the day he came to the island. We're back fence neighbors. I was working in my garden when he was moving in and he came over and introduced himself."

"So you live right behind Walt's cottage?"

"I can see the back of his cottage from my back steps. He was the kind of neighbor everybody hopes to have. Kept his place looking good and was always willing to help a friend. Only fault he had was that he was a merciless poker player. You tell that kid he left the place to that he should have had a service for Walt, whether he wanted it or not. Some of us would have liked the chance to say goodbye."

"I will do that. And thank you for your comments, Mister Goff."

"Andy," he said.

"Thank you, Andy."

"You're very welcome," he said. I like that response. One of my pet peeves is people who say "no problem" instead of "you're welcome" when you thank them for something.

I put down the phone and walked into the living room where Al and Dave were chatting and half-watching the TV news. They were slumped down on the sofa and I stretched out in the armchair and was almost dozing when a reporter standing in front of a brick building in Hyannis said something that brought us all to attention.

"The missing woman's name is Dolores Brewster," the man holding a Channel Four microphone said. "Better known as Dolly."

19

A CASE OF SHORT VS. NEAR

"They left off the Daffy," Al said.

"Shush," Dave said. "Listen."

The reporter was saying that Dolores Brewster was not in her room when her niece, Doris Brewster, of Oak Bluffs, arrived at the Hyannis hospital for a visit. "A search of the ward where Ms. Brewster was being treated failed to locate her. A search of the entire hospital ensued, and Ms. Brewster, who is eighty-three years of age, still was not found. Authorities were notified and they have asked that anyone with knowledge of Dolores Brewster's whereabouts contact Hyannis police at this number ... or Hyannis hospital officials at this number." The appropriate 800 numbers were flashing on the screen.

"Notice he didn't say it was the mental ward that couldn't find her?" Al said.

"Shush," Dave said. "Listen."

The reporter went on to explain that Doris might have been in Hyannis to inform Dolores of the death of her son, Teddy Brewster, who had been found dead at a Chappaquiddick campsite on Wednesday. "The cause of Mister Brewster's death is unknown, pending the results of an autopsy to be conducted by the Dukes County medical examiner," he said. "This is David Hudson, Channel Four News."

"If Dolly turns up dead, I'm saying the hell with this whole thing and going back to good old Minnesota," Dave said. "This place gives me the creeps."

"More likely she'll turn up walking on a road, heading for only she knows where," I said.

"I hope you're right," Al said. "I also hope this doesn't result in us having to stay here any longer than Tuesday."

"I don't see how it could," I said. "It's got nothing to do with Walt."

"You didn't see how we could be stuck here until Tuesday, either. You seem to be a little bit nearsighted these days."

"I believe the term you're looking for is shortsighted, but I plead not guilty to both."

"At least now we know why Dorie isn't answering her phone," Dave said.

"The woman at the hospital was right," I said. "Question now is: when will Dorie get back to the island? She'll probably stay on the Cape until they find Dolly."

"That shouldn't be too long," Al said. "I mean how far can an eighty-three-year-old woman with dementia get, all alone in a strange place? Somebody's bound to see her wandering around looking like a lost sheep."

At eleven o'clock, when we watched the news again, Al's question was still unanswered. Anyone seeing Dolores Brewster was again asked to call either the police or the hospital. This time the story was accompanied by a mug shot of Dolly, which they said had been obtained from her son, Toby Pilgrim, who had come to Hyannis from his home in Edgartown to participate in the search. "Guess Toby won't be answering his phone to give you his thoughts about his brother Teddy very soon," Al said.

"Shut up and go to bed," I said.

The one person who was answering a phone call Sunday morning was Martha Todd. I called her before breakfast and learned that her father had spent a comfortable night in our bed, and that she and her mother shared a not-so-comfortable night in our foldout sofa bed.

"So your dad's doing okay?" I said.

"He feels a hundred percent better. He gets up and walks around the house, but he's only supposed to be on his feet for a few minutes at a time. He's always been very independent but he seems to enjoy being served breakfast in bed by two doting women."

"What about his state of arrest?"

"We haven't told him about that yet. And nobody from ICE has coming calling."

"So ICE is cooling it?"

"Linda's trying to chill their case. She's asking a judge to issue an order to cease-and-desist with all legal action until Dad has fully recuperated from the surgery. That will give her time to dig into their records to find out why he's all of a sudden being arrested after all these years of complying with everything the government asked."

"It's the politics of the times."

"They still need a reason. Must be some glitch in the paperwork that they found when he was checked into the hospital."

I gave her the news about our missing Dolly. "Oh, god, that isn't going to keep you there longer is it?"

"Don't see how it could. She hasn't worked for Walt for a long time so she's not connected with the investigation of his murder in any way."

"But isn't the weird old guy you found dead in the tent her son?"

"Yes, but the only connection between his death and Walt's is that he was squatting on Walt's land. There's not enough story in that to keep us on the scene. Tomorrow Detective Gouveia in Oak Bluffs will tell us there's nothing new on Walt's murder and Doctor Newman in Edgartown will tell us whether Teddy Brewster died of a heart attack or a stroke. Then I will call Don O'Rourke and beg for a Tuesday airline ticket from Boston to the Twin Cities and he will have to say yes because he can no longer justify the cost of keeping us here."

"That's the ideal scenario," Martha said.

"It's the only scenario there is to be seen," I said.

"I hope you're not being nearsighted."

"You mean shortsighted, and as I told Al, I plead not guilty." As any lawyer will tell you, only a fool pleads his own case.

20

CALLING OUT THE ENEMY

With Toby Pilgrim and Dorie Brewster both unreachable on the other side of Nantucket Sound, I was in dire straits for a story to ship to St. Paul. I'd tapped out every known friend of Walt Jerome and I didn't know if Teddy Brewster had any living friends. I made a routine call to the Oak Bluffs police and was told, as expected, that Detective Gouveia was not in his office. It was Sunday on Martha's Vineyard and crime busting could wait until Monday.

With no additional friends of the victims available for interviews, I decided to try Walt's known enemies. I had looked up office phone numbers for both of the published casino boosters, Edward New-Moon of the mainland Wampanoags and Lysander Kraft, the Las Vegas developer. This seemed like the time to try them, Sunday or no Sunday.

I decided to start with the closer one. The answer was a recording telling me that the office was closed and that office hours were from 9 a.m. to 5 p.m. Monday through Friday.

That left me with the man in Las Vegas. Do developers work on Sunday there? Only one way to find out. I was startled when the phone was answered by a live, unrecorded male voice that said, "Yeah?"

"Hello," I said after recovering from the surprise. "Is Mister Kraft in?"

"This is Lysander Kraft," said the voice. "Who's this?"

I introduced myself and explained my interest in the death of Walter Jerome.

"What's that got to do with me?" Kraft asked.

"You wrote a letter to the *Martha's Vineyard Chronicle* in opposition to a column that Mister Jerome had written the previous week. I'm just calling to see if you'd heard that Mister Jerome is dead and if you had any reaction to his death."

"I read somewhere that he croaked, but I didn't know the guy or anything about him except that his column was full of crap."

"Are you aware that he was murdered?"

"Murdered? No, I didn't know that. Who killed him?"

"No one knows that yet. The Oak Bluffs police are working on the case. They haven't contacted you?"

"No. Why would they? All I can say is give my regrets to the guy's family and good luck to the cops. Like I said, I never met the man. Wouldn't know him if he walked in and stole a roulette wheel."

"But you disagreed with his position on the casino very strongly if I remember your letter correctly."

"I disagree with a lot of people. What's that got to do with somebody offing Mister ... what's his name? Jerome?"

I was getting nowhere very quickly. "I guess my main question was whether the Oak Bluffs police had contacted you about Mister Jerome," I said.

"Like I said before, why would they?" Kraft said. "Hey, wait a minute. Are you saying the cops are thinking that I had something to do with knocking off that dipshit column writer?"

"I'm not sure what they're thinking, but your letter was, as I said before, very strongly opposed to Mister Jerome's position, and it did get rather personal."

"So what am I supposed to have done to this Jerome character from three thousand miles away? Was he killed by a letter bomb?"

"Actually, he was poisoned."

"Oh, right. I mailed him a bottle full of arsenic that said 'drink me' on it. If those cops call me I'll tell them they can go fuck themselves."

"Actually, it *was* arsenic that killed him."

"Well, what a lucky guess by me? Hey, you ain't writing in the paper that I'm a suspect are you? I'll sue your ass from here to Timbuktu if you do."

"I'm only writing what you're telling me—that you didn't know the victim and that you sympathize with his family and that you weren't aware it was murder."

"What paper are you with again?"

"The *St. Paul Daily Dispatch*."

"I'll be watching it, Mister Michael. So be goddamn careful what you write."

"It's Mitchell. And I'm always careful, Mister Krapp." On that happy note, I ended the call with a smile.

"What's he sound like," asked Al, who'd been listening to my end of the conversation.

"Like an arrogant little prick," I said.

"Not a standup guy?"

"More like a holdup guy. But the kind of thief that steals your money legally."

"That's the worst kind. Did he also sound like the kind of guy who'd hire a hit man?"

"Yes, he did. But I don't think he did."

"Why do you say that?"

"Because I don't think he understood how much real influence Walt had on the island. Walt made him mad, but he basically kissed him off as a guest columnist who had it all wrong."

"So we're back to square one?"

"I don't think we ever left square one. This was strictly speculation based on a printed difference of opinion."

"Did he say the cops haven't talked to him?"

"He said that but he could be lying. I'll try to wheedle something about Kraft out of Manny Gouveia tomorrow morning."

"So what's next?"

"I write a story about my conversation with Mister Lysander Kraft, include some stuff saying that nobody knows anything about anything, you send the desk a picture of the ocean waves lapping at the shore and we go to the beach for the rest of the day."

And that's what we did, soaking up some late fall sunshine until returning in time for the five o'clock TV news, whereupon we learned that Dolly Brewster was still a missing person.

"How is she surviving without anybody taking care of her?" Dave said.

"I'm worried that she's not," I said.

The golden late fall sunshine in which we bathed on Sunday did not reappear on Monday morning. Low-hanging gray clouds covered the entire sky as we walked to Linda Jean's for breakfast. There wasn't even a patch of blue sky big enough to make a Dutchman's britches, as my grandmother used to say.

I had called said grandmother, and my mother with whom she lived, as I always do on Sundays and received their condolences for being "stuck out there on Martha's Vineyard." Can you imagine feeling sorry for someone who is being paid to spend his days at one of the country's elite vacation spots? Neither of them could imagine wanting to be anywhere other than dear old Minnesota, where they were both born and raised, and where they'd found husbands, borne their children and been widowed.

Not that I really wanted to be on Martha's Vineyard any longer. Martha Todd needed me at home and she'd told me so again when I'd called her right after talking to Mom and Grandma Goodrich. Neither Martha nor I had anything new to say about our current situations but somehow we talked for thirty minutes without stopping for breath.

My first call after breakfast Monday was my routine check with Detective Manny Gouveia about the Walter Jerome murder investigation. Gouveia was in his office and actually picked up his phone on the first ring, which was a good sign. His response to my question about progress was not so good. “I got nothin’ for the press at this time,” he said.

“Do you have any possible suspects, or even persons of interest?” I asked.

“We’ve talked to some people but I can’t say who.”

“Could one of those people be Lysander Kraft?”

“That arrogant little prick? Oh, shit, you did not hear that. I can’t say yes or no to your question.”

“I think you just said yes. I’ve talked to the charming Mister Kraft, too.”

“Are you stickin’ your nose in this case without talkin’ to me?”

“I’m calling all my possible news sources, including you, which is what reporters are paid to do.”

“You better not get ahead of yourself on this or you’ll wind up feelin’ sorry.”

“What if, instead of myself, I get ahead of you?”

“Not likely. But if you think you do, you damn well better let me know what you got or I’ll have your ass in a sling for withholdin’ evidence.”

“I always keep the police informed about what I know,” I said. “Just ask Homicide Detective Brown at the St. Paul PD.”

“I might just do that if you get in the way of my investigation,” Gouveia said.

“You’re welcome to call him. I’ll even give you his private number if you want it.”

“Not necessary. You got any more questions?”

“No, I guess not. Oh, yes, I do. Have you heard anything about the missing woman, Dolly Brewster?”

“Still ain’t found her as of an hour ago. It don’t look good; like maybe she walked off a dock into the water or somethin’. But that’s not an official statement.”

“I won’t report it as such. Thank you, detective. I’ll be talking to you later.”

“Have a great day,” said Manny Gouveia.

“Manny his usual cheerful and informative self?” Al asked when I put down my cellphone.

"He was Manny being Manny," I said. "But he did let slip enough to let me know he's talked to Lysander Kraft. Even got the same impression of him that I did."

"That was obscenely unfavorable, as I recall."

"You recall correctly. Now let's see what's happening with the big autopsy in Edgartown." I picked up the cellphone and punched in the Edgartown PD number.

Again it was answered by Officer Smithson. Again I asked for the chief. Again he was not in. "I think he's with the M.E. checking on Teddy Brewster's autopsy," Smithson said.

"That's what I'm trying to check on," I said. "Can you have the chief call me when he gets in?"

"I can give him your number but I can't promise he'll call you."

"Taking my number is a good start." I gave it and said goodbye.

"Have a good day," said Smithson. That's another of my pet peeves. Why are total strangers who don't give a hoot in hell about what kind of day you have always demanding that you have a good one?

I pondered what I knew about Walt Jerome. He was dead of arsenic poisoning from either his wine or his last meal, which had included fish. The only people I knew of who didn't like him were the Wampanoag casino backer and the potential casino developer. The only other person with a possible motive that I knew of was Teddy Brewster, who had brought Walt fish but was now dead of a cause that wouldn't be known until the results of an autopsy that seemed to be rather hurried were announced. I was at a stone wall with no way to climb over or go around it.

My cellphone rang. It was the Edgartown Police Department. I answered and was rewarded with the voice of Chief Morris Agnew. "Just want to let you know that we're having a press conference at one o'clock today to release the results of Teddy Brewster's autopsy," he said.

"Is it really that newsworthy?" I asked.

"Suspected homicides usually are," the chief said. "See you at one?"

"I'll be at the head of the line," I said after recovering from a momentary loss of jaw control.

"Have a good day," the chief said. Well, good or bad, my day was looking a lot more interesting than I'd imagined it would be.

21

DÉJÀ VU AGAIN

The crowd in the small Edgartown Police Station conference room was elbow-to-elbow by quarter to one. Along with the three of us, the room held Alison Riggs of the *Martha's Vineyard Chronicle;* a surly and silent young man Alison told us was from the *Vineyard Voice*, the island's other weekly; the TV team we'd seen reporting for Channel Four; an additional Boston TV crew from Channel Seven; and a young woman reporter from the *Cape Cod Review*, a daily paper that covered all of the towns on the Cape and the islands of Nantucket and Martha's Vineyard. It was warm and summerlike outside, and it was even warmer inside the room, where the body heat from the media animals pushed the temperature close to eighty degrees, and not everyone's deodorant was working one hundred percent.

"Hope this goes fast," Al said. "I've been in football locker rooms with better-smelling air."

"Don't kick about it," I said.

"Be a sport," Dave said.

Chief Agnew and Dr. Edward Newman stepped out of the chief's office at a minute past one and everyone began firing off questions. Agnew shook his head, held up his hands for silence and waited until the cacophony died before introducing the doctor. "Please hold your questions until after Dr. Newman finishes with his statement," Agnew said.

The doctor stepped forward and read from a sheet of paper. "This is the report of an autopsy on Theodore Ronald Brewster, also known as Teddy Brewster, age sixty-seven, whose body was found on Wednesday afternoon, October eleventh, in a tent on Chappaquiddick."

"Looked more like *seventy*-seven," Al whispered.

"That was my guess," I said.

"Hush," said Dave.

Dr. Newman kept talking: "The time of death is believed to be approximately twenty-four hours earlier, on Tuesday, October tenth, between noon and six p.m."

"Just the day before we found him," I whispered.

"The cause of death is found to be poisoning by the ingestion of arsenic." The doctor paused for dramatic effect after that announcement and several people obliged by gasping or murmuring something unintelligible.

"Turns out that what killed Walt *is* contagious," Al whispered during the pause.

"Almost an epidemic," I whispered.

"Hush," Dave said. "Listen."

"During the autopsy I found traces of red wine on the deceased's lips and a quantity of red wine in his stomach, along with substantial amounts of arsenic in his stomach and in his bloodstream," Dr. Newman said. He stopped again and scanned his audience, and the questions began to fly.

"Who'd want to kill him?" "Was the wine bottle with him?" "Were there any fingerprints?" "Could he have killed himself?" "Are there any suspects?"

The M.E. stepped back and motioned for the police chief to take over. Agnew stepped forward and again held up his hands for quiet. When the volley of voices ceased, he said, "Let me take these one at a time. First of all, I have no idea who would want to kill Teddy Brewster. Second, there was no wine or wine container anywhere on the premises or in the woods surrounding the campsite. When I examined the body in the tent, I saw what I thought might be red wine residue on his lips; that's why I called for the hurry-up autopsy and had the area thoroughly searched. There are no fingerprints and no suspects, and I doubt very much that Teddy or anybody else would choose arsenic as a method of ending his own life."

I waved a hand high above my head and Agnew pointed at me. "Do you believe there's a connection between this murder by arsenic and the recent murder of Walter Jerome by the same method?" I asked.

"We've set up a meeting with Oak Bluffs police to discuss that possibility," Agnew said. "The land upon which Teddy was camping was owned by Walter Jerome and subsequently by one of Mister Jerome's heirs, whom I believe is in the room right now." He looked toward where Dave was standing—or, rather, where Dave had been standing. At the mention of Teddy's connection with Walt, Dave had begun slipping through the crowd like an eel slithering out of a fisherman's grasping hand. He had reached the exit and was just closing the door behind himself when Agnew made his visual gesture.

All media eyes focused on Al and me. "I'm afraid you're wrong, chief," I said. "Elvis has left the building."

The *Cape Cod Review* reporter spun, wedged her way through the two TV crews and went out the door Dave had recently closed. The two TV reporters, with microphones in hand, bolted through the door behind her, followed by the two men bearing cameras. The reporter from the *Vineyard Voice* was next to depart, leaving Al and me alone with the chief, the M.E. and Alison Riggs.

I turned to Alison. "Aren't you going to chase him?"

"The next edition doesn't go to press until Thursday night," she said. "I've got three days until my deadline and I'm betting Mister Jerome will cooperate with me sometime during those three days."

"He's one of your designated three stooges," I said. "Maybe he'll only say 'nyuk, nyuk.'" I made a circular motion with my fist two inches above her head, air mimicking a favorite action of the real Three Stooges on film.

"I told you I was just kidding around about that cutline. Can't you guys take a joke?"

"I'm not speaking for Dave. He may be deeply hurt by your callous name calling."

"Well I'm willing to bet he's a better sport than you are. I'll be seeing you in Oak Bluffs for an interview either tonight or tomorrow." She turned toward Chief Agnew and asked if the press conference was over. He allowed as how it was, took the doctor by the elbow and disappeared through the door behind them.

"Thanks a lot," I said to Alison. "I had a couple more questions."

"Nyuk, nyuk," she said. She reached up and made a circular motion with her fist in full contact with the top of my head before turning away and following the troops out the door.

"Wasn't that sexual assault?" I asked Al.

"You should be so lucky," he said. "Let's see if we can rescue Dave." I followed him out of the room and out of the police station. Milling about in the small parking area in front of the building were the two Boston TV crews and the two local newspaper reporters who'd dashed out the door chasing Dave. Alison Riggs was getting onto a bicycle at the foot of the station steps.

"Where's Dave?" Al yelled.

"Don't know," said Channel Four.

"No sign of him," said Channel Five.

"Vanished," said the *Cape Cod Review*.

"Must be hiding in the van," Al whispered.

All the reporters except Alison, who was on her bike and rolling toward the street, began walking toward us.

"Let's get out of here," I said. We started walking briskly toward the van. The reporters started to walk faster. We broke into a trot and made it to the van several steps ahead of the Cape Cod woman, who was the fastest of the pursuers. As I've noted previously, she was young—probably just out of college and possibly a member of the women's track team.

"Get in quick," I said.

"It's locked," Al said. "You got the keys?"

"Dave has the keys."

We looked in the windows and banged on the doors of the van

but we saw nobody inside and the doors did not open. Seconds later we were surrounded by reporters and cameras.

"We're screwed," Al said. He banged on the right front door again.

It still did not open.

"Just act dumb," I said.

"No need to act," said Al.

22

MEDIA VS. MEDIA

Al and I became the unwilling subjects of a media event. Who were we? Where'd we come from? Why were we here? What was our relation to the Jerome family? Why were we involved with Teddy Brewster? How did we happen to find Teddy's body?

The last question, how we happened to find Teddy's body, came from the *Cape Cod Review* reporter, who had identified herself as Gretchen Miller. "You can read about that in detail in last Friday's *Martha's Vineyard Chronicle*," I said. I followed that endorsement by looking at the surly guy from the *Vineyard Voice*, whose weekly edition had already been on the newsstands at the time of the discovery. He promptly gave me the universal one-finger salute. I acknowledged the signal with a grateful nod. I had taken a dislike to the guy without having a tangible reason and now he'd given me one.

"Who do you think killed those men?" asked Channel Four.

"Not a clue," I said.

"Do you think the same guy killed them both?" asked Channel Seven.

"Yes, but that's purely a guess on my part. The cops may tell you something different after they meet and compare notes."

"Have you ever covered a murder before?" Miller asked.

"Way too many of them," I said.

"Including four others right on this island," Al said.

That was a mistake. It opened up a whole new round of questions about when those murders took place and who was killed and where were they killed and who were the killers. Only David Hudson from Channel Four, who had a fringe of gray hair at his temples, remembered the treasure hunter killings and nobody remembered the earlier set of murders involving two victims who'd been visiting the historic Martha's Vineyard Campground.

Young Ms. Miller allowed as how this was the first murder she'd ever heard of on Martha's Vineyard. "What do you do when you're covering a murder?" she asked.

"Same thing you always do," I said. "Talk to your police sources every day and look for new people with fresh information. It's called reporting."

I was facing the police station and, looking beyond the reporters and photographers standing in front of me, I saw the front door of the station open and a familiar face peer out. The face's owner waved a hand in a quick come-hither motion. The hand and face disappeared and the door went shut.

"Now if you'll excuse us, I've just remembered that I left something in the police station," I said. "I have to go back in and get it. Come along with me, Al. Nice talking to you folks. Have a good day." I couldn't resist uttering one of my pet peeve lines as I walked away from a group of people whose day—good, bad or indifferent—I didn't give a rat's ass about.

"What did you leave in there?" Al asked as we neared the front steps.

"A friend with a car key," I said. "Dave just stuck his head out the door and waved for us to come in."

"He's in the station?"

"What could be safer?"

"He was probably eating donuts while that mob was grilling us."

"Let's see if his story is full of holes."

We went inside and found Dave standing in front of the duty officer's desk. And yes, he was in fact munching on a donut—one with chocolate frosting no less.

"Welcome to serenity," Dave said.

"How'd you dodge the troops that were chasing you?" I asked.

Dave pointed to a door opposite the door to the conference room. "I ran like hell and hid in the jail," he said. "No questions asked in there."

"And they gave you donuts?" I said.

"That was the officer here at the desk. And this was the last one in the box. Sorry."

"You'll be the sorry one of if you run off and leave us to face the music again," Al said.

"I'm sure you guys did a wonderful job of dancing to the tunes, what with your journalistic experience and all."

I peeked out the front door. There were no bodies standing in the parking lot and the Channel Seven truck was just turning out onto the street. "Olly, Olly oxen in free," I said. "If you don't come now, you're it."

During the drive back to Oak Bluffs, I called Don O'Rourke at the *Daily Dispatch* city desk and told him about the autopsy report on Teddy Brewster. He asked if the police thought the two murders were connected and I said that they would be meeting to talk about that possibility later today.

"What did Don say?" Al asked when the phone conversation ended.

"He wants a story right away," I said.

"That's all?"

"Oh, yeah, one other thing: He wants us to stay for at least one more day. No flight home until Wednesday."

"Damn," said Al.

"My sentiments exactly. I hate to think what Martha's going to say."

Al turned to Dave, who was driving. "What are you going to do?"

"I guess I'm staying with you," Dave said. "Walt was my uncle and you guys are here because of me."

"Good choice," I said. "We'd have locked you in a closet if you'd tried to go home."

"All for one and one for all," he said.

"Ah, yes," I said. "The three stooges of Chappaquiddick."

When we reached Oak Bluffs, we made another trip to the car rental office.

"One more day," Dave said to Marty.

"I could give you the weekly rate and back it up to yesterday," Marty said. "It's twenty bucks a day cheaper that way."

"One more day is all we need," Dave said. "Just extend us one day at the daily rate."

"That'll be $129, plus the tax."

"That's the way we're going to do it."

"You're the boss," said Marty.

For more than a dozen years now I have been attending an Alcoholics Anonymous meeting with the same group in the same church basement on Grand Avenue in St. Paul every Monday night. I had not sought out a substitute meeting on our first Monday on the Vineyard because I didn't feel a need to interrupt the pleasant time I was having with my wife and best friends at a world-famous vacation spot. Now it was Monday again, and after the Teddy Brewster bombshell and the beleaguered session with the news media I felt the need for either a drink or the reinforcement of an AA meeting.

A meeting seemed like much the wiser choice, so I scanned our copy of the *Chronicle* to see if any were available. I was fortunate enough to find one listed for a church only a few blocks away in Oak Bluffs. It was an early meeting—6:00 p.m.—so I told Al and Dave that I'd be late for supper and hiked off to the church.

I arrived just as the meeting was about to begin. All the chairs were filled, but a man rose quickly, dragged a metal folding chair out of a closet and set it up for me. I thanked him, sat down and scanned a circle of faces that truly were anonymous to me. All except one, that is. Seated directly opposite me on the other side of the semi-circle was Alison Riggs.

Our eyes met, but Alison gave no sign of recognition and we both quickly looked down at our laps.

Some fifteen minutes later, when the moment seemed appropriate, I rose and said, "My name is Mitch and I am an alcoholic. I came here tonight because I am far from my home and my wife, and I've had the kind of a day that used to call for several rounds of bourbon on the rocks." I went on to explain my purpose for being on Martha's Vineyard and talked about the stressful events of the day. When I sat down again, it felt like a five-hundred-pound anvil had been lifted off my shoulders.

As I left the building after the meeting, I felt a hand touch the back of my left shoulder. I turned and was not surprised to find Alison Riggs half a step behind me.

"I was going to come and see you guys right after the meeting," she said. "Would that be okay with you?"

"Of course," I said. "And we won't tell anyone where we met."

"That was my next question. Or my next request, actually."

"You're one of the youngest people I've ever seen at one of these meetings."

"I got started early in life. Booze in high school; more booze and some pot in college. Lots of booze on my first job, from which I was fired for always being late or absent because of hangovers. I quit smoking pot on my own. That was easy because the smoke made me gag. But I couldn't give up the lovely floaty feeling I got from the alcohol. Finally, when my fiancé asked for his ring back, I decided it was time to get a grip on myself and I went for treatment. AA has kept me on the straight and narrow ever since."

"Did your fiancé come back?"

"While I was drying out he found somebody else. I see you're wearing a ring."

"Met her after I'd been sober for almost two years," I said. "Before that I was the town drunk, and the town was St. Paul, which has more than 300,000 people."

"I'm impressed. But not in a positive way."

"The positive way was the same as yours, through expert treatment and regular attendance at a wonderful chapter of AA."

When we were a block from the cottage I suggested that I go ahead and she come trooping along a few minutes later. She agreed, and the three of us were all sprawled in rocking chairs on the front porch—I was munching on leftover pizza—when she walked up the steps and said, "Hi, stooges, you got a minute to give a girl a story?"

"Nyuk, nyuk," I said.

23

STORM WARNING

We pulled up a rocking chair for Alison and she sat facing us with a notebook and a ballpoint in her hands. Dave offered her a paper cup of wine and she politely refused, saying she never drank while she was working. Or any other time, I said to myself.

We told her about our ordeal with the media in the police department parking lot and Dave answered several questions about himself, his uncle and his long-distance relationship with said uncle.

We gave Alison everything we knew about both murders and about the entwinement between Walt and the three Brewster family members. She couldn't get it into print until Friday, by which time we'd be back in St. Paul, but she'd have a leg up on the surly guy from the *Vineyard Voice* in the weekly duel between Martha's Vineyard's two newspapers.

When the conversation ended, Alison rose from her chair, we got up from ours, and she shook hands with each of us in turn. I was last in line and she gave my hand an extra pat, which didn't go unnoticed by my ever vigilant photographer pal.

"What was that about?" he asked when she was gone.

"What was what about?" I said.

"The little love pat on the hand."

"Who knows? Maybe Alison likes me best. It wouldn't surprise me; I'm a very likeable person when I'm not the one asking the questions."

"I report everything I see to Martha, you know."

"So report that I shook hands with a pretty young female reporter, just like you and Dave did. And speaking of Martha, I need to call her and see how her dad is doing."

"Hope he's not in jail."

"Me, too. I didn't know you could be arrested for having a heart attack."

"We live in heartless times," said Al.

Martha Todd said much the same thing when I called her a few minutes later.

"ICE is on a rampage to arrest more immigrants and get them out of the country," she said. "A story in the paper said their arrest rate is up fifty percent. They watch hospital admissions for people with African or Muslim-sounding names and go in and arrest them and look for something to charge them with after the fact. Linda is defending a couple of others besides Dad. One is a single mother who was driving to daycare with two little kids in baby seats. She was arrested after a minor traffic stop—she rolled through a stop sign the way a lot of people do, and the next thing she knew she was in handcuffs. The cop had called ICE while he was sitting in his squad car checking her driving record."

"What happened to the babies?"

"They were hauled off to Social Services, screaming their lungs out. Social Services eventually got them to their grandparents after a day full of phone calls and paper shuffling. And Linda got the mother out of jail, so the family is together with a court hearing coming up. Linda says the charge is bullshit, just like Dad's."

"What is he charged with, other than occupying space in an American hospital?" I asked.

"There's some technicality with his paperwork that they're trying to use to deport him," Martha said. "Linda says it's so minor that it could be a typographical error. You know, like you see in the newspapers."

"Not our newspaper."

"Oh, of course not. I meant the Minneapolis newspapers, where there's less quality control."

"And less reporting excellence."

"Less modesty, too, I assume."

"Much less. *Daily Dispatch* reporters lead the world in modesty."

"Some *Daily Dispatch* reporters have much to be modest about," she said.

"None that I know of," I said. "But modesty is a trait worth boasting about."

We continued chatting in this vein of silliness for another five minutes before making kissy sounds and saying good night. I felt better than I'd felt all day.

Dave turned on the TV news at eleven o'clock and we learned that Dolores Brewster was still missing on Cape Cod. The reporter did a brief standup interview with Toby Pilgrim, who was still in Hyannis helping with the search. This meant I wouldn't be talking to him about his half-brother's death before my next deadline.

"I hope nothing bad has happened to Dolly," Dave said. "I hope there isn't somebody out to get everyone connected to Uncle Walt."

"If there is, you could be next. But don't worry; we've got your back," Al said.

"I couldn't feel safer if I had an armed Secret Service guard on both sides of me. But I'm not going anywhere alone and I'm not drinking wine from any bottle but my own until they catch whoever is pouring the vintage with arsenic in it."

On that positive note, we went off to bed for what we were sure would be our penultimate night on Martha's Vineyard. I dreamt of swimming very slowly toward Hyannis in the cold waters of Nantucket Sound and woke up shivering. A chill breeze was blowing in through my open window, which faced the water I'd been dreaming about. I got up and closed the window down to a two-inch crack. It felt like Tuesday would not be a beach day.

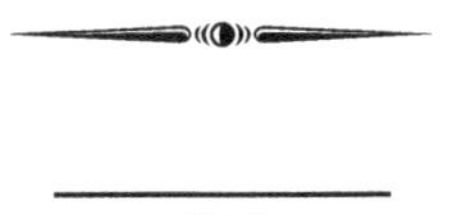

Tuesday definitely was not a beach day. As we left the cottage for breakfast, we found that the balmy warmth and sunny sky of Monday had been replaced by a temperature in the low forties, with a sharp wind blowing in from the water, underneath a low, solid ceiling of battleship gray.

"Nor'easter comin'," said the woman greeting customers and handing out menus at Linda Jean's. "Prob'ly hit right about supper time or a little later tonight."

"Are nor'easters really bad news?" Al asked. "We're not from around here."

"Nor'easters can cause all kinds of damage," she said. "Lotta wind and lotta rain. Prob'ly shut down the ferries for a while."

"Oh, don't say that," I said. "We've got to get to the airport in Boston tomorrow."

"The big Steamship Authority ferries that carry cars won't ever shut down, will they?" Al said.

"All depends on the sea state and the time," she said. "Better not give up your hotel room too quick." She handed us three menus, pointed to a table we could occupy and turned to greet a couple behind us.

"Just what we need," Al said. "A storm that shuts down the goddamn ferry."

"Hope the roof on your cottage is good and strong," I said to Dave.

"It's stayed on through a couple of hurricanes," Dave said. "It should make it through a mere nor'easter."

When we'd finished eating and were on our way out of the restaurant, I swung the door open and found myself face to face with a cute red-haired woman with a bright white smile. Directly behind her was an exact copy of face, hair and smile. Only the clothing was different; the one in the lead wore a short gray skirt and the other wore crisp white slacks.

"Ima and Ura," I said.

"You got that right," said the one closest to me.

"Which of you is which?" I asked.

"Neither one of us is a witch," said the other one.

"I mean, who's Ima and who's Ura?"

They pointed at each other. "She is," they said in unison.

"I give up," I said, holding the door open and backing up to give them room to enter. They bounced in and said "hi" to Al and Dave. I let the door swing shut and turned to look at the Jewell twins. Hoping my memory was accurate, I pointed to the one wearing the short gray skirt and said, "You're 'a da one dat's Ura."

"You gotta dat right," she said. "Gooda for you'a."

"How come you guys are still here?" Ima asked. "I thought you'd be long gone by now."

"Complications," Dave said. "We're leaving tomorrow."

"Better go off-island today like we are," Ima said. "Ferries might not be running tomorrow."

"Oh, don't say that," I said. "We need to get home."

"Well, we've got business in America tomorrow but we're catching a ferry today and staying in a motel overnight," Ura said. "You'd be smart to do the same thing."

"You have business in *America*?" I said.

"That's what we islanders call the mainland," Ima said.

"Well, we tourists have business here today," I said. "Have a nice trip to America."

"Thanks. We'll send you a postcard from Boston," Ura said. "You'll probably still be here when the mail comes Thursday. Bon non voyage." The closing door kept us from responding to that non-acceptable nugget of negativity.

"They've got to be wrong about the ferries shutting down," I said on the way back to Dave's cottage.

"I don't know," Dave said. "The twins seem to be singing the same tune as the greeter at Linda Jean's."

"Well, we need to play stop the music," I said. "Before we think about bugging out, I have to come up with a story for Don O'Rourke, which means I need to talk to both the Oak Bluffs and Edgartown investigators about the other set of twins—the twin killings of your Uncle Walt and his squatter pal, Teddy of Many Names."

"Think we should extend the car rental for another day?" Dave asked.

"Not yet," I said. "Let's hold off until we know for sure that the ferry will shut down."

"Which may be too late to change the plane tickets," Al said.

"That's Don's problem," I said. "We're on the paper's time, remember?"

"Speak for yourself," Dave said. "I think I'm still paying for my ticket and any penalties that go with the changes."

"Between plane tickets and car rentals you'll have to be tapping into your inheritance fortune to pay the credit card bill," Al said.

"I might just do that," Dave said. "Be a good way to test the Jewell sisters' withdrawal system. See how efficient they are."

"They said it would take five days to get money from the fund to you," I said.

"Five days would do it. I'd have the money in time to pay off the credit card," Dave said. "If we get stuck here for another day by the storm I just might give them a call. Do you remember what they call their business?"

"Wasn't it twin something?" Al said.

"No, it was double something," I said.

"That's it; Double Your Money," Dave said.

"Deuce of a name," Al said.

"Maybe I'll pull out twenty thou and take Carol on a trip to Hawaii," Dave said.

"Can we come along?" I asked.

"Not on my twenty thou," Dave said. "I can't give you free bedrooms there."

We had reached the cottage and it was time for me to put on my working face. I booted up the laptop, picked up my cellphone and called Oak Bluffs police. Guess what? Detective Gouveia was in a meeting. I left the requisite message and called Edgartown police.

Guess what? Chief Agnew was in a meeting. "It wouldn't be with Oak Bluffs police by any chance, would it?" I asked the woman who'd answered the phone.

"Not authorized to answer that," she said, not realizing that this was an affirmative response.

"Okay," I said. I gave her my number and asked her to have the chief call me when the meeting with Oak Bluffs was over. She did not challenge my assumption—merely wished me a good day and hung up.

"Think their combined brains will solve the murders before the ferries stop running?" Al asked.

"Two heads are better than one," I said. "Between them, they might know something about each victim that gives them the name of the killer."

"On the other hand, dead men tell no tales."

The phone in the kitchen rang. Dave picked it up. I heard him say "why," and then, "Okay, we'll be there."

Dave put down the phone and turned to Al and me. "The Edgartown cops want to talk to us," he said. "Sounds like they want to know where we all were at the time Teddy Brewster was taking his last drink of wine."

24

MORE Q'S AND A'S

In the Edgartown police station, they put us in three separate rooms with three different investigators. Dave was interviewed by Edgartown Police Chief Morris Agnew, Al was questioned by Edgartown Detective Aaron McGee and I drew my old buddy, Oak Bluffs Detective Manny Gouveia, as interrogator. He sat facing me across a metal table in a narrow room that served as the Edgartown PD's interrogation room. A tape recorder sat on the table between us. He informed me that the session would be taped and I shrugged my shoulders in a "so-what?" gesture.

"You don't really think any of us had anything to do with poisoning Teddy Brewster, do you?" I asked.

"I'm askin' the questions here, Mister Mitchell," Gouveia said.

"Just trying to save you some time, detective," I said.

"We conduct our investigations by eliminatin' people who might have been involved," he said. "You three ain't been eliminated yet."

"Well, by all means, let's get on with the elimination then."

"That's what I'm tryin' to do. How about for you to stop talkin' and to start answerin' my questions?"

I swallowed the urge to ask how I could answer his questions without talking and merely nodded my head in submission.

"Okay, then," he said as he turned on the tape recorder. "Where was you on Sunday, October eighth, and what was you doin' all day?"

I had to run the days backward through my head. Was Sunday, the eighth, the day we went to Chappy and first met Teddy? Yes, it must have been. God, that was nine days ago; our third day on Martha's Vineyard. Had we really been here for twelve days? What had happened to "just a few days?"

"We had breakfast at Linda Jean's, all three of us and our wives," I said. "Then we drove to Chappaquiddick to check out the woodland that Dave inherited from his uncle, Walter Jerome. All six of us went. We planned to hit the beach after looking at the land. You don't think we and our wives poisoned Teddy that day, do you?"

"Like I said before, I'm askin' the questions," Gouveia said. "Did you see Mister Brewster that day?"

"We did. He crawled out of his little tent and stood up nearly naked with a nasty-looking knife in his hand and told us to *git off this proppity*, quote and unquote."

"What was your response to that?"

"I had no verbal response. Dave did most of the talking. He informed Mister Brewster, who eventually identified himself as Teddy Kennedy, that he, Dave, was the new owner of the property and told him, Teddy, that he would have to move his tent and his vehicle off the property because he, Dave, planned to sell the land."

"How did Mister Brewster respond to that?"

"He said he had squatter's rights and would take Dave to court if he tried to sell what he called the *proppity*."

"How did Mister Jerome respond?"

"He told Mister Brewster that if he did not vacate the property he would have the Edgartown police remove him."

"After that, did Mister Brewster say he'd get off the property?"

"He did not. He repeated his threat to sue. Then he made a move toward us with the knife, so we got back in our van and drove to the Edgartown police station, where we met Chief Agnew. We told him about our encounter with Teddy Kennedy and the chief informed us of the man's real name, Teddy Brewster. The chief also told us that Mister Brewster sometimes called himself Teddy

Roosevelt and that he might actually try to sue Dave because he had a cousin who was a lawyer."

"Yeah, that's right. Toby Pilgrim is a lawyer."

"Except the so-called cousin, Toby Pilgrim, is actually a half-brother."

"How do you know that they're half-brothers and not cousins?"

"I'm a reporter. I ask questions, just like you do."

"So what else did Chief Agnew say to you?" Gouveia asked. "Did he say he'd kick Teddy, uh, Mister Brewster, off the property?"

"It sounded like the chief hoped he wouldn't have to do that," I said.

"Did he say he wouldn't never do that?"

"No."

"So did you go back to Chappy and talk to Mister Brewster again that day?"

"No. We went back to Oak Bluffs, had a happy hour on the porch, went to dinner and came back and watched the Red Sox lose a playoff game to the Indians on TV. Then we all went to bed. End of story." I put my hands on the table, ready to push back and stand up.

"Not quite," Gouveia said, motioning me to remain seated. "Where were you on Tuesday, October tenth?"

"Isn't that the day the M.E. thinks Teddy Brewster was killed?

Gouveia's face flushed red. "Like I said a dozen times already, I am askin' the questions here. Where were you and what did you do that day?"

"Okay, let me think a minute," I said. "As I recall, that was a really busy day. I think it started with breakfast at Linda Jean's. Yes, I'm sure it did. I remember that morning because it was the first time we didn't have to wait in line outside the restaurant."

"Lucky you."

"Well, it was good because we were kind of on a schedule. Dave and Cindy had an appointment to meet with Walt Jerome's lawyer, Richard Rylander, that morning. It wasn't a beach day, so the other four of us tagged along, which kind of flustered Rylander."

"Did Rylander let you sit in on a meetin' with his clients?"

"Actually, Walt was the official client, and he was in no shape to protest."

"Very cute, Mister Mitchell. So how long was you there?"

"Long enough to be introduced to Walt's financial advisers, the Jewell sisters, Ima and Ura. There was paperwork to sign with them in order to transfer Walt's IRA fund to Dave and Cindy. When that was finished, we walked back to the cottage, and who was there waiting for us but Detective Manny Gouveia, who insisted that Dave go with him to the police station for questioning."

"I was doin' my job. What did you do while I was interviewin' Mister Jerome?"

"Let me think," I said, trying to recall what happened on which day. "Okay, I remember. Al and I walked over to Walt's next door neighbor, whose name is Ozzie, and chatted with him about anything he might have seen the day Walt was poisoned."

"Why did you question the neighbor about that?" Gouveia asked.

"Because we were working on a news story for our paper. I'm a reporter and Al's a photographer, remember?"

"I do remember you two gettin' in the way when I was investigatin' a homicide back a few years ago."

I was pretty sure he also remembered us solving the case before he did, which was the reason for his attitude. "Nine years ago, to be exact," I said. "Anyhow, we talked to Ozzie for a while and then went back and sat on the porch waiting for you to bring Dave back."

"After that, did you go back to Chappaquiddick to talk to Mister Brewster?"

"No. Actually we went to the Vineyard hospital to talk to Walt's housekeeper, Dorie Brewster. The receptionist and the head of security at the hospital can vouch for the amount of time we spent there."

"Why did you want to talk to Ms. Brewster?"

"As you very well know, she's the one who found Walt's body and called 911. Her first-hand account was background for my story."

"Where did you go after that?"

"Back to the cottage. We had a happy hour and listened to the tape of Dave's meeting with Dorie."

"He taped that?"

"He did. So that all of us could hear what she said."

"That might be against the law, Mister Mitchell."

"Dorie knew she was being taped and the tape was not quoted verbatim in my story. There's nothing illegal about it."

"That remains for me to check out with the district attorney. So what else did you do that day?"

"It was close to dinner time when we finished listening to the tape. We had a quick happy hour, went to the City, Ale & Oyster for hamburgers, took a short walk to shake them down and then went back to the cottage. We turned in early because we planned to get up early the next morning to pick up and scatter Walt's ashes and get on a ferry in time to catch a bus to the airport."

"The Boston airport?"

"Yes. We had tickets to go home to Minnesota that day."

"But you're still here. Why is that?"

"Boss's orders. He told Al and me to stay a while longer to continue covering the investigation of Walt's murder. *Now* end of story?"

"No way. Now let's talk about Wednesday, October eleventh. Tell me where you went and what you did before you had your happy hour that day."

That, of course, was the day we found Teddy's dead body in his tent.

"That was another busy day," I said. "As I just said, we were supposed to go to Vineyard Haven, get Walter Jerome's ashes and scatter them in a place he'd directed, catch the 1:15 ferry in Oak Bluffs, get on a bus to the Boston airport and fly home. As it turned out, our boss in St. Paul ordered Al and I to stay a couple of days longer to cover the story of Walt's murder, and the funeral home didn't have the ashes ready to scatter, so Dave had to stay an extra day also. We walked our wives to the ferry and they went home without us."

"So what did you do the rest of the day?"

"I'm sure you know that we went to Chappy to see if Mister Brewster was still squatting on Dave's land and we found his dead body in the tent."

"Was you surprised to find him dead?"

I stared into Gouveia's eyes for nearly a full minute before I answered. "Oh, no, he'd called us from his tent and said he was dying, please come pick up the body. Of course we were surprised, for god's sake."

"Just answer the questions, Mister Mitchell. Ain't no need to get snotty."

"Ain't no need to ask that kind of question, detective."

"I'll decide what kind of questions to ask, Mister Mitchell. My next one is: what did you do when you found the body in the tent?"

"We called the Edgartown cops and told them where we were and what we'd found. We talked to them when they came and we followed them to the station when they left and we gave them our statements when we got there."

"What did you do after that? Was it time for another happy hour?"

"Actually, we talked to a reporter named Alison Riggs, and I suggested that she call you and ask about Walt Jerome's murder. When we got back to Oak Bluffs we all called our wives and told them about finding the body. I don't remember having a happy hour that night."

"Why not? I'd think that Mister Jerome would be happy that his problem with Mister Brewster was solved."

"You can think what you like, but Mister Jerome is not the kind of person who rejoices in somebody's death, problem or no problem. Are we done now?"

"I believe we are," Gouveia said. "You're free to go, but I'd like for you to call me before you leave the island."

"I guarantee I'll be calling you for a report on your progress in solving the murders of Walt Jerome and Teddy Brewster. Which reminds me, what progress have you made?"

"We've prob'ly cleared a possible person of interest in the Brewster homicide, which is yourself. If your friends are lucky we'll have cleared two more."

"And?"

"And nothin'. That's my answer."

"So you've made no progress except to clear three people who you knew damn well weren't involved in either murder?"

"Talk to Chief Agnew or Detective McGee. Maybe they got something I don't have."

"I will. But I've got one more for you. Have you got any idea what might have happened to Mister Brewster's mother, Dolly Brewster?"

"That ain't my jurisdiction," he said. "That's Hyannis's problem."

"Do you think her disappearance could be linked to the murders of Walt Jerome and Teddy Brewster?"

"I don't think about her disappearance at all. Like I said, that's Hyannis's problem."

"Doesn't your curiosity as a detective ever extend across Nantucket Sound?"

"I only deal with what's in my town. Only reason I'm sittin' here now is that Chief Agnew sees a link between his homicide and mine, and he asked me to help with the interrogation."

"Are you saying you don't see a link between the two?"

"No, I ain't sayin' that. If I didn't agree with the chief I wouldn't be here."

"So you do see a link?"

"I said I agree with Chief Agnew. Now how about you haulin' your butt outta here? Your buddies are prob'ly waitin' for you."

"I'll be checking with you tomorrow morning just before we leave," I said. "We'll be going on the 10:30 ferry."

"I don't think you will," Gouveia said. "There's a nor'easter comin' and the ferries won't be runnin' till a lot later in the day."

"Don't say that. I don't want to miss that flight."

"You don't wanna be on a ferry on fifteen-foot seas in eighty-mile-an-hour winds either." He got up, went to the door, opened it and turned back toward me. "Have a good day," he said, and walked away. He left the door open behind him, and left me again wondering why people who don't give a good goddamn in hell about what kind of day you might have always order you to have a good one.

I followed Gouveia out of the room and found Al, Dave and Chief Agnew standing near the front door. "Everybody eliminated?" I asked.

"Is that what we are?" Al said.

"So said Detective Gouveia," I said.

"Are we eliminated, chief?" Al said.

"Whatever you want to call it," Agnew said. "You're all free to go, but before you go back to Oak Bluffs you might want to go out to Chappy and take down that tent. There's a nor'easter coming and it might get blown away."

"So let it blow," Dave said. "Why would I care?"

"You'd care because there's a hundred dollar fine for littering and we wouldn't have any problem locating the current owner of that tent if we found it somewhere it didn't belong."

Dave sighed. "Well, blow me down. I guess it's Chappy for us. Come on guys."

We got into the van, drove to the On-Time ferry, made the crossing and drove to the clearing in the woods. The Landrover stood in its usual parking spot, but the ground was flat and bare where we'd last seen the tent.

25

STORMY WEATHER

"Must have blown out into the woods," Dave said. The wind was swirling around in the underbrush and swishing through the pines, but it didn't seem strong enough to blow away a tent that had been staked in all summer.

"Let's look around for it," Al said. "Don't want you to get hit for another hundred bucks."

"God knows I've spent enough money this week," Dave said.

"It's been almost two weeks," I said.

"Feels like two months," said Dave.

We split up and traipsed through the underbrush looking for the tent. When we reconvened in the clearing twenty minutes later the tent was still missing.

"Okay, now we've got a missing tent as well as a missing Dolly," Al said.

"You think somebody stole the stupid tent?" Dave said.

"Who'd steal a ratty old thing like that?" I said.

"Maybe the same guy who'd poison a ratty old man like Teddy," Al said.

"At least they didn't take the Landrover," Dave said.

"Actually, taking the Landrover would have been a service," I said. "You're going to have to move it and park it somewhere before you can sell this land."

"Wonder if there's a junkyard on Chappy," Dave said.

"Land's too expensive here to waste it on a junkyard," I said.

"Want to move it now?" Al said. "You could drive it to Oak Bluffs and we'll follow in the van."

"Wonder where the key is," Dave said.

I opened the driver side door and looked inside. "It's in the ignition," I said. "Guess old Teddy wasn't worried about anybody stealing it."

"Why would somebody take the tent and leave the Landrover?" Al asked.

We soon found out why. Dave slid into the driver's seat and turned the key. There was no sound from under the hood. "Battery's dead," Dave said.

"If there is a battery," Al said.

"Pop the hood," I said.

Dave searched under the dash for the hood release and finally found it. The hood sprang loose and Al raised it all the way. "There is a battery. Looks pretty shitty but we could give it a jump and see if it's got any life. Are there any jumper cables in the van?"

I opened the tail gate of the van and saw nothing in the cargo space. I raised the carpeted floor of the cargo space and discovered a doughnut-style spare tire, a lug wrench and a jack. No jumper cables.

"Guess we can't do it today," I said.

"This old wreck can sit here until next summer as far as I'm concerned," Dave said. He removed the key from the ignition, then changed his mind and stuck it back in. "Maybe I'll just call somebody today and have them tow it."

"Cheaper than flying out here again," Al said. "Assuming there is a junkyard anywhere on Martha's Vineyard."

"You can ask your friendly naked lawyer about that. Let's get back to Oak Bluffs so I can write a story about the island cops having no clues about two homicides and the mainland cops having no clues about a missing woman with Alzheimer's," I said. "We're producing so little in the way of copy and photos that Don's sure to let us get on that plane tomorrow."

"If we can get to the airport," Al said. "People keep telling us the storm will knock out the ferry service."

"I'm ready to swim for it," I said.

"Good luck paddling against the wind," Al said. "I assume the wind comes from the northeast during a nor'easter and we're south of the Cape."

"Well, blow me down, I'll just have to paddle harder."

"Might be a good idea for us to get in the van and get back to Edgartown before the On-Time Ferry shuts down," Dave said. "The wind is picking up right now."

"Which means it'll be letting us down tomorrow," Al said.

The water in the channel between Edgartown Harbor and Nantucket Sound was noticeably rougher on the ferry ride back to Edgartown proper. In Oak Bluffs, white caps as wide as our living room dotted the water, waves as high as my chin were crashing onto the beach and the American flag above the cottage porch steps was flapping so hard it sounded like rapid-fire gun shots. Swimming to the Cape, which was not a realistic option for me on the calmest of days, did not look like a viable plan for even a trained English Channel swimmer.

Don O'Rourke was not pleased with the story I wrote as I sat on the porch with the wind blowing my hair straight back. Not even the first-person account of us being questioned by the police satisfied him. His return email said, as I had predicted, that we were not producing enough real news to warrant our staying on Martha's Vineyard any longer.

I replied that we might not have a choice and gave him the weather report and the dire predictions from long-time island residents about a probable ferry shutdown. He suggested that we get off the island today and spend the night in a motel room on the mainland. I asked if the paper would pay for this room. He said yes. I said we'd try to do that and he said fine, have a good day. I said it wasn't looking all that great and he said to call him when we were safely on the mainland. At last, here was somebody who actually did care about what kind of day we were having.

I felt something wet spray across my face and I looked up from the computer on my lap to see that it was raining. The drops were slanting sideways at a forty-five-degree angle and blowing onto the porch. This was going to be a very uncomfortable ferry ride.

I got up and went inside. Al and Dave were in the living room watching the national Weather Channel on TV. "What's the word?" I asked.

"Nor'easter coming to New England," Dave said. "Give you something to write about besides arsenic and old men."

"What the heck makes a nor'easter a nor'easter?" I said. "Minnesota readers won't know what I'm talking about."

"Search me," Dave said. "I have no clue why this storm has got a special name."

I needed to find the answer but I didn't know where to look. "Maybe Dave's naked lawyer could tell you," Al said.

"Ah, yes, he should have the bare facts," I said. "Dave, what's his number?"

Dave gave me both Dick Rylander's office and cellphone numbers. I tried the office and got his voice mail. I had better luck with the cell. "Hey, Dick, this is Mitch Mitchell, Dave Jerome's friend. We're leaving the island today to get ahead of the storm and we've been wondering why this kind of storm is called a nor'easter. Can you tell me that?"

"It's because of the location of the storm," Rylander said. "Most of our storms come from the north or the west. A nor'easter comes up from the southwest and spins counterclockwise, so the winds blow into the northeast."

"*Into* the northeast and not *out* of the northeast?" I said.

"Right. Cold air from the north that gets pushed south by the jet stream and meets warm air from the Gulf of Mexico, and the storm floats north, getting stronger as it goes. That's why New England generally gets the worst of it."

"Why the funny abbreviated name with the 'th' left out? Is that the way New Englander's have always pronounced it?"

"I don't know where that contraction came from, Mister

Mitchell. That's not really New England speak. Your traditional Yankee would just drop the 'Rs' and say 'nawth-eastah.'"

"That's what I thought," I said. "Thanks for the explanation. And Dave says thanks for your help with the legal stuff."

"Oh, you're very welcome," Rylander said. "I just hope you guys get home okay. You're smart to leave today; there won't be any ferries tomorrow until the wind dies down."

I explained nor'easter and nawth-eastah to Al and Dave and then went online looking for motels in Falmouth, where the ferry would be landing. The first five I checked had no vacancies. The sixth had one room with two beds. It also had taxi service from Falmouth Harbor. I suggested to Dave and Al that they could share a bed.

"Or you could sleep in a chair," Al said.

"If anybody sleeps in a chair it won't be me," I said.

"We can flip for it," Dave said. "Book the room and let's get going to the ferry."

"As long as it's you that we flip," I said. I booked the room for $129, plus the tax, and put it on my credit card, thinking that this was a number I'd heard somewhere before. I made a note to myself to put this on my expense account for the reimbursement promised by Don O'Rourke.

We packed our gear into the van and drove it back to the rental office through the windblown rain. As we checked the vehicle in, Dave pointed out to Marty that our total bill, plus the tax, added up to two-hundred dollars less than what it would have been for two weeks at the weekly rate.

"You didn't have it for two full weeks," Marty said.

"That's my point. We didn't need it for two full weeks."

"You're the boss," Marty said.

Wearing an inadequate assortment of foul weather gear we had found in the cottage's hall closet, we took our bags out of the van and plodded through an increasingly heavy rainfall to the Steamship Authority Terminal, which was two uphill blocks away. The gusts of wind that took turns hitting us from the side made it impossible to walk in a straight line.

We staggered like drunks up to the front door of the ticket office and stood under the eaves with the wind and rain at our backs. On the door was taped a handwritten sign that said: *All Oak Bluffs ferries now leave from Vineyard Haven.*

"What the hell?" Al said.

"Makes sense," Dave said. "Look at the water out there." Huge, white-capped waves were rolling through the unsheltered ferry slip at the end of the wide open pier where the Steamship Authority boats docked. "I think the docks in Vineyard Haven are in a harbor where the water's a lot calmer."

"So how do we get to Vineyard Haven without a car?" I asked.

"Taxi," Dave said. He had turned around and was pointing to the curb where two enterprising cab drivers were sitting in their seven-passenger vans. We hustled toward the leading van and the driver popped out to help us load our bags and clamber into the seats.

"Lots of business today?" I asked as the driver pulled away from the curb.

"Been keepin' busy," he said. "Oak Bluffs shut down after one boat this morning so we been makin' a lotta trips to Vineyard Haven."

The fare was ten dollars when we piled out of the cab at the Vineyard Haven terminal. I gave the driver a twenty and said, "Keep the change." Another item for my expense account. Through the rain we saw a ferry in the landing slip as we went to the terminal to buy tickets.

The waiting room was full of people in various types of wet clothing, but nobody was in the ticket line so I stepped up to a window at the counter. "One," I said to the agent behind the counter.

"Sorry, we're closed," the agent behind the counter said.

"What do you mean closed?" I said. "There's a ferry out there with people standing in line to get on it."

"Sorry, sir. That boat's sold out and there won't be any more today."

"How can that boat be sold out? It looks like it would hold a thousand people."

"Maybe it would, but the Coast Guard says it can only safely carry so many cars and so many people, and that's all we can put on her."

"So we're stuck here, even though there's open space on the ferry?"

"You're not alone," he said, pointing around the room and then waving toward the front door. Outside, about two dozen people were huddled under the awning at the foot of the front steps.

"I guess it's back to Oak Bluffs," I said to Al and Dave.

"Hope we can get a cab before dark," Dave said. "I assume that's what those people outside are waiting for."

"Maybe we'd have better luck with a bus," Al said.

We went out the back door and walked to the glass-walled, three-sided shelter for bus passengers, which was on a miniature traffic circle half a block from the terminal. The shelter, which rattled and vibrated in the wind like a wet dog shaking itself, was packed like the proverbial can of sardines with women and children. About a dozen wet and miserable looking men stood in the cold, slanting rain outside the shelter. We joined the group of dripping *les miserables* and hoped there'd be a number thirteen Oak Bluffs/Edgartown bus in sight before we melted, froze, blew into the harbor or drowned.

Fourteen minutes went by before a bus with the number thirteen flashing above the windshield penetrated the curtain of rain and stopped in front of us. The doors opened, front and middle. No one stepped off. Apparently the word about the cancellation of ferry service had gone out.

We joined the pack of people squeezing to get onboard the bus, hoping there'd be room for all three of us. We made it through the door and up the steps, deposited our money in the box beside the driver, grabbed onto steel poles and stood by the second row of seats. Seven more men got on and all of us standing in the aisle were shoved farther toward the back. At last the doors closed with a whooshing sound, and we started toward Oak Bluffs with a jerk that almost toppled the standees like a row of dominoes.

When we got to the Oak Bluffs stop we had to push our way to the exit because of course the people between us and the door were staying on the bus all the way to Edgartown. There was water spraying over the seawall as we walked to the car rental agency to once again renew the van. We found the lights off and the door locked at the agency. A placard in the window said CLOSED.

"Shit!" yelled Dave, who almost never let a curse word pass through his lips.

"Double that," Al said.

"Make it three," I said.

Off we went, the three stooges, slogging through the rain and wind toward Dave Jerome's eight-hundred-thousand-dollar cottage, which I had hoped never to see again. I was wearing a waist-length plastic rain jacket and a sailor hat with the brim turned down. My unprotected khaki pants were as soggy as a dishrag in a sink full of suds and my feet were squishing in my saturated canvas walking shoes. As a final insult, water was running off the downturned brim of the sailor hat and drizzling down my neck into the rain jacket. All three of us were leaning ninety degrees into a wind that blew clouds of rain drops into our faces with a force that stung like needles.

"Here's to our vacation in paradise," Dave said, raising a paper cup of wine after we'd all taken hot showers and put on dry clothes. Al and I joined the salute, Al with wine and me with my standard can of ginger ale. The rain was pounding against the living room windows and the cottage would occasionally shake from an extraordinary blast of wind.

"I don't suppose you can get a refund from that motel in Falmouth," Al said.

"Their website said no refunds," I said.

"If you called them and cancelled, they could probably rent the room again and maybe they'd give you a refund."

"And maybe pigs will fly."

"Hey, in this wind that could happen. We might have shakin' bacon."

"Or stork pork," I said.

The only thing on Boston TV was the storm, which was fine with us because the storm was our only interest. In addition to the ferries not running, Boston's underground transit system was being flooded, houses in several coastal cities were sliding into the sea and Logan International Airport was closed until further notice. Our next day's flight was certainly among the thousands that were being cancelled all up and down the east coast.

The only food left in the cottage was half a box of Triscuit and part of a block of cheddar cheese. We demolished both of them for our supper and continued to watch the TV weather reports. I tried to call Martha but I couldn't get a signal on my cellphone. On the TV screen, a man standing perilously close to a seawall over which mountainous waves were splashing was trying to make himself heard over the roar of the wind when the screen went dark and the room went black.

"Guess Mother Nature is telling us it's bedtime," Dave said.

"You can't fool Mother Nature," I said.

"She's one mean mother," said Al.

26

MAROONED

Sleep did not come easily that night. I'm not sure which was more effective at keeping me awake, the occasional shudder of the cottage when hit by a particularly robust gust of wind or the constant hammering of the raindrops against the window panes five feet from my bed. Normally when I have trouble dropping off I turn on a bedside lamp and read until I feel drowsy. Without a functioning lamp—I had found my way to bed by the light of a candle but I didn't choose to read by one candlepower of illumination—this option was not available.

What was available, in addition to tossing and turning, was an opportunity to think. As I lay in total darkness with no visual distractions, I ran through everything I knew about the murders of Walter Jerome and Teddy Brewster. First of all, the killings had to be connected, which eliminated the angry readers of Walt's anti-casino column as suspects. Why would such a person also kill a slightly loopy man in his late sixties who couldn't possibly affect the placement of a gambling casino?

Who else was there? I could understand Teddy poisoning Walt if he felt a threat of eviction, or Walt wanting to be rid of a pest like Teddy, but the former was far-fetched and latter was impossible given Walt's prior departure from this veil of tears.

And how did the disappearance of Dolly Brewster fit into this scenario? Did it fit in at all or was it mere coincidence? Was somebody systematically doing in the Jeromes and the Brewsters? Were Dave Jerome and Dorie Brewster and Toby Pilgrim all on some psychopath's hit list?

I had just concluded that I really knew nothing that would help identify the killer when I finally drifted away into dreamland. Fortunately, I did not find any Brewsters, Jeromes or Pilgrims waiting there.

When I woke at a few minutes past seven, the cottage was no longer rocking in the wind and the window panes were no longer being strafed with liquid bullets. The sky was still heavy with gray clouds, but they were releasing only a drizzle, not a downpour.

I reached over and flipped the switch of the lamp on my bedside table. The bulb remained unlit. We were still without power, which was no surprise. I hadn't imagined that electrical repairmen would be working on fallen wires through the night's intense forces of wind and rain. Still, I had to test the lamp. Human nature, I guess, like the need to confirm the message conveyed by a sign that says "wet paint" by testing its tactility with a finger.

I found Al and Dave already in the living room when I arrived there. The major topic under discussion was whether or not the restaurants on Circuit Avenue would have power. If they were out, we had a real problem with breaking our fast because without electricity we couldn't even boil water to make a pot of tea.

"It's barely raining," Al said. "We could walk over and look."

"Let's not get wet unless someone's open," Dave said. He went to the kitchen, thumbed through the pages of the directory beside the phone and found the number for Linda Jean's. He called on his cellphone and got an answer. Their power had been restored fifteen minutes ago and they would be open in another fifteen. The world was looking brighter.

Our next question was about the ferry service. Could we possibly get to the mainland in time to catch our flight in Boston? Dave called the Steamship Authority. This answer was not as welcome. "The earliest they expect to restore service is one o'clock this afternoon," Dave said. "That's about two and a half hours too late for us."

"I'll call Don," I said. It was an hour earlier in St. Paul but I knew our city editor would be at his desk. "City desk. What have you got?" was the way he answered the phone.

"Bad news is what I've got," I said. "This is Mitch. Because of the storm, we can't get a ferry off this island in time to catch our flight."

"Don't worry about it. I've got an email from Delta that says the flight is cancelled and that passengers can't reschedule until tomorrow. You might be stuck there until Friday. If you look at the news on TV this morning you'll see that airports along the entire east coast were closed last night and the flights across the whole country are backed up."

"I'd like to look at the news on TV but we are currently without the current that's required to operate a television set."

"You're power is out?"

"Went out in the middle of last night's news. This island could have blown farther out to sea and we wouldn't know about it."

"Haven't seen anything like that. As long as you're stuck there, give me a piece on your experience in the storm and have Al send some pix of the damage. Can you explain to Minnesota readers what the hell a nor'easter is?"

"Believe it or not, I can."

"Do that. Later on today I'll see what I can do about flying you home. Probably won't be able to reserve seats until tomorrow."

"I'll fly home standing in the aisle if they'll let me," I said.

"Probably not. They might be an Air Bus, but they don't have straps for standees to hang onto," he said. "Anyhow, send me something that people might read."

I relayed all this information to Al and Dave, and we got back into our rain gear, which hadn't totally dried, and started for Circuit Avenue. As we walked, I punched in my home number and Martha answered by saying, "Are you okay? I saw on TV that you had an enormous storm out there. They said something about there being no Easter, which made no sense to me."

I explained about nor'easters to her, assured her that we were physically fine and asked her about her dad.

"Would you believe it? Those bastards from ICE came around wanting to put an electronic tracking bracelet on his ankle, but Mom wouldn't let them in the house." she said. "Like the man's going to run away somewhere four days after a heart attack that almost killed him. Mom locked all the doors and called Linda, and she got a judge to issue an order for ICE to leave Dad free under his own recognizance."

"You're keeping Linda pretty busy."

"Like she needs more business. And she's doing it pro bono at that. I feel terrible about this whole mess, including getting Linda involved."

"You have to use all your resources, and Linda is a prime resource."

"I know that, but it still doesn't feel good."

"Any idea when this will get resolved?"

"Not really. Do you have any idea when you're coming home? I hear there's millions of people waiting for flights because of the ... what did you call it?"

"Nor'easter," I said. "For some reason that my source of information couldn't explain, they drop the T and the H from the word northeaster. And as far as getting home, Don is trying to book a flight for tomorrow. It might be midnight. Who knows?"

"Just so you get here," Martha said. "I don't care what time it is."

"Me, too. We're now at the door of our favorite restaurant so I'll say I love you and goodbye for now."

"Love you, too," she said. We both made kissy sounds to finish the call.

We were the restaurant's first customers of the day, and we obeyed a sign that instructed us to seat ourselves at a clean table. No problem there; all the tables were clean. A slender, thirtyish blond woman named Angie, who had served us at least half a dozen times, came to us with coffee pot in hand.

"We barely had time to get this hot," Angie said as she filled our cups.

"How long was your power out?" I asked.

"Went out sometime after we closed last night and came on a little after seven."

"So nothing spoiled?" I was thinking about the sausage I intended to order with my eggs.

"Oh, no. We've got a generator that kicks in and keeps the cooler cold," she said. "Nothing ever spoils in there. It's just that we don't have little things like lights and griddles and computers when the power is out."

I trusted her and ordered the sausage. While we ate, we talked about what we could do for a story and pictures. We decided to rent the van again and take a tour of the island so Al could get some good storm damage shots. I would write about our experience with the sold-out ferry and include an explanation of the word "nor'easter."

"Speaking of damage, did you check around the cottage this morning?" I asked Dave.

"I walked all the way around it and didn't see anything serious," he said. "Lot of sticks in the yard, and one big branch down in back, but the shingles on the roof all seem to be where they belong."

When we finished eating, we walked down the hill toward the harbor and the car rental office. We found a long portion of the low-lying east-west street under water, which forced us to walk up the hill toward the Steamship Authority office, circle around behind the bicycle, moped and car rental offices and approach our target from the seaward side. We found the office surrounded by two feet of water, but Marty had laid some wooden planks from the top step to the edge of the pool and we were able to wobble our way in. Marty did not seem surprised to see us.

"Back again," Dave said in a cheery voice. "Missed the last ferry that went out. Glad you've got power so you could be open for us."

"Ain't no power yet, but I got a generator runnin' so's I can process credit cards," Marty said. "You want the same van?"

"Unless you've got something cheaper," Dave said.

"All the same price unless you want a Mini-Cooper convertible. I can give you a heck of a deal on that little number."

"We'll take the van, thank you."

Because the air traffic situation could possibly keep us on the Vineyard until Friday, we had decided to rent the van for two more days—today and Thursday—at the daily rate of $129, plus the tax. Dave had done some calculating and discovered that he had already spent a total of $1,419, plus the tax, for eleven days of van rental. Two additional days would up that total to $1,617, plus the tax, which was $117 more than he'd have paid for two weeks at the $750, plus the tax, per week price. He was hoping Marty would not be aware of this.

"You're now spendin' more than the two-week rental fee but you still ain't had the car for two weeks," Marty said as he wrote out the slip. "This makes it thirteen days."

"We never thought we'd need the car for anywhere near two weeks, so it would have been foolish for us to take the weekly rate," Dave said.

"You're the boss," Marty said.

Before beginning our island tour, I called Oak Bluffs police and Officer Molina answered the phone. I identified myself and asked for Detective Gouveia. "The detective's not here," said Molina. "He's got a problem at home."

"Can I reach him there?" I asked.

"I can't give you his home number but I can give you his cell."

"Good enough." He gave me the number, I called it and Manny Gouveia answered with, "Yeah?"

"This is Mitchell," I said. "Anything new on the Jerome homicide?"

"Yeah, the killer called me and confessed." He paused, waiting for my reaction. When I offered nothing, he continued. "No, Mister Mitchell, I ain't got nothin' new except a pickup truck with a big fuckin' tree on its squashed down cab roof and chunks of glass from its windows scattered all over my driveway. I don't think I'm gonna have time to solve your friend's uncle's homicide today." He switched off without even wishing me a good day.

"Manny's having a bad storm day," I said, and told Al and Dave about the squashed pickup.

"Shall we truck on down and help him?" Al said.

"I don't think seeing us would pick up his spirits," I said.

Next I called Edgartown police and asked for Detective McGee. He was at his desk, but his response to my question about Teddy Brewster was equally negative, although it was given in a more polite way. "I just don't have any leads," he said. "Teddy didn't have any enemies that I know of. And I don't know if he had any friends outside his family except Walt Jerome. There's nobody I can talk to until they all get back from the Cape."

"Any word on the missing Dolly?"

"Still missing as far as I know. The TV news reports can probably tell you more than I know about that one. I just hope she was some place safe from the storm."

"Okay. I'll watch the news as soon as our power comes back."

"Good luck with that. There's power lines down all over the island."

We began our island storm tour with a trip to Edgartown, where we found a crew of men trying to disengage a large sailboat from a dock upon which it was tipped. Then we headed to the airport, where we found a crew trying to free a small single-engine plane from a fence it had been blown into. We went next to the harbor at Menemsha, where puddles of water rippled on the dock. Along the roadsides we saw dozens of downed or tipping trees and several fallen power poles. Every low spot was filled with water and Dave crept through the pools at idle speed because he wasn't sure how deep they were.

Back at the cottage, I wrote a story, running my laptop on battery, and Al sent half a dozen of his most dramatic images to the city desk. Don O'Rourke's email response to both the story and the pix was complimentary for the first time in many days.

"Couldn't get you a flight until Friday," Don said at the end of the email. "Take off time is 5:30 p.m." This was disappointing but not unexpected. That's why we'd taken the van for two days instead of one.

"Should have no problem making that," I replied. I should have signed it "Warren Mitchell, staff writer and eternal optimist."

27

AFTER THE STORM

We were sitting on the deck, consuming happy hour drinks and snacks and discussing what to do about the evening repast, when Dave noticed that the lightbulb in the lamp above our heads was lit. "Power's on," he yelled. We bounced up and scurried into the living room and turned on the TV to see what was on the five o'clock news.

The scene was shifting from one reporter to another as the cameras showed storm damage at eight sites, starting on Cape Cod and moving north along the shore of mainland Massachusetts all the way to the New Hampshire border. There were no scenes from Martha's Vineyard. "Guess their camera crew missed the last ferry to the Vineyard," Dave said.

Dave was about to switch channels when we heard a reporter standing in front of a red brick school building say, "There was one positive result of the storm here today in Hyannis, and that was finding a missing person."

"Leave it on," I said.

"An elderly woman who had been missing since Saturday, after apparently walking out of Hyannis Hospital, was spotted by a sharp-eyed lady in the storm shelter that had been set up here in the gymnasium of this high school," the reporter said. He turned and put the microphone in front of a middle-aged woman wearing a Red Sox cap. "It was Marian Alfonso who spotted the missing woman."

"Yes, I seen this elderly lady sitting at a table eating soup and I said to myself, I've seen that face on the TV," Marian Alfonso said. "I recognized her from the picture that I seen on your news program. I went right over to the gentleman in charge of the shelter and pointed her out and said to him that she looked like the missing woman from the hospital psych ward that everybody was looking for."

Reclaiming the microphone, the reporter said, "The woman has been identified as Dolores Brewster, a hospital patient suffering from symptoms of dementia, who has been the subject of a widespread search in Hyannis for four days. Ms. Brewster was accompanied at the shelter by another elderly woman who told police that last Sunday afternoon she found Ms. Brewster sitting on the beach near a small, rather primitive summer home the woman has there. She said Ms. Brewster told her that she was walking to her son's home to visit him but had lost her way when the sun went down. The woman, who has not been identified, said Ms. Brewster looked hungry and thirsty, so she took Ms. Brewster to her beachfront home, which has no electricity and no telephone.

"She said she was taking care of Ms. Brewster, intending to notify police on Tuesday, when emergency volunteers patrolling the beach warned her about the approaching storm. The volunteers said the house, which is an eighty-year-old wooden structure, might not survive the expected high winds and tides, and escorted both her and Ms. Brewster to the shelter in the school. Ms. Brewster has been returned to the hospital and reunited with family members who came from Martha's Vineyard to join in the search. This is Charles Goodwin, reporting live from Hyannis, Channel Seven." A true New Englander, he pronounced "Charles" without the inclusion of the letter "R."

"So it sounds like Dolly's okay," Dave said. "At least she is according to Chahles."

"That's good news," I said. "At least that eliminates the theory about Dolly's disappearance being part of a plot to wipe out all the Brewsters and their friends."

"Whose theory was that?" Dave said.

"Mine."

"That's crazy. Who'd kill an old lady with dementia?"

"Same person who'd kill two old men with arsenic."

"He's got you dead to rights, Dave," said Al.

"I still think it's crazy. With that theory, I could be in line to be killed."

"I was thinking that, too," I said. "I had you in line right after Dorie."

"The only thing I'm in line for is a humongous credit card bill for my extended stay on this vacation paradise," Dave said. "I can't put Carol's and my air fare, the cost of several days of extra meals and the van rental on an expense account for somebody else to pay."

"We could probably charge a couple of days of the van to the *Daily Dispatch*," Al said. "We've been using it for story purposes."

"Not worth the mixed-up paperwork," Dave said. "My name is on all the receipts."

"You could do what you were kidding about," I said. "Tap into your new inheritance."

"I'm seriously considering that. It would leave my savings account undamaged and provide a test of the Jewell sisters' proclaimed efficiency."

"So, give Double Your Money a call," I said.

"I'll do that right now." He took out his wallet, dug out the card the Jewell twins had given him and called the number. After four rings, it went to voice mail and instructed him to leave a message, which he did.

"They were on their way to the Cape," Dave said. "Must not be back yet."

"Obviously they didn't miss the last ferry off the Vineyard," I said. "Isn't there a cellphone number on that card?"

"No. Guess they don't want to be bothered outside of office hours."

"Well, there's strike one against their efficiency."

"I'll try again tomorrow morning. See if they're back."

After hamburgers at City, Ale & Oyster, I worked up the courage to call Martha Todd and tell her we wouldn't be home until Friday.

"That would be this Friday, October twentieth, during this current year of our lord?" Martha said.

"Be our good lord willin' and the crick don't rise again," I said.

"That would be special," she said. "I'll mark it on my calendar with a gold star."

"You're in a pleasant mood. More problems with ICE?"

"What else? The bastards notified my dad that he must have a one-way ticket to Cape Verde by a week from today. He's recovering from a heart attack, for god's sake, and they're ordering him to get on an airplane and fly for twelve or thirteen hours to a place where he has no home and no family. He's been in this country for sixteen years and has actually been approved for a green card. The only reason he doesn't have it is because there's a huge backup because of a personnel shortage caused by budget cuts, with that money probably going to the knuckleheads at ICE who are trying to clear the country of people with dark skin."

"What did Linda say about this ridiculous order?"

"She's going before a judge tomorrow to request that the order be rescinded. She will argue that Dad is legally eligible to remain in this country because of the pending green card."

"Will she win?"

"Who knows? You'd think the green card approval would clinch it, but you never know what a judge will decide."

"Wish I was there to hold your hand through all this."

"You'd be holding a lot more than my hand, sweetie. All I can say is you'd better be on that airplane Friday."

"Wild horses couldn't keep me from making that flight. If the ferries aren't running I'll paddle to the mainland in a kayak."

"Well, there's certainly no other reason for you to stay there. I've been reading your stories, and I haven't seen reports of any progress by the cops on Walt's murder—or the other guy's either."

"Both Oak Bluffs and Edgartown are totally stumped," I said. "These might have been the perfect crimes."

"Fifty years from now someone on his death bed will confess to those two killings," Martha said.

"I wish I could be there to report on it."

"You can read about it in the rocking chair in your nursing home. What about the two people you thought might have killed Walt?"

"Wouldn't make any sense for either of them to kill Teddy, and Teddy was killed exactly the same way Walt was."

"A copycat maybe?"

"I suppose that's possible. But why kill Teddy at all? I'd really like to talk to Teddy's half-brother when he gets back from the Cape. See if he knows anybody who might have hated Teddy. Maybe I can catch him tomorrow or Friday before we leave."

"Good luck with that. Just do not miss that Friday flight."

"Like I said, wild horses couldn't keep me from that airplane."

Little did I know that wild horses would not be needed.

28

HELLO, HOUSTON

Thursday morning we slept in until after eight, put on jeans and sweatshirts because the temperature had dropped to near freezing, ate a leisurely breakfast in the usual restaurant, took a long walk on the bike path toward Edgartown and returned to the cottage to relax.

While relaxing, I called Detective Manny Gouveia in Oak Bluffs and Detective Aaron McGee in Edgartown. Neither had anything to offer beyond the standard "our investigation into the murder of (Walter Jerome) (Teddy Brewster) is continuing at this time." With a sigh, Gouveia asked me how soon we'd be leaving Martha's Vineyard. McGee didn't seem to care how much longer I would continue to pester him and told me to have a good day.

After relaxing some more with a novel by the (sadly) late Vineyard author Philip Craig, I called both Toby Pilgrim's home and office numbers and left messages asking for return calls.

Dave also got busy on the phone, calling Double Your Money's number. There was still no answer other than the voice mail, so Dave left another message asking for a return call. Next he called his syndicate and explained that he was still stuck on Martha's Vineyard because of the huge storm and would need another two days of down time before creating his next set of cartoons. "They're not happy," he said after the syndicate call.

"Who is?" I asked as I punched in the *Daily Dispatch* number. Don

O'Rourke certainly was not when I told him I had zero progress to report on the Walt Jerome murder story. "Do you have any theories of your own?" he asked. "Not that we could print them; I'm just wondering."

"None of my theories hold water," I said. "And we've had a lot of that."

"You and your twin will be able to get to that plane Friday? No more big storms coming?"

"Not that I've heard of. We should be back in St. Paul in time for supper on Friday."

"Good. I'll expect to see you Monday morning. Don't bother calling again unless you've actually got something we can print."

"Whatever," I said. "See you Monday."

At noon we turned on the Boston news to see if there really were no more major storms headed our way. Naturally we had to wait through a long string of automobile, miracle medication and furniture commercials. Our patience was rewarded, not by an immediate weather report, but by a live interview of a woman in her eighties who was introduced as the Good Samaritan who had sheltered Dolores Brewster after finding her on a beach.

The highlight of the interview was when the reporter sought to confirm the fact that the woman, whose name was Grace, had no electricity and therefore no television set in her beach cottage. "Wouldn't have a television even if I had the electric," Grace said. "Television is the tool of Satan."

When the reporter recovered control of his jaw and tongue enough to form words, he quickly said, "Thank you, Grace. This is Charles Goodwin reporting live, Channel Seven." The scene switched instantly to the main studio, where the camera caught both anchors laughing like two kids in a cluster of clowns.

"Poor Charles stepped into a bucket of crap," Al said.

"Reporters doing live interviews should be like lawyers and only ask questions for which they've checked out the answer," I said.

"I liked that moment of spontaneity," Dave said. "It was so ... spontaneous."

We made sandwiches for lunch and ate them on the porch, still wearing jeans and sweatshirts. No shorts and T-shirts on this day. After we'd tossed our paper plates into the kitchen waste basket, Dave called Double Your Money again. Again he got the voice mail. This time he didn't leave a message.

"When are these hotshot businesswomen coming back to tend to their business?" Dave said. "There ought to be some way to get in touch with them when they're away from the island. What if somebody needed their money right away?"

"Good luck with that," Al said. "Remember, they said it will take five days for them to process a request and move it through the office that actually doles out the money."

"Why the hell do I have to go through the twins to get to the office that actually doles out the money? Why can't I call the people who handle the money directly?"

"Because Ima and Ura are agents working for whatever the investment firm is," Al said. "Without agents like the Jewells, the main office would have to field hundreds of buy and sell requests every day. They'd need a huge staff, so they pay transaction fees to agents like the Jewells, who deal with the customers and decide which funds to tap."

"Well, these particular agents aren't doing their job," Dave said.

"Why don't you try calling the folks who handle the money?" I said. "That might wake up the twins to the fact that they need to be available when they're not on the island. Do you know who they're connected with?"

"I'm sure it's in the paperwork somewhere among all that crap I had to sign. I'll get that stuff out and see if I can find a name and a number. I hope it didn't go home with Cindy."

It took almost fifteen minutes for Dave to paw through the stack of papers he'd acquired and find the ones pertaining to Walt's investment fund. "Here it is," he said at last. "Hennessey and Houston. They're headquartered in Atlanta, Georgia."

"Call them," I said.

"Put your phone on speaker so we can hear what they say when you bypass their agent," Al said.

The call was answered by a recorded voice that assured Dave that his call was very important to Hennessey and Houston and then listed a menu of button-pushing choices. Dave pushed zero to speak to an operator. Said operator asked him with whom he wished to speak and Dave thought a second, then chose Mister Houston. After three rings a woman answered and said this was Mister Houston's office, how could she help.

"You can connect me with Mister Houston," Dave said.

"May I tell him who's calling?"

"David Jerome. Tell him I'm the new owner of the Walter Jerome account."

"Thank you. One moment, please."

About thirty seconds later a man's voice said, "This is Vernon Houston, how may I help you?"

Dave identified himself as Walter Jerome's nephew and the inheritor of the account. Houston said, "Oh, I'm so sorry to learn of your uncle's passing. One moment please while I bring that account up on the computer."

We waited, and got a shock when he returned. "Mister Jerome, this account is still in the name of Walter Jerome."

"It was transferred into my name last week," Dave said. "I signed all the papers with your agents in Oak Bluffs. Didn't that get into your computer?"

"There's nothing here that shows a change in ownership. And looking at this account reminds me that I discussed my question about this account with his local agent about three weeks ago."

"What question is that?"

"I'm afraid I can't discuss it with you unless you can prove your identity."

"How the heck do I do that?"

"Let me see if you're listed as a person to call in the event of an emergency or the death of the owner. Hold on for another moment, please."

Dave held, looking worried and muttering, "This is crazy. Why the hell didn't those women put the paperwork through?"

When Houston came back, he said, "The account does list David Jerome as an emergency contact. Can you give me your social security number and your date of birth, please?"

Dave rattled off both and asked again about the question.

"I grew concerned about the large amounts being withdrawn in rapid succession," Houston said. "I talked to his local agent, a Ms. Jewell, I believe it was, who explained that he was transferring the money to another account held by a different investment firm. I wanted to confirm that fact with Mister Jerome because it wasn't like him to act in such a reckless manner. But I wasn't able to get in touch with him. He didn't respond to an email or return a phone message, and I finally tried the old-fashioned way. I sent him a letter and an account statement by post office mail, but I still haven't received a response. And now you tell me that he's deceased, so I understand why he hasn't responded."

Dave's eyebrows rose like the morning sun. "What kind of withdrawal amounts are we talking about?" he asked.

"The account has been drained down to a balance of one-hundred dollars and thirty-one cents," Houston said.

Dave's face blanched underneath his Vineyard tan and he sucked in a gallon of air. "Did you say one-hundred dollars and thirty-one cents?"

"I did."

"Houston, we have a problem."

"I thought we might," Houston said. "That's why I was trying to contact Mister Jerome."

"I have documents given to me by Double Your Money showing a balance of more than five-hundred-thousand dollars in that account," Dave said.

"That was at its peak value a couple of years ago," Houston said. "There have been regular withdrawals that took the balance down to about three-hundred-thousand before the start of the recent major withdrawals that virtually closed Mister Jerome's account with us."

"How can I withdraw some of my money?"

"I think you need to find out where your uncle moved the money to," he said.

"How do I do that?" Dave asked.

"His local agent should have that information."

"Then why didn't she give me that information? Why did she give me papers in your name instead of the name of the new account?"

"You might want to ask the agent that question," Houston said.

"You don't have any information on where the new account might be?"

"Absolutely none. Mister Jerome withdrew the money the usual way, through his agent, and didn't discuss anything about the switch with either me or Mister Hennessey. Only the agent can help you with that."

The color was slowly returning to Dave's face and I could sense his shock turning to anger. "You don't suppose the agent withdrew the money without my uncle's knowledge, do you?" he asked.

"I would hesitate to accuse anyone of doing such a thing," Houston said. "It would certainly be unprofessional and it could very well be unlawful depending on where it was deposited."

"But it is possible?"

"It is. You might wish to consult a lawyer before you talk to Mister Jerome's agent."

"I'll consider that. Thank you for the advice, and for the information. I may be getting back to you for more."

"I'll gladly answer any questions that I can, Mister Jerome. If you've no more questions now, I'll say goodbye."

"Nothing I can think of at the moment. Goodbye, Mister Houston."

"Have a good day," Houston said.

Dave's face had turned to scarlet when he put down the phone. "Have a good day? I should have a good goddamn day after what he just told me? What the hell is he thinking?"

"It's a habit," I said. "Everybody says it automatically without thinking about what's going on at the time. If you called your lawyer and said you wanted to make out a will right now because your doctor had just told you that you only had eight hours to live, he would give you an appointment and end the conversation by saying have a good day."

"Whatever," Dave said. "The rest of my *good* day is going to be spent hunting down the Jewell twins and finding out what the hell happened to Uncle Walt's money. Did they move it on their own, and if so, why? And why didn't they tell me when I was signing all those papers?"

My train of thought was moving on an ugly track. "Whoa down for a minute," I said. "Stop and think about a possible scenario. Suppose your Uncle Walt blows off the phone message from Houston, thinking it's one of those aggravating callers begging for a donation of some sort, and suppose he deletes Houston's email without answering it, either accidentally or on purpose because he doesn't recognize the sender's email address and assumes that it's spam. Then he receives an envelope in the snail mail from Hennessey and Houston and decides to open it and read it because he does recognize the return address on the envelope. Suppose your Uncle Walt didn't make those withdrawals that he sees in the letter and he calls Double Your Money and asks what the hell is going on. And suppose Ima or Ura says it's all an unfortunate case of miscommunication and says that she'll come to the house to explain it. And suppose she shows up bearing a nice bottle of wine to help smooth things over."

"Oh, my god," Dave said. "You're thinking that—"

"I'm thinking that we just got handed a reason to stay on Martha's Vineyard until a lot of questions are answered."

29

WHAT NEXT?

We needed a plan. Should we take this news and our suspicions to Detective Manny Gouveia in Oak Bluffs? Or should we conduct an interview with Ima and Ura on our own? If we did the latter, should we play dumb about the monetary withdrawals or should we confront them with our knowledge? How would they react to being accused of larceny and murder?

And what about the case of Teddy Brewster? Could the Jewell twins also have killed him? If so, why? We decided not to tackle that question until we had confirmed our theory about the murder of Walt Jerome.

It didn't take us long to eliminate the Manny Gouveia option. Because of his firm desire to have us leave the island we couldn't see trying to work with him until we possessed hard evidence to present. What kind of hard evidence could we come up with?

"I wonder if Houston's letter to Uncle Walt is still here in the cottage," Dave said.

"If the twins really did poison Walt, they might have found the letter and stolen it," Al said.

"Or the cops might have swept it up when they ransacked the place for evidence," I said.

"Hey, remember the papers that were on the coffee table when we got here?" Al said. "I took pictures of the whole room, including the mess on the table. Let's see what we got." He picked up his camera and scrolled through the images he had taken since arriving on the island.

"Here we are," he said. "Here's a couple shots of the table. Let's download them into your laptop and blow them up as big as we can."

I dragged out the laptop and Al downloaded the two images. Expanded to full screen on the computer, we were able to see that one of the type-written sheets of letter-size white paper contained a list of financial figures. The sheet partially covered a sheet that bore a letterhead. We made out the letters "ssey and Houston."

"Bingo!" Dave said.

"Now, where's the original?" I said. "Is it in the boxes of stuff that went to Gouveia's office or did Martha put it through the paper shredder in Walt's den when she cleaned up the living room?"

We dashed for the den, bumping each other and tripping each other like the real Three Stooges. Alison Riggs would have been laughing out loud.

Dave got to the shredder first and hoisted it onto the small wooden desk.

"Careful," I said. "If it's shredded in there we don't want to mess up the strips."

Dave gently pried open the lid. "It's empty," he said. "Either it was never in here or the cops emptied it out when they searched the place." We already knew that the search party had scooped everything from the waste basket, the desk top and the desk drawers.

"One way or another, shredded or whole, the cops must have it," Al said.

"Wonder why Ima or Ura, if it was Ima or Ura, didn't take it with her," Dave said. "Why'd she leave it on the table?"

"Because of Dorie," I said. "Remember she heard a noise from the back of the house? That was the killer. She was in the kitchen washing the wine glasses and didn't have time to go back to the living room and grab everything before running out the back door."

"You've decided for sure that the killer was a she?" Al said.

"I think there's a ninety-nine percent chance that it was one of the Jewells."

"Working from that starting point, what do we do next?" Dave said.

"The first thing we have to do is get Don to cancel tomorrow's flight," I said. "Then we have to call our wives and tell them we need to stay here for a couple more days."

"Telling that to Carol ain't going to be easy," Al said.

"It'll be a piece of cake compared to me telling that to Martha," I said. "She's in a frenzy over what ICE is doing to her sick dad. I might have to go home to her and leave you guys to deal with the twins."

"Oh, no, you don't," Al said. "You're the investigative reporter going after a story. I'm just the photographer who provides the visual accompaniment to your Pulitzer quality prose. We're all in this together."

"Like the motto of the Three Stooges," Dave said. "One for all and all for one."

"That was the Three Musketeers," I said. "And I hope we're as sharp as their swords."

"We're all in this up to the hilt," Al said.

"I get your point," I said. "But I'm afraid Martha might be ready to cut my throat."

"Why don't you start with a call to Don, and tell him to cancel those tickets because we have a real lead on the murder story?" Al said. "That way you and I can at least tell our wives that Don has ordered us to stay."

"Spoken like a true musketeer," I said. "Here goes."

I thought Don would be pleased to learn that we had a probable breakthrough on Walt Jerome's murder, but he was not overjoyed. "We're not exactly overstaffed here, you know," he said. "Unless you have something spectacular, you would be much more useful here in St. Paul next Monday. The Jerome story has gone stale as far as our readers are concerned."

"I think it will be spectacular," I said. "We just need time to prove our theory. We have a suspect—two suspects, in fact—who had both the opportunity and a very strong motive to kill Walter Jerome."

"What's the motive?"

"About three-hundred-thousand dollars. Maybe more."

"That is strong. People have been killed for a hell of a lot less than that. How long will it take you to break the story?"

"It depends on how soon we can talk to the suspects. They're away from the island just now and we don't know when they're coming back."

"What are the cops saying?"

"They don't know what we know, and we aren't telling them until we have solid evidence to give them."

"So you and your twin are playing the Lone Ranger and Tonto again," Don said.

"We're thinking of it as the Three Musketeers," I said. "Dave is still here and is hanging on until the end. Remember, it was his uncle who was murdered."

Don was silent for a moment before he said, "I'll give you until Monday. I'll rebook your flight for Tuesday afternoon, and you and your twin will be on that flight come hell or high water, story or no story, and you both will be in this office, bright-eyed and bushy-tailed, on Wednesday morning. Understand?"

"Aye, aye, captain," I said. "If we break the story earlier, can we get an earlier flight?"

"Talk to me when that happens," Don said. "I'm not holding my breath." I heard the receiver go down, ending the call without anybody saying, "Have a good day."

My phone had been on speaker so Al and Dave had heard both ends of the conversation.

"Sounds like he has very little confidence in your investigative ability," Al said.

"He called you my twin, so take that for whatever that's worth," I said.

"Okay, twin brother reporter, what's next in our three musketeers' adventure in crime solving?" Al asked.

"We call our wives and break the news," I said.

"You first," Dave said.

"All together," I said. "Remember all for one and one for all?"

We separated to make our calls. As I walked away I asked Al to ask Carol to reach out to Martha. "She needs a shoulder to cry on," I said.

Martha's response was what I expected, only louder. "You've *GOT* to be kidding! You're staying out there until Tuesday?"

By the end of this explosion I was holding the phone three inches from my ear.

"It's my job," I said. "I'm covering a murder story. You know I'm a reporter."

"Your office is in St. Paul. You should do your reporting in St. Paul, not from some godforsaken island fourteen hundred miles away."

"Your office is in St. Paul, but you've gone away for several days at a time to do trials in Duluth and godforsaken Fargo, 250 miles away."

"Don't try to confuse me with facts. I need you here Monday to hold my hand while Linda argues Dad's case before the judge."

"They won't let you in to listen, will they?"

"No, but I need somebody to hold my hand outside the judge's chambers."

"If we get a break, I might get the story done in time to catch an earlier flight. We just don't know when the suspects will be available to talk to."

"You really have living, breathing suspects? Plural?"

"Last seen they were living and breathing. We're pretty sure it's Ima and Ura Jewell."

"Why on earth would they commit murder?"

"We think they drained Walt's IRA account and that he found out about it and called them on it. Maybe he threatened to report it to the police."

"That would certainly be a motive."

"A very common one. Now tell me, how's your dad doing?"

"He's feeling better and he's up and walking for a few minutes every day. We haven't told him about what ICE wants to do with him, but I have a feeling that he knows we're hiding something from him. If Linda loses her argument Monday we'll have to break it to him."

"Linda never loses, does she?"

"Not very often, thank god. If she does, and the judge allows the deportation, she's going to argue that Dad should have at least six weeks to get over the heart attack before he flies. That will give her time to muster another line of defense for an appeal."

"Common decency would be to allow him to recuperate before sending him on a fourteen-hour flight to a country he hasn't seen in sixteen years."

"We're talking ICE, Mitch. Those people don't know the meaning of common decency."

We chatted for a few more minutes, told each other how much we loved each other, made kissy sounds and said goodbye. I rejoined the other two stooges/musketeers and they reported the receipt of equally unhappy responses. One for all and all for one.

Now we needed to formulate a plan. "Houston suggested contacting a lawyer before talking to the twins," Dave said. "Do we want to discuss this with our bare-ass buddy Dick Rylander?"

Both Al and I voted an unadorned no because of Rylander's ongoing association with the Jewell twins. "He might even be in on the swindle," I said.

"What about Dorie's brother? He's a lawyer," Dave said.

Another double negative. "Total stranger," Al said. "We've got no idea how smart or how competent he is."

"So it's just us against the twins," Dave said. "No cops; no lawyers."

A double affirmative. Then we sat down in a triangle and derived a plan so convoluted that, looking back on it later, I can't imagine how we ever expected it to succeed.

30

THE PLOT THICKENS

It was a two-part plan.

Part one involved me as the main character. I won that honor as the active stooge, I mean musketeer, over Al because I was the reporter doing the story and I was equipped with a miniature tape-recorder. That's the logic he and Dave used to convince me, and it did seem reasonable at the time.

My job was to contact the Jewell sisters and tell them I wanted to open an investment account through them because I was impressed with how well Walter Jerome's plan had done. This would get me into their office for a conversation, and it would possibly provide us with the name of the new firm holding Walt's IRA, if such a firm existed. If my money was put into an account with good old Hennessey and Houston, we would have additional reason to believe that Walt's funds had been transferred into the Jewells' personal account, probably far offshore and identified only by number.

Part two of our master plan would put Dave onstage. He would call Double Your Money and tell them he had some questions about the account he'd inherited from Walt and would like to discuss them in person. The Jewells' response to that request would determine when and how to bring Detective Manny Gouveia into the action.

Simple, right? And foolproof? We were sure that it was.

The first step was to find out if Ima and Ura had returned to the Vineyard. I called their number and discovered that they had not.

I left a message saying that I'd decided to stay on the island for a couple more days and would like to talk to them as soon as possible about setting up an investment account. I left my cellphone number and crossed my fingers that they would come back before we had to get on a flight to St. Paul.

Our next step was to return to the car rental office and renew our lease on the van. The pool in front of the building had been reduced to a puddle and we were able to bypass Marty's temporary boardwalk and step over the water to get onto the front steps.

"Think you might want to take the seven-fifty weekly rate this time?" Marty asked. "I can back date it one day."

"We only need it through Monday," Dave said. "That's only four more days. That adds up to only $516 at the daily rate."

"Plus the tax," Marty said.

"Plus the tax," Dave said.

"And next Monday you might decide you want it for three more days, which would add up to a week."

"That won't happen," Dave said. "We're turning the van in for the final time on Monday afternoon, come hell or high water."

"You're the boss," Marty said.

"You maybe shouldn't have said that about high water," I said as we drove away. "What if we get another nor'easter and are stuck here because the ferries don't run?"

"We rent bikes or ride the bus if we need transportation," Dave said. "A damn hurricane couldn't blow me back to that office for another go round with Marty."

"You're the boss," I said.

My cellphone rang at nine o'clock Friday morning while we were walking back from breakfast on Circuit Avenue. Seeing that it was a 693 number, which is the Martha's Vineyard exchange, I stepped away from Al and Dave before answering. In a voice so cheery that it would inspire a dying man to rise from his pallet and shout "life is good," the caller identified herself as Ima Jewell.

"Ura and I just got back on-island on the last ferry last night," she said. "We got your message and we'd love to talk to you about setting up an account through us."

"Great," I said. "As I said, I'm only here for a couple more days so I'd like to do it today if you're available."

"I think we can do that. Let me look at the calendar. Hang on just a sec."

I hung. She returned in about thirty secs and suggested two o'clock. I agreed and asked for an office address.

"We work out of our home," Ima said. "Are you familiar at all with Edgartown?"

"Not much. I know how to get to the On-Time ferry, the police station and the newspaper office."

"We're on South Water Street. Just pretend you're going to the On-Time ferry but stay on Main Street all the way to the very last cross street, which is South Water. Take a right on South Water and we're about three blocks up, on the left side of the street. Big old white house." She gave me a house number and said I should have no problem finding it.

"One more thing," she said. "Be sure and bring your checkbook. There's a minimum deposit of a thousand dollars to open an account."

"Okay," I said. As I put away my phone, I was wondering if I had that much in my checking account. Actually, it didn't matter. I was planning to stop payment before that check arrived at the bank.

It was Friday, so we picked up a fresh copy of the *Martha's Vineyard Chronicle*. At the bottom of Page Two was a report on the island's two murders under an Alison Riggs byline. She had learned no more from the Oak Bluffs and Edgartown police than we had. The Thursday edition of the *Vineyard Voice* had been equally devoid of new information. It made me feel a little better to learn that the island police departments hadn't given the local press anything that they hadn't told me. We were all in the same (empty) boat.

We decided to combine my visit to Double Your Money with a trip to Dave's property on Chappy to see if the Landrover had been removed. With the help of the Edgartown police, Dave had located a junkyard on Chappaquiddick. He'd called the owner, who'd said he knew where "poor old Teddy" had been camping and he'd have no problem removing the Landrover. Dave gave the man, who said his name was Eddie, his credit card numbers in exchange for a promise to remove the vehicle. "I give you a special deal," Eddie said. "I tow that old junker for a hundred bucks."

Dave had agreed to that price, only to find out later, when he called the cops to thank them for their help, that the going rate for towing a vehicle that distance was fifty dollars. Now we were going to Chappy to make sure that Dave had received the service he'd purchased on Eddie's "special deal."

We took the usual thrill ride as the forward-most vehicle on the On-Time ferry and were on our way to Dave's little slice of Chappyland when Al pointed to the left and yelled, "Look!"

We looked and we saw a small junkyard that we had not noticed in passing on our previous trips. Dave slowed almost to a stop and we all took a long look at the wrecks lined up beside a low wooden shed. We did not see the rusty old Landrover.

Dave resumed normal speed. "Bet the robber hasn't moved it," he said. We turned off the blacktop and bounced through the woods and were almost at the clearing when we encountered a heavy black flatbed truck emerging from that spot. Perched on the rear platform of that truck was Teddy's Landrover.

"Timing is everything," Dave said. He stopped the van, got out and went to discuss the situation with the truck driver. It was decided that the truck was closer to the clearing than our van was to any wider space behind us, and that the truck driver was the more skilled at driving in reverse in a narrow space. Therefore, the truck driver backed his load up about a hundred feet so we could proceed forward and get into the clearing.

"Are you Eddie?" Dave asked through the open window as we sat beside the tow truck.

"No, I'm Joey," the driver said. "Eddie's my old man."

"Well, tell your old man that I appreciate you towing the Landrover, but I that I found out how special his special deal is."

"You're an off-islander, ain't ya?"

"I am," Dave said.

"Don't tell him that I told you, but Eddie always gives off-islanders this kind of special deal." With that, Joey stepped on the gas and drove slowly away.

Dave turned the van around and we followed the truck back to the blacktop road. We passed Joey and tooted the horn as he was turning into the driveway at the junkyard. Al suggested that we follow Joey in and demand a fifty-dollar refund from Eddie, but Dave shrugged it off. "I got enough problems without getting into a pissing match over fifty bucks," he said.

"Actually, he should be paying you for giving him the Landrover," I said. "With a new battery it will run, and he can use it or sell it."

"I'm just happy to get rid of the damn thing," Dave said. "Let Eddie think he's the slickest robber since John Dillinger."

It wasn't quite two o'clock when we cruised past the Jewells' address on South Water Street. Ima had described it as a big old white house, and it was every bit of that. It was painted white with black shutters and trim, it was old—a plaque above the front door said C. 1790—and it was big—three stories topped by a widow's walk that overlooked Edgartown harbor.

"Not bad for two young women working at home," Dave said.

"Nice view of the harbor," Al said. "Looks like their ship came in."

"I wonder how much of it was paid for with stolen cargo," I said.

"That's what we're setting sail to find out," Al said.

Dave drove south for a couple of minutes, turned around in a driveway and arrived back at the Jewells' big old white house at a minute before two. The arrangement was that they would go downtown for a cup of coffee and return to pick me up at 2:45.

"Have a good time polishing up the Jewells," Dave said.

"Whatever you do, don't drink any wine," Al said.

"I'll show them my AA membership card," I said.

A scallop shell-shaped brass knocker as big around as a softball was attached to the door. On the frame beside the door was a doorbell. I chose the knocker, rapped three times and stood back. The door was opened by a smiling redhead wearing a hot pink, knee-length beach cover-up. Not quite what you'd expect for a business meeting, but at least it was more than Dick Rylander had—or had not—been wearing in our initial encounter.

"*Entrez vous*," she said. "Nice to have you."

"Nice to be had," I said, meaning both the good and not-so-good definitions of the sentence.

31

FUN AND GAMES

Inside the house I was greeted by a second smiling redhead in a knee-length beach cover-up. The only difference was the color of the dress; this one was bright yellow.

"Know which one of us is which?" asked the lady in pink.

"Does it matter?" I asked. "You're both looking very bright and beautiful."

"Ooh, flattery will get you nowhere," said Ms. Pink.

"Or maybe everywhere," said Ms. Yellow with a wink.

"Okay, I give up," I said. "Who's who?"

"You give up too easy," Ms. Pink said.

"I'm just not good at guessing games."

"Okay, quitter. Pink is for Ima and yellow is for Ura," said the one in yellow. "Together we make pink lemonade."

"Sweet lemonade, I'm sure. Do you play this game with all your clients?"

"Oh, you should see some of the games we play," Ima said.

"We like to have some fun with our clients," Ura said. "Especially our male clients."

"Especially our *young* male clients," Ima said. Another wink.

"Come on into our office," Ura said. She turned and I followed her through a living room as big as a tennis court—the furnishings included two sofas, a stone fireplace and a grand piano—into a den that held an executive desk with a flat screen personal computer, three oak filing cabinets, a brown leather-upholstered sofa and three matching overstuffed chairs.

Ima waved me into a chair facing the desk and I sank deeply into it. "Make yourself nice and comfy. Can I get you something to drink? A glass of wine maybe?"

"No thanks." I hoped I hadn't said it too vehemently. "I'm fine. Anyway, I don't drink anything alcoholic."

"You're missing out on one of life's great pleasures," Ura said.

"And one of life's great horrors, if you happen to get addicted," I said.

"Oh, I get it," Ura said. "You're one of those temperance freaks. Okay, no wine for Mitch. How about a glass of lemonade or some water?"

"Nothing, thanks," I said.

"Okay," said Ima, who had seated herself at the desk. "Let's get down to business and leave the pleasure for later."

Ura plopped into the chair next to mine and for the next half hour we talked straight business. We talked about my income, my expenses, my age, my financial goals and my long-range plans. We also talked about Martha Todd's income, her expenses, her age and her financial goals. I had no clue as to what her long-range plans might be, but I was assuming they included me.

Would this be a joint account? If so, they'd need Martha's signature. We decided to start with my name only and add Martha's after I got back to St. Paul and discussed it with her. "This is kind of a spur of the moment thing on my part," I said. "But you two seem to have done so well by Walter Jerome that I didn't want to miss this chance."

"Oh, poor Mister Jerome," Ima said. "I read in the paper that they think he was murdered. Who would do that to a sweet old gentleman like him?"

"I have no idea," I said. "And apparently the police don't either. Can you think of anybody who might have hated him or had a grudge against him or had any other reason to murder him?"

"No, nobody that I can think of," Ima said. "Like I said, he was a sweet old gentleman. We loved working with him."

"Did he join you in a glass of wine?" I was getting on thin ice here but I couldn't resist.

Ima didn't bat an eye. "Oh, yes, he was always ready to raise a glass."

"No temperance talk from him," Ura said. "He could party with the best of them."

"Chug it right down did he?" I said.

"Bottom's up was his motto," she said.

How interesting, I thought. A fast drinker wouldn't catch any possible taste of arsenic until most of it was down the hatch.

Ima had been tapping away on the computer and now she printed out some papers and spread them on the desktop for me to sign. She explained what each form was and why it was needed. I signed them without giving them much of a read, but I examined them closely enough to determine where my money would be invested. It was with Hennessey and Houston.

After everything was signed, Ima asked for two checks, one for at least a thousand dollars and one marked VOID to authorize the automatic withdrawal of a hundred dollars a month from my checking account. These automatic withdrawals were to be deposited directly into my new investment fund for the purchase of stocks or bonds. I wrote a check to Hennessey and Houston for a thousand, scribbled VOID on another, and handed both to Ima.

"Okay," Ima said. "We're done with the business and now we can get going with the pleasure."

"What sort of pleasure are we talking about?" I asked. I was hoping for the pleasure of bringing Walter Jerome's murder back into the conversation.

"Remember, we said we like to play games?" Ura said. "Now we're going to play one with you."

"I'm not much of a game player."

"I think you'll like this one," Ima said. "It's a guessing game."

"And there are no losers," Ura said. "Even if you guess wrong you get a prize."

I looked at my watch. It was 2:41. "I should be going," I said.

"Not before you play our game," Ima said. "You just sit there in that chair. We're going to go into our bedroom and when we come out we will be dressed exactly alike, and you are going to try to guess which one of us is which. Doesn't that sound like fun?"

"I couldn't even do that when you weren't dressed alike."

"This will get you looking at us harder," Ura said.

"A lot harder," Ima said.

"Okay, I'll play your little game. But I can't stay around much longer."

"You might change your mind about that when you see what's next," Ima said.

Off they went, out of the den and into a bedroom somewhere down the hall. I sat in the chair wondering how I was going to figure out who was who if they were dressed exactly alike. I couldn't think of anything I'd seen to differentiate them. There were no distinguishing marks or scars. No giveaway tattoos on either one. Even their hair styles were exactly the same, right to the last stray wisp of red. They both were wearing the same kind of sandals and displaying identically pedicured toenails that were painted the same shade of purple.

I had closed my eyes and was trying to picture them in my mind when I heard two voices in unison shout, "Ta da!"

I turned to look and almost tumbled backward out of the chair. The twins were standing in the doorway, side by side, with their arms linked together at the elbows and their legs spread so that their feet were shoulder-width apart. They were, indeed, dressed exactly alike. Both wore an evenly distributed covering of tan that had been produced by unobstructed exposure to the summer sun, and nothing else. Both displayed a pair of firm, round breasts tipped with stand-up magenta nipples. Both had flat, muscular tummies that curved smoothly into their pubic playgrounds. Their identical bikini wax jobs left a wide-enough fringe of curls to prove they were genuine redheads.

My eyes must have been bugging almost out of my head when the one on the left asked, "So, Mitch, who do you think is who?"

I half fell and half staggered out of the chair, shook my head and said I didn't have a clue.

"How about a closer look?" the one on the right said. They walked toward me until they were almost within arm's reach. "See anything you like?"

I swallowed hard and said, "Lots. But I can't say who is who, so I guess I lose."

"Remember? We said there are no losers in this game," said Lefty.

"Look closer," said Righty. "There is one teeny tiny difference, but you wouldn't have seen it when we were all covered up."

My armpits were beginning to feel wet. I looked down at my watch instead of the enticing wall of sun-tanned flesh standing before me. It was 2:47. The van should be parked out in front. I could get to it by making a run for the door. But two naked beauties were standing between me and that door.

"I'm stumped," I said.

"Oh, I'll bet it's a lot more than a stump," said Righty.

It was beginning to respond in the normal male fashion to the sight of two naked females. The flow of perspiration into my armpits increased and I could feel my face going from warm to hot. If it got any redder it would glow like a traffic light. "This is a great game, ladies, but I really should be going," I said.

"Oh, not until we've played the next part of the game," said Lefty.

I knew I shouldn't ask, but I did. "What's that?"

"*You* go into the bedroom and take off all *your* clothes and *we* come into the bedroom and try to guess who *you* are," Lefty said. They both broke into such a robust round of giggles that their breasts jiggled and bounced in identical jiggles and bounces.

I was beginning to enjoy the show but I knew it had to stop. "My friends are waiting for me outside," I said. "I have to go right now."

"Let'em wait," Lefty said. "Look real close at these." She cupped her breasts in her hands and thrust them toward me. "Then look at hers."

Numbly, but not without pleasure, I obeyed. After scanning both pairs of sun-tanned globes three times, I discerned a difference. Lefty had a tiny gold stud in her left nipple and Righty had an identical decoration in her right nipple. I pointed at the studs, being very careful not to touch any of the surrounding territory.

"Okay, so, who do you think is who?" Lefty said.

"You're Ima," I said, taking a wild guess.

"Right you are," she said. "Now let's go get you undressed for the next part of the guessing game."

They separated and came around the chair. They each took one of my arms and started tugging me toward the bedroom. "Actually, our part of the game is guessing the size of you know what," Ura said.

There was a time before I'd pledged myself to Martha that I would have played this game with pleasure, but I was really sweating now. A drop rolled off my forehead and down to the tip of my nose. "Please, I'm a happily married man. I can't play any more of this game."

"Oh, Mitchy, don't be a party pooper as well as a temperance freak," Ura said. "If you need help getting those clothes off we're right here to ... give you a hand." With that, she pulled down the zipper on my fly. "When you're all undressed you'll get the grand prize."

Stupidly, I had to ask. "Just what is the grand prize?"

"Us," they said in unison. "In a three-way pile on top of the bed."

That did sound grand, and I was now in full male response to the intense titillation, but no way could I accept it. I could never again look at Martha without feeling guilty if I let this crazy game reach the climax the Jewell twins had in mind. I had to find a way to get out of there with my clothes on and my marriage vows intact.

32

FOR WHOM THE BELL TOLLS

We were at the open bedroom door, and I was still protesting, even with a silky-smooth, warm, bare female breast pressed against each sweaty arm, when the doorbell rang.

"Who the hell is that?" Ima said.

"It's got to be my friends, wondering why I haven't come out," I said. "I told you I had to go. They're here to pick me up."

"Oh, damn it!" Ura said. "The game's over ... unless your friends want to play."

"Not likely," I said. "They're both happily married, too."

"Just our luck," Ima said. "Here we are ready to have a ball with a real stud muffin and the muffin stealers arrive. Okay, go, Mitchy. Go with your goddamn friends." They let go of my arms and continued into the bedroom.

"Don't forget your copies of the paperwork," Ima said as I hustled toward the front door.

"And don't forget to zip up your pants," yelled Ura. I heard them both making sounds like a sit-com laugh track behind me.

My mind was total mush by this time, but thanks to the reminders I managed to get my fly zipped over a diminishing protrusion and the paperwork gathered before opening the door to find Al standing there with his hand reaching toward the bell button for a second ring.

"About time. What's going on? Still busy?" he asked.

"You won't believe how busy," I said. "Get me the hell out of here."

I pushed past Al and headed at a gallop toward the van. "Jesus, what did they do to you?" Al asked as he trailed along behind me.

I opened the right front door and practically dove headlong into the passenger seat. Al got in back and I started babbling about guessing games and naked dames as Dave pulled away from the curb.

"You should have called us in," Dave said when I paused to take a breath. "We could have had a mixed quintet."

"Oh, I'm sure you'd have come romping in and whipped off your clothes and leaped onto a pile of naked females with no thoughts of Cindy," I said.

"Yeah, well, that might have slowed me down I guess, but I could have had fun looking at the pile."

"We really would've been three stooges to get into that kind of trap," Al said. "Imagine the blackmail those two little bandits would have on us. There might even be a camera in the bedroom. I can just hear them chirping, 'Better keep on paying, dude, or we'll show this movie to your wife.'"

"No problem, Al. We could have added blackmail to the charges when we send them up for murder," Dave send.

"*If* we send them up for murder," I said. "I got what I was after and now it's up to you to get the clincher."

"Are they still using Hennessey and Houston?" Dave asked.

"They are. I don't think there's any second home for Walt's investments beyond Double Your Money's bank account, which is probably located somewhere in the Cayman Islands."

"I wonder how many other accounts they're sucking dry," Dave said. "It's a great scheme. Tell your client it takes five days to get a withdrawal from Hennessey and Houston when it really has to come out of your account because you've stolen it from the client. It's better than a Ponzi."

"Their mistake was pulling so much so fast from Walt's account that it worried Houston and caused him to question Walt," I said. "They either got really greedy or they needed a big bundle for something."

"Or maybe when Walt had his heart attack last spring they were afraid he would pass away and leave them without a way to get at the money that was willed to me," Dave said.

"Whatever," I said. "What you need to do is get one or both of them to admit they stole the money while you're wearing my mini tape recorder." That was part two of our master plan.

"Okay, I can see several reasons why they might have stolen Uncle Walt's money, and why they had to shut him up," Dave said. "But what I can't figure out is why they would also kill Teddy Kennedy Roosevelt Brewster. He sure as hell didn't have a big investment account to steal from."

"Or maybe he did," I said. "Just because he was a little nutty and lived like a homeless hermit doesn't mean he had no money. I should ask his lawyer half-brother, Toby Pilgrim, about that possibility."

"Having that kind of money would make Teddy eccentric instead of a little nutty," Al said. "Ain't that the way it works?"

"That's right," I said. "Weird people with a ton of money are always called eccentric. Howard Hughes, for example. Lived as an unbathed recluse with millions in the bank, but news reports always identified him as the eccentric Howard Hughes, not as the nutty as a fruit cake Howard Hughes."

When we were settled in again at Dave's Oak Bluffs cottage, I punched Toby Pilgrim's office number into my cellphone. A recorded message informed me that Attorney Pilgrim's office hours were 8:00 a.m. to 4:00 p.m., Monday through Friday, but in an emergency he could be reached at his mobile phone number. It was 3:42 p.m. Apparently Attorney Pilgrim had chosen to cut his work day a few minutes short. Well, who could blame him? It was Friday, after all, and he must be tired after spending several days hunting for his missing mother.

I decided that this was an emergency and tried the cellphone number. A voice mail message said that Attorney Pilgrim could not answer his phone just now and instructed me to leave a message. I left yet another message on yet another phone. Such is the life of a reporter.

I didn't have to leave a message for Martha. She called me with a report on her father versus ICE. Dad was feeling better and Linda L. Lansing was working on her argument for Monday's judicial hearing. Dad still had not been told that ICE wanted him out of the country.

"I would think that Linda's best argument would be that deporting a man who has already been approved for a green card would be basically stupid," I said.

"Welcome to today's America," Martha said. "Stupidity in the name of trying to get rid of immigrants is no excuse. So what's new with you?"

My responding narrative about signing up for an investment account with Double Your Money was brief and to the point. I saw no need to include the irrelevant parts of the meeting, such as the dual disrobing of my hosts and their foiled attempt to drag me into a threesome in the bedroom.

"So now you have an account for them to steal from?" Martha said.

"I've already stopped payment on the check through the miracle of online banking," I said. "The folks at Hennessey and Houston are going to wonder what the hell it's all about."

"They'll be calling Double Your Money to find out."

"Not until next week. By then we'll have enough evidence to hand the Jewell twins over to Manny Gouveia, and we'll all be back in St. Paul rockin' in our babies' arms."

"I hope it works that way. What if the Jewells don't tell you anything?"

"Then we'll give Manny what we have and come on home and forget about it."

"You promise you'll be on that plane Tuesday?"

"I'd swear it on a stack of stylebooks if I had a stack of stylebooks."

"Walt must have had one somewhere that you could swear on. Anyhow, be sure to call me after Dave's session with the Jewells."

"You bet your diamond ring I will." We made kissy sounds and signed off.

To my utter amazement, Toby Pilgrim returned my call at 9:30 Saturday morning. I told him who I was and why the three of us were on Martha's Vineyard. I said I was sorry about Teddy Brewster's death and asked the obvious question.

"No, I have no idea why anyone would poison Teddy," Pilgrim said. "Sure he was an oddball, but this is Martha's Vineyard. Oddballs are a dime a dozen here."

I had thought about several ways to ask the next question and decided to be brief and direct, with no mention of an investment fund. "Could it have been for his money?"

"His money? Are you serious? The man owned a tent, a beat-up Landrover and the clothes on his back. His only income was his Social Security check and an occasional twenty bucks he mooched from me and never paid back."

"No bank savings account or investment account?"

"Oh, please! The man didn't even have a checking account. His Social Security came to a PO box and he cashed the check at the grocery store."

"How'd he pay for his trip to Florida every winter?"

"Saved a few bucks from each summer check, and he got a hand-out from Walter Jerome when he was ready to leave. Anyhow, he tucked it all into some hiding place out there in the woods. Didn't anybody find a stash?"

"We didn't. Maybe the police did. Have you talked to them?"

"I've got an appointment with Detective McGee for this afternoon. I'll be sure to ask about the money."

"His tent disappeared. Could his travel money have been hidden there?"

"Who knows? He didn't tell any of us where it was. I always

figured it was somewhere in the Landrover. If the cops haven't found any money, I'm going out to search it."

"The Landrover is at the junkyard on Chappy," I said. "Dave had it towed."

"Oh, shit, you mean Eddie has the Landrover?" Pilgrim said.

"'Fraid so."

"Thanks a whole hell of a lot. I'll probably have to get a warrant to search it, especially if Eddie thinks I'm looking for money."

"Sorry. Dave just wanted that rust bucket off his property. We never thought about it being a piggy bank."

"Well, I'll have to wait until Monday and get a warrant and have it in my pocket in case Eddie gives me a hard time. Were you going to tell me where the Landrover was or were you going to let me wonder where the hell it went when I got to Teddy's camp? And you say somebody also took the tent?"

"The tent disappeared between the time we found his body and when we went back there last Tuesday. We thought the wind might have blown it away somewhere, but we couldn't find it out there in the woods."

"I sure as hell hope the money wasn't in it. I mean it wasn't much, but my cousin Dorie could use it. She ain't making all that much at the hospital."

"I hope you find the money," I said. "Let me know what happens. This number is my cellphone so you can call me anywhere."

"Okay. And if I don't find it I suppose I could always sue your friend Dave for moving the Landrover without my permission."

"Or Dave could sue you for leaving the Landrover on his land without his permission. He did order Teddy to take his stuff and get off, you know."

"No, I didn't know. And if the order wasn't in writing it doesn't mean shit to me. Your tow-happy friend actually stole my vehicle. Whatever Eddie paid him for it, he should give to me.

"My friend paid Eddie to haul it away. You should reimburse my friend."

"Oh, that's right, you're off-islanders. Eddie gave your friend one of his special deals, didn't he? Well, too damn bad, but I ain't reimbursing anybody that dumb. Nice talking to you, Mister Mitchell. Have a good day." With a beep, the call ended.

I was sure he meant that good-day wish from the bottom of his heart.

"Teddy's brother is going to sue you for stealing his Landrover," I said to Dave.

"Let the bastard sue me," Dave said. "I'll countersue to collect rent for all the time the old fart camped on my property and parked his junker there."

"He thinks Teddy's travel funds might be hidden in the junker."

"That's between him and what's his name out at the junkyard. ... Eddie, was it?"

"Eddie it was. Apparently he's a hard-ass to deal with."

"He's a highway robber; we know that for sure."

On Sunday afternoon, I called my mother and my Grandma Goodrich, better known as Grandma Goodie, who live together in a farmhouse near the little town of Harmony, in southeastern Minnesota. I have been observing this ritual for more years than I can count, even though it almost always gets me a lecture on my religious failings from Grandma Goodie. The previous Sunday's call had been very brief and I'd been feeling guilty about cutting it much shorter than usual. This time I vowed to absorb the full lecture on my failure to attend any church services.

"Glad to hear you're still alive," my mother said. "We've been reading your stories and it seems like everybody out there is getting poisoned."

"Not everyone," I said. "Only two so far. And I don't drink wine anymore, so I think I'm safe."

"I certainly hope you're safe. Wouldn't want to have you spoil your vacation out on that fancy rich man's island by getting killed.

So does this call mean that you're on your way back home?"

"It means I'll be home Tuesday night. I think we've finally solved the original murder case out here—the one involving Dave's uncle—and most likely the second one, too."

"So they've arrested the killer then?"

"No, but we're planning to expose them on Monday."

"Them? It took more than one person to poison an old man?"

"Two old men, actually. And we think the poisoning was done by a pair of twins."

"Well, don't let them poison you then."

"No chance. It's Dave Jerome who's sticking his neck out this time, not me or Al."

"Couldn't you just let the police handle it?"

"The police are stumped. We're tricking the killers into giving us evidence to take to the police."

"Sounds crazy to me," Mom said. "Hope none of you get hurt then. Anyhow, I'm going to give the phone to your grandmother now."

She passed the phone to Grandma Goodie, who immediately asked if I'd been to church today. I told her I was in a strange place and didn't know where to go.

"I know where you will go if you don't start taking care of your spiritual life," she said. "It'll be a really strange place. And a really hot one, too."

"I'm counting on your prayers to keep me out of that," I said. "I know you have a lot more clout with the almighty than I'll ever have."

"I'm eighty-eight years old. You can't count on my prayers much longer, Warnie baby." I have been Warnie baby to her since the day my given name was chosen.

"Oh, come on. You're good for at least twelve more years. I'll be bringing the cake to your hundredth birthday party."

"Don't want to live to a hundred unless my mind stays clear. If I can't remember things and can't talk sensible I'd rather be with the lord."

I managed to change the subject to baseball—the Minnesota Twins were in the playoffs and she was watching every pitch on TV—and we ended the conversation with the usual profusion of verbal hugs and kisses. All was forgiven for my brevity the previous week, but I was instructed to look for a church service in the evening. Good luck with that.

I put away my cellphone and went into the living room to join Al and Dave in a rehash of the second half of our foolproof plan to trap the Jewell twins. We had the rest of the day free to lollygag about until Dave went into action Monday morning.

33

THE BEST LAID PLANS ...

The second half of our foolproof operation went into effect shortly after another fine breakfast Monday morning. I was going to miss those bountiful breakfasts when I left the Vineyard, but I wasn't going to miss the additional four pounds they'd put on me after I'd lost three at home on a month-long morning diet of peanut-butter toast and coffee.

Dave called Double Your Money at a few minutes past nine and put his cellphone on speaker so Al and I could hear both ends of the conversation. Ima Jewell answered. Dave said he wanted to talk about the investment account he'd inherited from his uncle.

"You must be happy with it," Ima said. "Your buddy, Mister Mitchell, opened one with us just last Friday on your recommendation."

"Yes, he did," Dave said. "But Mister Mitchell has gone back to Minnesota, along with Mister Jeffrey, and I've come across something that I want to discuss with you. It might change my future recommendations."

"That sounds kind of serious."

"It is kind of serious. Can you come to my place? I've turned in my rental van because I'm leaving first thing tomorrow morning." I mentally crossed my fingers, hoping she wouldn't suggest taking a taxi.

"So you need to see me today? At your house?"

"That's right. Sorry about that, but you can pick any time that's convenient for you."

She was quiet for a moment. "I guess I could make it early this afternoon. Say one-thirty?"

"That'll work. Do you know where the cottage is?"

"I think I can find it," Ima said. "We've gone there the last three years to do our annual review with Mister Jerome because he didn't want to drive into Edgartown traffic anymore."

Dave recited the address and gave her directions from Ocean Park in case she'd forgotten. She thanked him and said she'd see him at about one-thirty. "Have a nice day," she said as she ended the call.

"I believe I will," Dave said to us. With a Cheshire cat grin on his face, he said, "She took the bait—hook line and sinker."

"She didn't sound too enthusiastic about it," Al said.

"Good that she's a little uncomfortable," Dave said.

"Be interesting if she shows up with a bottle of wine," I said.

"I'll have to tell her I don't drink alcohol."

"She already knows that I don't. She'll think we're all what she called temperance freaks."

"I'll tell her it's okay to go ahead and drink without me."

"That'd be fun," Al said. "She'll have to come up with a fast excuse."

"I almost hope she does bring wine," Dave said. "Anyhow, I'd better go hide the van before we forget about it. Can't have it sitting in front of the house when Ms. Jewell arrives."

"Sure hope she can find the place, not having been here since last year's review," I said.

Now we were looking at a four-hour wait. What could we do to while away the time until Ima Jewell's arrival at 1:30?

We started by going over the details of our plan again. It was simple enough. Dave would have my mini-recorder hidden in his shirt pocket when he opened the door for Ima. He would turn it on after they'd finished the "hello, how are you, come on in" routine and lead her into the living room. Al and I would be hiding back in the kitchen, where we could hear the conversation. If at any time we sensed that Dave was in danger, we would charge out of the kitchen and through the dining room to the rescue. All for one and one for all.

We took a walk. We sat on the beach. We bought roll-up sandwiches, roast turkey salad with walnuts and cranberries, at the Reliable Market on Circuit Avenue and ate them on a bench in Ocean Park. I desperately wanted to talk to Martha but we had an iron-clad rule against calling each other at work. Neither Al nor Dave chose to break into their wives' workdays either.

We went back to the cottage and rehearsed the plan again. Dave would tell Ima that he had attempted to withdraw money from the account and had found it reduced to one-hundred dollars and thirty-one cents. Without accusing Ima of either theft or murder, he would quietly ask where she had re-invested the money and when he could make a withdrawal.

What happened next would depend on Ima's response. If she said the money had been moved to a different fund, he would ask for the name, address and phone number. If she hemmed and hawed, he would press for an answer. If she threatened Dave in any way, Al and I would make our grand entry. She'd be faced with all for one and one for all.

The minutes dragged by at the pace of a laconic turtle until at last the clock read 1:15. After reminding Dave to be sure and turn on the recorder, Al and I adjourned to our hiding place so there would be no rush if Ima Jewell arrived early. Dave picked up a book that he'd just finished reading, took a seat on the front porch and began reading the book again.

The minutes ticked by. One-twenty. One-twenty-five. One-thirty. One-thirty-five. At one-thirty-eight we heard a car door slam. "She's here," Al whispered. "Hope Dave remembers to turn on the recorder."

"I'm sure he will," I said. "I reminded him to remember. Remember?"

"Oh, that's right. I forgot."

We heard Dave greeting Ima Jewell on the porch and heard them exchanging how-are-yous on their way to the living room. "Have a seat," Dave said.

"Thanks. I hope you haven't had lunch," Ima said. "I brought along some lobster rolls and a nice bottle of burgundy."

Al and I looked at each other and his mouth formed an "O."

We heard paper rustling. She was taking the wine and lobster rolls out of a bag.

"Thanks for thinking of me, but I've already had lunch," Dave said. "I couldn't eat another bite, not even lobster."

"You're definitely not a New Englander," Ima said. "If you were, you could eat lobster right after a full turkey dinner. How about I pour us some wine? There must be a corkscrew in the kitchen. I'll go out and open this and bring you a glass."

"No, that's okay," Dave said. "I'm really not much of a wine drinker, and when I do it's always white. I just don't care for red."

Al and I looked at each other and nodded in approval.

"Well, looks like I struck out all the way around," Ima said. "I'll put all this back in the bag."

"Sorry," Dave said. "If I'd known you were bringing lobster rolls I'd have held off on lunch. And if you want to have some wine while we talk, feel free to open it."

"I never drink alone," Ima said. "My daddy told me that that can lead to problems." The paper rustled as she put the wine back into the bag. "So, Mister Jerome, let's get down to business. What's this problem that you want to talk about?"

"Please call me Dave. The problem is ... well, I wanted to pull some money out of Uncle Walt's account—the one you had switched over to me. But you and your sister were off-island and I had no way to reach you, so I took a flyer and called the broker listed on the paperwork you gave me. Hennessey and Houston. I talked to Mister Houston, and he said the account balance was only one-hundred dollars and thirty-one cents. His explanation was that you must have transferred the money to another firm. Is that what happened?"

There was a moment of silence before she answered. "Yes, that's what we did. We moved it because we think we can earn more with a new broker."

"But all the paperwork you gave me is with Hennessey and Houston. Don't I have to get some new documentation?"

"We were going to get that to you but we haven't had the opportunity. We were off-island for several days, as you know. We planned to mail you some new documents back in Minnesota. You shouldn't have gone to Hennessey and Houston, Dave. You should have waited for us."

"Well, I wanted to get started on it, and I was afraid I'd be back in St. Paul before you two got back on the island. If I'd had your cellphone number I'd have called that."

"I'm sorry we didn't give you that, but we don't generally like to do business when we're off-island and don't have our files with us. If you want me to, I'll start on the process today and you'll get your check in St. Paul in five business days."

"What's the name of the new broker?"

Al and I looked at each other. We both raised our eyebrows.

"That really doesn't matter," Ima said. "You won't be corresponding with them anyway."

"I'd just like know," Dave said. "In case they contact me. So I don't blow them off as a robo-call or trash mail."

"You'll get all that information when I send you the new paperwork. How much do you want to withdraw?"

"What if I withdraw all of it?"

"That would be foolish. The taxes would eat up an enormous chunk if you did that."

"Didn't the taxes eat up a big chunk when you withdrew it and transferred it?"

"No, it's an IRA. As long as you transfer the money directly to another retirement fund it won't be taxed until you make a withdrawal."

"Okay, what's the name of the new fund?"

"What difference does it make? It's not a big deal."

"I'm new at this. It is a big deal with me. What's the problem with telling me the name?"

"I said you'd get it when I send you the new paperwork."

"Why not tell me now? Again I'm asking, what's the problem with that?"

"There is no problem. Now how much money do you want?" Her tone was sharper, at the edge of anger.

"I want to know where my money is," Dave said. "And you seem to have no answer to that. Is that because the money is somewhere that it's not supposed to be?"

There was definite anger in Ima's next reply. "Are you suggesting that we've done something improper with your funds?"

"I'm suggesting that you're dodging my question about their whereabouts, which arouses my curiosity."

"They say that curiosity killed a cat, you know."

"Did curiosity also kill my Uncle Walt?" Dave said.

Al and I turned to each other and whispered, "Whoa!"

"What do you mean by that?" Ima said. "Are you suggesting that Ura and I had something to do with your uncle's heart attack?"

"Wasn't a heart attack," Dave said. "Somebody poisoned his wine. Maybe a nice bottle of burgundy."

"This is crazy. You're talking crazy. How can you even suggest such a crazy thing?"

"Tell me where the money is and maybe my craziness will fade away."

"I don't have to sit here and listen to this shit. If you want to withdraw some money tell me how much and I will get out of here right now."

"You're not soothing my crazy bone, Ms. Jewell."

"I'm not a psychiatrist, Mister Jerome. I believe you seriously need the kind of help that I can't give you."

"You can give me the location of my money. That's all I want from you right now."

"You called me here just to accuse me of stealing your money and, my god, killing your uncle?"

"I did. Prove me wrong."

"You're making a serious mistake, Mister Jerome. You need to drop this talk and allow me to conduct my business in a normal, sane manner."

"And what if I don't drop this talk? What if I ask the police to investigate the transactions from Hennessey and Houston to wherever you sent the money?"

"You will never do that, Mister Jerome."

Al and I looked at each other. and nodded toward the doorway to the dining room. It was almost time to move.

"I think I just might do that," Dave said.

"This says you won't," Ima said.

"Jesus, what the hell is that?" Dave said.

Al and I looked at each other. We both took a step forward. We both stopped when a voice behind us said, "Enjoying the show?"

We both spun around, and we found ourselves facing Ura Jewell. In her left hand was something that looked very much like a revolver.

34

GANG AFT A'GLEE

"Shall we join them?" Ura Jewell said, motioning toward the living room with both her head and the nasty little weapon in her hand.

Al and I walked slowly out of the kitchen, through the dining room and on into the living room, with Ura close behind us. In the right hand of Ima Jewell, who stood facing us, was a shiny object that looked like the instrument nurses use to give patients their tetanus shots. The business end was pointed toward Dave, who stood with his back toward us.

"Welcome to showdown time," Ima said as we entered the room.

This caused Dave to turn around. He did a spontaneous double take and pointed at Ura. "Where'd she come from?" he asked.

"Don't know," I said.

"Back door," Ura said.

"Back door was locked," Dave said.

"Old fool Walter told us where he hid the spare key," Ura said. "Bragged that nobody would ever look where he hid it."

"Where was it?" Dave said.

"Under the next door neighbor's back porch. Old fart there is so deaf he'd never hear anybody looking for the key."

"So why were you sneaking in the back door?" I asked.

"Backup," Ura said. "Like in the cop shows. We were expecting trouble because you guys are about as subtle as the Three Stooges but only half as much fun. Only thing we weren't sure of was how many of you would be here to put the squeeze on Ima."

There we were again—being likened to Larry, Moe and Curly. "What made you suspicious?" I asked.

"Well, first of all, Mitchy boy, you called us, all hot to open an account, and it had to be done right away because you were only going be here for two more days," Ura said. "Then the next day Davey here calls us and wants to talk about a problem with his account, and he says you two have already left the island, and that the meeting has to be here in this house because he no longer has wheels. We figured he could be lying about you two going off-island a day early, and that the three of you might be planning to spring something on Ima when she came. But we weren't sure about that, so Ima decided to meet Davey one on one while I snuck in the back and listened to the conversation. I very quietly slipped in the back door and stood behind the two of you, who had supposedly gone off-island, while you were exchanging funny faces and little backstage whispers."

"I guess we were a little clumsy," Dave said. "So what's with the shots needle?"

"It's loaded with thorazine," Ima said. "A shot of this would have put you to sleep long enough for this house to catch fire and burn you to a crisp before the firemen got here. If you were lucky, you wouldn't wake up while you were on fire. That was Plan A, for if you were here all by yourself. Plan B was for Ura to come in the back door with the gun in case the other two knuckleheads were still here. So, Plan B is now in effect."

"Okay, now you have all three of us here at gunpoint under Plan B," Dave said. "What are you going to do next? Be hard to pass off three people dead of gunshot wounds as normal in a burning house."

"You're right about that," Ima said. "So we're going to take you for a boat ride. And unfortunately for you, the boat is going to blow up and burn. And being big macho men, you'll have paid no attention when we warned you to be sure to put on the life vests."

"And your story will be that you did survive the accident because you were wearing life jackets?" I said.

"Our story will be that we weren't even aboard," Ura said. "Our story will be that we loaned you the boat—it's called Double Your Fun, by the way—and it turned out to be too much for you Minnesota landlubbers to handle. You got way out away from the island and somehow the boat caught fire and the fuel tank exploded. Overboard the three of you went, into the cold October water of Vineyard Sound. And, sadly, without life vests none of you were able to make it to shore."

"Wait a minute," Al said. "How will you two make it to shore?"

"We tow a rubber dinghy with a little outboard motor behind the Double Your Fun. While you're splashing away, we'll be putt-putting away—back to Edgartown. After a couple of hours we'll get concerned that something might have happened to you and we'll report the boat missing."

"You're going to drown us out there?"

"Sad, isn't it—three lives lost in a tragic boating accident. But think about me and Ima. We'll be losing a very nice boat."

"I'm taking all this as a confession that you stole my uncle's money and murdered him," Dave said.

"You seem to have stumbled onto that fact by not following directions, Davey boy," Ima said. "If you hadn't bypassed us and called Hennessey and Houston you wouldn't have found out the account was empty, and you'd all be going home fat, dumb and happy to your wives."

Before I could object to being called fat, Dave asked, "How did Uncle Walt find out about you taking the money?"

"That damn Houston got worried that Walter was getting senile and doing crazy things with the money. When Walter didn't respond to an email, Houston sent him a letter asking why he was pulling his money away, and included a copy of the account transactions. When Walter read that stuff he called us and demanded an explanation. I tried on the phone to convince him that we'd only transferred the money to a different, better IRA, but he demanded that we bring him some kind of documentation to show what we'd done. He said he would go to the police or the attorney general if we didn't."

"So you came to see him with a bottle of poisoned wine?"

"I came hoping that I could convince him that his money was safe," Ima said. "We've been meeting here with Walter for several years to review his account and sometimes suggest some changes, like more bonds and less stocks, stuff like that. He always had a bottle of burgundy out on the table and we always drank to his continued prosperity. This time I brought the wine, along with a little something to add to it if he continued to threaten us with a call to the law."

"And he wouldn't back down?" Dave said.

"He was furious about the withdrawals we'd made and he was convinced that we'd been stealing his money all along. Actually, we were just sort of borrowing it, like we do with all our clients. Any time he wanted a withdrawal, we took it out of the interest-earning account we'd set up for ourselves and sent him a check that had the Hennessey and Houston logo printed on it."

"Where is this account?"

"Where you're going, there's no need for you to know, Davey, old boy."

I interrupted their little chat with a question. "Did you also kill Teddy Brewster?"

"I hated to do that but I didn't have any choice," Ima said.

"Why? What was the reason to kill Teddy?"

"Teddy knew about Walter's problem with the account. He told Teddy that we'd been stealing from him, and a couple days after Walter died Teddy came to see us and said he was going to the police with what Walter had told him unless we brought him five-hundred-thousand dollars in cash."

"Blackmail."

"Right. I told Teddy I'd come to his camp on Chappy and bring him a down payment. I took along a bottle of our special burgundy to celebrate our agreement and he took a nice big swig. You know the rest."

"Not everything. His tent disappeared. Did you take that?"

"I discovered that I'd lost an earring out there. I went back and couldn't find it on the ground so I was afraid it was in the tent and someone else might find it. I took the tent home so I could search it in the privacy of my basement."

"Did you find the earring?"

"No. The damn thing might still be out there. I'm going back for another look tomorrow. I won't have to worry about you guys catching me, will I?"

"Enough of this chatter," Ura said. "Our SUV is parked out in front. Time to load up and take you guys to the Double Your Fun. March!" She gestured toward the front door with her gun, and like sheep on a slaughterhouse runway we formed a line and marched.

The SUV was a white Cadillac Escalade ESV, the biggest model they make. I wondered why two petite women needed a vehicle with all that space. Maybe it was for showing off to prospective clients—an advertisement of their money-making skill.

As we moved toward the Caddy, I looked up and down the block, hoping to see someone we could yell to or run toward. Not a soul in sight.

When we reached the SUV, we were herded into the second row of seats. Ima got behind the wheel and Ura sat in the front passenger seat, turning toward us with her gun aiming at the level of our heads. Ima started the engine and the big vehicle began to move.

"You're driving us to Edgartown?" I asked.

"No," Ima said. "Ura brought the boat over to Oak Bluffs. We're just going down to the harbor here and you're going to walk aboard like nice little boys. From there it will be bon voyage."

Five minutes later we were parked next to the dock in Oak Bluffs harbor and Ura was opening the door for us to exit. When we were out, she pointed toward a white cabin cruiser with "Double Your Fun" painted on the stern in gold letters edged in black. Apparently white was their favorite color for all means of transportation.

Double Your Fun was a substantial boat, bigger than your

average runabout, with the controls in a cockpit forward of an open stern lounge and an enclosed dining and sitting area amidships on the main deck. It would, indeed, be a serious sacrifice to lose this boat in a trade for our lives.

"Keep your mouths shut and get your butts on that boat," Ura said. It occurred to me that Walt Jerome's money might have paid for that thirty-foot hole in the water.

The dock on that side of the harbor is about the length of three city blocks. The inland third is filled with dockside restaurants and an assortment of tourist traps that includes T-shirt shops, a souvenir vendor, a jeweler, a bakery and a Christmas specialty shop. The next third is occupied by a fleet of rental cars and the outer third is a black-top parking lot used by cars and tour buses greeting incoming ferry passengers from two ports on Cape Cod and one in Rhode Island.

The harbor water on the inward third has space for private yachts, a para-sail business, a cluster of rental jet skis, a pirate ship for little kids and a walkway out to a docking place for ferries going to and from Hyannis. Next come slips for medium size boats, the harbor master's office and docking space for several small commercial fishing boats. Nearest the harbor mouth is a large landing area for the Island Queen, and for a couple of smaller boats that carry freight and newspapers, along with a few passengers, to the island from Falmouth.

The twins had tied the Double Your Fun up parallel to the dock beyond the vacant Island Queen berth, closer to the mouth of the harbor and as far from the cluster of dockside restaurants and shops as she could get. The inflated rubber dinghy, their escape vessel, was bobbing gently in the ripple behind the Double Your Fun.

This end of the dock was deserted. The fishing boats had been emptied of the morning's catch and the Island Queen had made its final run of the season on Columbus Day. The other end was almost as quiet. All of the seasonal water sports facilities had shut down and only a couple of shops and one of the restaurants were still open for business. There were only about a dozen shoppers and gawkers on that part of the sidewalk.

With Dave in the lead, we started to walk single-file toward the white boat, followed by the Jewell twins. Ura held her gun low, tucked tight against her hip, where it wasn't visible to the people milling about on the sidewalk about two blocks away.

A few steps from the boat, Dave stopped and turned around to face us. "This is nuts," he said. "Why are we marching to the boat like lambs to the slaughter? I'm not going another step. If you want to kill me, you'll have to shoot me right here, with all those people watching." He pointed toward the group at the other end of the harbor.

"Nobody's watching," Ura said. "Get your ass moving or I will put a slug in it."

She was right, no one was watching. That is, no one was watching until Dave began waving his arms and yelling, "Hey, everybody! These crazy women are going to shoot us right here on the dock where you can see them do it. Come and watch the firing squad. Come and watch them kill us."

Half a dozen heads turned in our direction.

"Shut up and move your ass," Ima said.

Instead, in the spirit of all for one and one for all, Al and I joined Dave in the arm waving and shouting. "The Jewell sisters are going to shoot us," we yelled. "Come and watch the Jewell sisters shoot us." More heads turned and several men started walking in our direction.

"Okay, Ura, go ahead and gun us down," Dave said. "You've now got a nice crowd of witnesses to testify at your trial."

"You bastard," Ura said. She raised her gun and aimed it at Dave's head. Dave did a belly flop onto the blacktop surface of the parking lot while Al and I split and ran in divergent directions. I ducked behind a pickup truck, heard a shot and looked back. Dave was still lying on his belly on the blacktop. Ima was climbing over the side and into the stern of the boat. Ura had undone the bow line and was running toward the stern line.

I ran to Dave, who was on his hands and knees by the time I reached him. "Are you okay?" I said.

"Yah, she missed me," he said. "I heard it buzz past my head."

Al joined us and asked the same question. Dave got to his feet and brushed some sand off his hands. His palms were red and raw from scraping them on the blacktop when he dove.

A boat motor roared and we looked toward the Double Your Fun. Ima was at the controls and the boat was moving away from the dock, heading toward the mouth of the harbor. Ura was standing in the stern waving goodbye with the gun in her hand.

Several men joined us and began asking questions. We pointed toward the boat and said they'd planned to kill us.

"I've got a boat here, do you want to go after them?" one man asked.

"Hell, no," Dave said. "They've got a gun and they've already shot at me once."

"You should call 911," another man said.

"I'm doing that right now," Al said. He had his cellphone in hand and was punching in the magic numbers. While he was telling the officer who answered what our emergency was, we were watching the Double Your Fun roar out of the harbor at full throttle, with the black rubber dinghy bouncing on a gusher of water churning behind them.

"Don't they know this is a 'no-wake' area?" asked a man who had just joined our group. "They could get a ticket for that."

35

WHITHER THE JEWELLS

"Which way did they go?" was the first question asked after we had explained the reason for our call to the two police officers who arrived five minutes after the Double Your Fun left the harbor.

There were three options: a forty-five-degree angle to the right, which would take them to Hyannis; a sharper angle to the left, which was the route to Falmouth; or a hard left, the way to several harbors in Rhode Island. A fourth option, a hard right, would take them out into the Atlantic toward Europe, but nobody was considering that one. The Double Your Fun was big, but it wasn't built to be an ocean-going vessel.

The problem was that none of us could agree on which of the three likely options the sisters had taken. Nobody in our group had kept a steady eye on the boat after it passed the end of the breakwater and plowed into the waves of Nantucket Sound. There were votes for all three options, along with a majority chorus of "I don't really know."

"Do they really have weapons?" was the next question.

That we could answer without a doubt. We'd definitely seen one, and it fired real bullets.

"Then we'd better get the Coast Guard involved," said the officer whose name tag read Sgt. Walker. "The harbor master ain't gonna go chasin' after anybody that's armed."

"You got that right," said a man who'd just joined the party. "Good afternoon, gentlemen, I'm John Lamoille, the harbor master for whom this officer spoke. Now, what's the problem and who's got the guns?"

Dave, Al and I overlapped each other in our explanations so badly that Lamoille held up his hands in a plea for silence. "One at a time, please, gentlemen; one at a time," he said.

We gave the honor to Dave, who fired out words like a machine gun as he told Lamoille who he was, why we were here and what the Jewell twins had done.

"We've got their confession on tape," I said when Dave finished. "Which reminds me, you can turn it off now, Dave."

Dave reached into his shirt pocket and brought out the recorder. "Oh, shit! I forgot to turn it on."

Fifteen minutes later we were in the Oak Bluffs police station, where we were ushered into the office of Detective Manny Gouveia. The word had gone out to the Coast Guard, which had agreed to organize a search for the Double Your Fun. Again the question had been asked, and gone unanswered, about which direction the Jewell twins' boat had taken after leaving the harbor.

Gouveia greeted us with all the enthusiasm of a swimmer encountering the shark from the movie "Jaws." "I suppose you're gonna tell me you've solved Walt Jerome's murder."

"We have," Dave said. "And we were almost the killers' next victims."

Gouveia did not look as if he'd consider this to be a tragedy. "Hard to believe those beautiful little girls would do such a thing," he said.

"They told us all about why they did it and how they did it," Dave said. "And they admitted killing Teddy Brewster, too."

"I don't suppose you got any of this on tape?"

Dave's face turned red. "It's my fault we didn't. But you've got the testimony of three of us who heard the confession and were about to be executed by those beautiful little girls."

Gouveia dug into a desk drawer and came out with three legal-size note pads. He dealt them to us like big yellow playing cards, pointed to a coffee mug full of ballpoint pens and said, "All three of you write out your statements—everything the girls said and did—without talkin' to one another. I'll be back in half an hour to get them." He rose and went out the door, closing it none too gently behind him.

"How do you like that?" Dave said. "The guy's pissed off because we solved his murder case for him."

"He's not the type who appreciates help from the sidelines," I said. "Seems to be a matter of pride with him."

"They say that pride goeth before a fall," Al said.

"Maybe that's it," Dave said. "Manny's afraid he'll get demoted for being outsmarted by a group of amateurs."

"The three musketeers, no less," I said.

"No longer the three stooges," Al said.

We raised our fists at arm's length and shouted, "All for one and one for all."

The door opened and the head and shoulders of a woman in a blue police uniform appeared in the opening. "Everything okay in here?" she asked.

We lowered our fists.

"Everything's great," Dave said.

"Just fine," I said.

"Four-oh," said Al.

The officer's head and shoulders disappeared and the door closed.

"Guess we better get to work on our statements," Dave said.

"We can celebrate later," I said.

"Where do we start?" Al said.

"Sorry, Manny says we can't talk to each other," I said. "You'll have to find your own starting point."

"I'm starting with Ima's arrival at the cottage, but I'm not saying that loud enough for anyone to hear me," Dave whispered.

"Nothing heard, nothing gained," Al said.

I sat in Manny Gouveia's chair and placed my yellow pad on his desk, Dave plopped into a wooden chair facing the desk with the pad in his lap and Al stood in front of a five-foot-tall filing cabinet and laid his pad on top. We wrote in silence for the next twenty minutes, the only sound being a flutter when one of us flipped over a page and started on a new one. We finished within a few seconds of each other and stuck our pens back in the coffee mug. A couple of minutes later the door opened and Manny Gouveia strode in. "Finished?" he said.

"All done," we chorused.

"Did'ja sign every page?"

We all groaned, took pens out of the coffee mug, scribbled our names on the bottom of every page of our documents and returned the pens to the coffee mug.

"Okay," Gouveia said. "You can go now. But don't leave the island until I say so."

"Whoa, when might that be?" I said.

"Depends on when I need to talk to you some more. Might be tomorrow, might be next week."

"We have plane tickets for Tuesday."

"Well, ain't you lucky? I'll be sure to keep that in mind durin' my investigation of this very *uncomplicated* case."

"We'd appreciate that," Dave said.

"Have a nice day," said Manny Gouveia.

We hustled out the door and were turning the corner around the end of the police station when we almost collided head-on with a woman trotting briskly in the opposite direction. She stopped when she saw us. "Okay, what the hell's going on?" asked Alison Riggs.

"What do you mean by going on?" I asked.

"There's chatter everywhere, on the police radio, the harbor master's radio and the Coast Guard radio," she said. "And now

I meet the three … uh, the three of you coming from the police station."

"And you think that we, of all the people on this island, who you were just about to refer to as the three stooges, might have information of interest to the Martha's Vineyard news media?" I asked.

"Oh, don't give me any crap. Just tell me what's happening."

"Come with us to my cottage and join us in a cold libation while we tell you about our day," said Dave.

"After that, you can ask Manny Gouveia for the official police version," I said.

"Fair enough," Alison said. "It's not like I've got a daily deadline."

"That reminds me, I do have a daily deadline," I said. "But these two musketeers can fill you in while I type my story."

"Musketeers?"

"No longer stooges," Al said. "At least not today."

36

LOST AT SEA

The first thing I did when we reached the cottage was call the *Daily Dispatch* city desk, hoping that Don O'Rourke was still there. My wish was granted; I caught him during the changing of the guard from the day shift to the night watch.

"Stop the presses," I said.

"Oh, please," Don said. "They don't even say that stupid line in movies anymore. What have you got that's so press stopping?"

"A first-person encounter with Walter Jerome's killers."

"Did you say *killers*, plural?"

"I did. Two beautiful, sweet-looking twin females who also tried to murder yours truly, Al Jeffrey and Dave Jerome in a triple-header."

"I hope they missed all three of you."

"We're all safe and sound, although Dave has some battle scars on his hands from dodging a bullet. They're not sore enough to keep him from drawing cartoons."

"Good god, what happened?"

I rattled off a quick summary of the day's events. This was the third time around, counting my written statement, and I was getting quite good at it. Don was duly impressed with both our detective work and our ballsy method of escape.

"Any pix of the killers?" he asked.

"I think Al might have some from an earlier, much more amicable, meeting. I'll check, and have him send you anything he's got."

"Okay. Whatever. Start writing. I'll tell Walt you've got a page one piece coming."

"There is some bad news," I said.

"What's that?"

"The detective in Oak Bluffs says he might hold us here past our Tuesday flight time."

"Screw the Oak Bluffs detective," Don said. "I'm not cancelling any more bookings. Get off that island and on that airplane Tuesday or you can find your own way home."

I relayed Don's ultimatum to Dave and Al, along with his request for any pix Al had of the Jewell sisters.

"I did sneak some shots on my cellphone the day Dave signed those bogus financial papers," Al said. He pulled out the phone and scrolled through some images. "Yeah, here they are. Trouble is I can't remember which one is Ima and which one is Ura."

"Won't make any difference to readers in Minnesota," Dave said. "Just take your pick and nobody will know any better than you do."

"Good thinking," Al said. "I'll call this one Ima and this one Ura."

Dave and I examined his choices. "I think it's the other way around. I think Ura was wearing the white frilly blouse," Dave said.

"Are you sure it wasn't Ima in white?" I said.

"I wouldn't bet my entire fortune of one-hundred dollars and thirty-one cents on it, but I think Ura had the white blouse and Ima was wearing blue."

"I'll yield to the discerning eye of an artist," Al said. "Ima in blue and Ura in white. Off they go to the *Daily Dispatch*."

Off they went, and off I went to my bedroom to write my story while Al and Dave continued to entertain Alison Riggs with their descriptions of the day's events. I could hear her reacting verbally to each new revelation as I pecked away on my laptop. "Really?" "Oh, my god!" "No shit?"

When I'd finished and emailed the story to the *Daily Dispatch*, I desperately wanted to call Martha and tell her about our little adventure. It was close to five o'clock on the Vineyard, but it was an hour earlier in St. Paul, which meant she was still at work. I fought the urge to break our iron-clad agreement about no working-hours calls and started toward the living room to join the story tellers and their bedazzled one-woman audience. Before I got there my cell-phone rang. It was Martha.

“Greetings,” I said. “All done with the day’s labors so early?”

“All done with our day in court so early,” she said. “The judge heard Linda’s arguments on my dad’s deportation case this afternoon.”

“And was the judge convinced that Linda was correct?”

“Don’t know. He took the case under advisement and said he would give her his decision within forty-eight hours. That means Wednesday at the latest.”

“Does Linda think she convinced him?”

“She’s not sure. He’s one of those judges that never changes his facial expression, so you can’t get a reading on what his reaction is. You could describe a bloody axe murder and the piece by piece dismemberment of the body to this guy and he wouldn’t so much as blink an eye.”

“Inscrutable.”

“Face like a stone. Hope his heart’s a little softer. Anyhow, what’s up with you? Coming home on schedule or did you run into something new and crazy?”

“I thought you’d never ask. The answer to both questions is yes.” I went back to my bedroom, sat down on the edge of the bed and described my day. Her responses were remarkably similar to Alison’s.

Alison was giving goodbye hugs to Al and Dave when I returned to the living room. Hugging is a much more common expression of both hello and goodbye in New England than it is in Minnesota, where fathers and sons of Nordic or Germanic descent have been known to greet each other with a hand-shake after a separation of ten years. I marched forward to receive my hug, and I made her promise to keep me informed on the search and eventual (I hoped) trial of the Jewell twins.

"I suspect the police and the prosecutor will keep you informed on the trial," she said. "You'll all be subpoenaed to testify as the prosecution's star witnesses."

"Oh, goody," Al said. "Another Martha's Vineyard vacation."

"We could give Marty a thrill by renting a car at the weekly rate," Dave said.

"You're the boss," I said.

"I'll treat you to lobster rolls at Linda Jean's the day you arrive," Alison said. She gave us a farewell wave and went out the door.

"Now what?" Al said after the door closed behind Alison.

"Now we turn in the van for one last time," Dave said. "I assume you're coming with me to say goodbye to Marty."

"Maybe he'll give us a hug," Al said.

"I'll hug Marty when hell freezes over," said Dave.

Marty was his usual helpful self when Dave handed him the van key. "You sure you don't want to keep it for another day, just in case something unexpected comes up?" he said.

"Nothing's coming up, unexpected or unbelievable," Dave said. "We're taking a taxi to Vineyard Haven tomorrow morning and we will be on the 9:30 ferry, come hell or nor'easter."

"Or Detective Gouveia," I said.

"You're the boss," Marty said. He handed Dave a receipt and did not offer a hug.

The Boston five o'clock television newscast led with the Coast Guard's search for the Double Your Fun. The anchor gave a brief rundown of the Jewell sisters' alleged crimes, accompanied by film of a Coast Guard cutter leaving the harbor at Woods Hole to search the waters between Martha's Vineyard and Cape Cod. As of that time, there had been no sighting of the Double Your Fun.

A spokesman for the Coast Guard said that if the fleeing boat wasn't located within an hour the search would be expanded to the area between the Vineyard and Rhode Island. He added that the duty helicopter was busy airlifting a fishing boat crewman who'd had an attack of appendicitis thirty miles offshore. By the time the med-evac flight was completed, it would be too dark for the chopper to start looking for the Double Your Fun.

Authorities at all ports on Cape Cod and in Rhode Island had been alerted and police were standing by. The Coast Guard spokesman said he was confident that if the Jewells evaded the search at sea they would be apprehended anywhere they attempted to dock or moor their boat. He warned the public not to approach the Double Your Fun because the occupants were armed and considered dangerous.

"Damn right they're dangerous," Dave said, looking down at the scabs on his palms.

I did not sleep much that night. As of the eleven o'clock news, the search for the Double Your Fun had been unsuccessful. When I did doze off, I dreamed of people on huge boats carrying guns, and woke up expecting to see Ima and Ura come charging into my bedroom with pistols and hypodermic needles in both hands.

At six o'clock, I gave up trying to sleep, got out of bed and took a shower. When I emerged from the bathroom Al was waiting to get in. "You couldn't sleep either?" he said.

"Slept like a log," I said. "A log being chopped to pieces with a chain saw."

"If you had opened your laptop, you could have logged off."

I went downstairs and turned on the early morning news. After sitting through some chatter about the weather around Boston, an on-the-spot report of a late-night shooting in South Boston and another long stream of automobile, miracle medication and mattress commercials, I learned that the Coast Guard was resuming its hunt for the Double Your Fun and that the helicopter would be joining the cutter in the morning search. The theory was that the twins had gone toward Rhode Island and would be trying to sneak into a mooring in one of the harbors there.

Al joined me as the newscast was morphing into more commercials and Dave appeared a few minutes later looking as drawn and bleary-eyed as I felt. "Linda Jean's," he said. "Coffee."

We secured every window and locked every door on the cottage and dragged our luggage with us to Circuit Avenue. We planned to get a taxi after breakfast and go directly to the Steamship Authority ferry landing in Vineyard Haven harbor. We had to be on the 9:30 ferry in order to catch the bus that would take us to Boston's Logan International in time to check in for our flight to the Twin Cities.

We were greeted by Angie, the smiling, attractive, middle-aged woman who had served us breakfast a dozen times. "Looks like you guys are going somewhere," she said as she led us toward an empty table.

"Home," I said. "We're finally going to see our wives again."

"Be careful with your homecoming celebrations," Angie said. "There's a name for couples that get too exuberant after a long separation."

"What's that?" I asked.

"Parents," she said as she turned and went to get our coffee.

The coffee, along with plates full of omelets, pancakes, sausages and whole wheat toast, revived us to the point where we could speak and think again. We were examining our checks and computing our tips when Dave's cell phone rang.

"Caller ID says Oak Bluffs police," he said.

"Don't answer it," Al said.

We were all staring at the ringing phone when Angie returned to pick up our credit cards. "Shouldn't you answer your phone?" she asked.

"No way," said Dave. "And if anybody from the police department comes in here looking for us, you have not seen us this morning."

Angie's eyes opened wide. "My god, what have you guys done?"

"Nothing. That's why you haven't seen us."

"We need to catch a ferry without any delays," I said. "That's why we didn't stop here this morning."

Dave's phone went to voice mail and he played it on speaker. "Mister Jerome, this is Detective Manny Gouveia," said an all too familiar voice. "I need for you and your two friends, Mister Mitchell and Mister Jeffrey, to be at the Oak Bluffs police station at nine o'clock this mornin' to discuss the written statements you provided us with yesterday."

"We need to get out of Oak Bluffs," I said.

"Fast," said Dave. "He's only three blocks away and he comes here for coffee."

37

ON THE RUN

Al picked up his phone, pulled a card with a taxi service's number on it out of his shirt pocket, and made the call. He arranged to have a taxi meet us in front of a store named Good Dog Goods, which was straight up Circuit Avenue, about three blocks in the opposite direction from the police station. Catching the taxi there instead of at Linda Jean's would double our distance from Detective Manny Gouveia.

Angie returned with our credit cards, we hastily wrote down outrageous tips, signed the checks and started dragging our luggage toward the door. Angie caught us before we got outside and insisted on giving each of us a farewell hug. "I'm going to miss you guys," she said. "Have a safe trip home."

"The most dangerous part is getting to the ferry before Detective Gouveia realizes we aren't joining him at nine o'clock to answer questions," Dave said. "When we don't show up, he'll go to the cottage looking for us. When he finds out we're not there, he'll come here."

"Sorry, but I haven't seen you guys since yesterday," Angie said.

"Thanks. You'll probably be seeing us again next summer."

We hustled along the sidewalk toward the Good Dog Goods, weaving through late-season tourists looking in store windows, reading menus on restaurant doors or staring at cell phones held in their palms. The latter were the most dangerous, as they were oblivious to our approach and would not vary their course to avoid us.

The taxi, a nine-passenger van, arrived at the store a minute after we did. The driver helped us pile our bags into the back and within minutes we were starting the three-mile ride to Vineyard Haven. The late-autumn, mid-morning traffic was light and we arrived at the ferry terminal with time to spare. Too much time, in fact. The ferry wasn't in yet and we would have to wait at the terminal until we could board, which meant that Manny Gouveia would be looking for us while we were still on the terra firma of Martha's Vineyard.

Dave gave the driver a twenty-buck tip and informed him that we had never been in his vehicle. The driver looked at the picture of Jackson in his hand and nodded in agreement. "Hope you have a safe trip, even if I've never seen you," he said.

We headed directly for the boarding area, where a line was beginning to form. There were eight people and two dogs ahead of us.

"How long before Manny starts hunting for us?" Al asked.

Dave checked his watch. "It's ten-to-nine. The ferry's due in at nine but we can't get on until the people coming from Woods Hole get off. That should take anywhere from ten to fifteen minutes, depending on how big a load they've got this trip."

"Manny probably won't start looking for us until five minutes or so after nine," I said. "It will take him several minutes to check the cottage and several more to look at Linda Jean's. Then if he decides to try to catch us here, it will be another five or six minutes unless he turns on the siren and lights and drives like a madman through slow-moving traffic. We should be onboard and heading out to sea by the time he gets here."

We stood, shifting our weight nervously from one foot to another, watching for the ferry to arrive and trying to look innocent and inconspicuous to a state policeman who was standing nearby.

"Damn boat is late," Dave said at nine o'clock.

"Want to call the Steamship Authority and complain?" Al said.

"I'll let it go this one time."

"Discretion is the better part of valor," I said.

We were forced to be discreet for another five minutes before we saw the tall, broad shape of the Island Home loom up before us and slide into the slip. The bow opened and vehicles began to emerge. The portable pedestrian ramp was connected to an exit on the ferry and people began to straggle off. It seemed as if they were purposely going at a snail's pace to keep us from getting onboard.

At 9:15, Dave's cellphone rang. "It's the Oak Bluffs cops again," he said.

"Don't answer it," Al and I said in unison.

After the ringing stopped, Dave checked for a message. It was Manny Gouveia, saying we were late and he was still expecting us to come to his office. "You can keep right on expecting," Dave said.

"It'll be a long wait, Manny," Al said.

We handed the attendant our ferry tickets and started up the ramp at 9:25. Once onboard, we went to the upper deck and walked to where we could look back over the parking lot. Cars and SUVs and pickup trucks were still rolling onto the freight deck, two levels below us.

"Manny could be at the cottage by now if he's gone looking for us," Dave said. "But we should be well under way before he gets here."

The line of boarding vehicles came to an end. The boarding ramp was pulled back away from the ship. The three musketeers relaxed; we'd beaten Detective Manny Gouveia.

Dave snapped to attention. "Oh, shit!" he said, pointing to the parking lot. A Tisbury police cruiser was wheeling into the lot with blue lights flashing.

"Manny called the locals," I said. "We're toast."

The police cruiser rolled to a stop near the detached boarding ramp. The driver, a blue-uniformed police officer, got out and trotted toward the ferry. He stopped beside the state cop and they both looked up to where we were standing. The local cop pointed at the closed boarding ramp and appeared to be asking the ground crew to reopen the ramp.

The ferry's horn let forth a blast of sound so loud that all three of us jumped. And the ship began inching slowly away from the gesticulating police officer.

"Whatever you do, don't wave bye-bye," Dave said.

Instead, we exchanged high-fives and headed for some seats in a celebratory mood. However, that mood vanished when Al said, "What if they call the cops on the other side, in Woods Hole? What if they grab us there and put us on the next ferry back to the island?"

"We can't let it happen," I said.

"How can we sneak past them?" Al said. "Even if they don't catch us as we're getting off the boat, it won't do us any good to out run them to the bus. They'll just follow us on and haul us off."

We spent the next thirty minutes discussing our options, which were extremely limited and not very likely to succeed. We decided that our best bet was to split up. We had seen a couple of people with heavy luggage walking off the freight deck ahead of the cars in Vineyard Haven. The cops most likely would be waiting to catch us at the bottom of the pedestrian ramp. If a sacrificial lamb went down that ramp, the other two might be able to sneak off the freight deck, scoot cross the parking lot and make it to the airport-bound bus. The question was, who would be the sacrificial lamb?

Dave volunteered for that unpleasant role. "This whole friggin' mess is my fault," he said. "You guys are only here because I asked you to keep me company on this trip. I should be the one to go back to the island and talk to Manny Gouveia."

"Actually, we should all stand together and refuse to go back," Al said. "Remember one for all and all for one?"

"Right. The three musketeers," I said.

"It'll be the three stooges again if we all go back," Dave said. "Didn't Don say that you two will wind up paying for your own air fare if you miss today's flight?"

"He did say that," I said.

"Think he meant it?" Al asked.

"Sounded like it."

"Well, I'm already paying for my ticket, so I won't be losing money if they send me back to Manny," Dave said. "And I've got a whole hundred dollars and thirty-one cents in an investment fund to help defray the cost."

"Ah, you rich guys have all the fun," Al said.

"I will make sure that I'm the very last person off the ferry," Dave said. "That will give you time to get to the bus stop. I just hope the bus is there so you can jump onboard without having to wait in the ticket office."

"I just hope they'll let us walk off with the cars," I said. "Our luggage isn't all that huge."

"One of us could hobble, like he's got a sore foot or a bum leg, and the other could be helping him along," Al said. "I'll be the hobbler."

"Have you ever hobbled?" I asked.

"No, but I've wobbled a couple of times after too many beers."

"Close enough. But you'd better look sober when you hobble or we may have a different kind of problem."

A voice over the public address system announced that we were approaching Woods Hole and that all drivers should return to their vehicles. Al and I wished Dave good luck and joined the stream of people going to the freight deck, dragging our luggage down two flights of stairs. When we reached the bottom, the huge doors in the bow were opening and we were minutes away from the end of the ride.

"Think we'll make it to the bus without being stopped?" I said.

"We'll either be bused or be busted," Al said.

38

THE ARTFUL DODGERS

There were four other passengers, all with multiple baggage items and monster suitcases, lined up with us to walk off the freight deck. The crewman directing traffic gave us the go-ahead and we started forward as a group. Al put on such a great show of hobbling that the crewman actually asked if he was going to be okay, and I replied that he had sprained his ankle but he'd be able to get to the bus with my assistance.

Once off the ferry and out of sight of the crew, Al's hobble healed itself and we took off at a brisk walk toward the ticket office. Looking back toward the Island Home, we saw two uniformed police officers and a state policeman standing at the foot of the exit ramp. They were speaking to every man who wasn't with a woman or a child as they came off the ramp.

"They've got to be looking for us," I said.

"Dave is toast," Al said.

"What'll we tell Cindy?"

"We'll tell her that Dave is a hero who took one for the team."

"Let's hope the team doesn't get grounded before game time. The bus isn't in yet and there's no place to hide."

Our only option was to duck into the ticket office and mingle with a small gaggle of people buying last-minute ferry tickets, sandwiches and coffee, and going to the rest rooms. We looked out the window at the Island Home and saw a line of people still coming down the passenger ramp. Dave was not yet visible and the cops were still there.

"They're going to have to sweep Dave off that ferry with the trash," Al said.

"A little trash talk might get him past the cops," I said.

Our view was momentarily blocked by a Peter Pan bus as it drove past the ticket office and stopped at its designated loading area. We were the first two people out the door and on the way to the bus. Of course we had to wait for about forty people to get off before we could climb aboard. While we waited, we kept the bus between us and the officers watching the ferry exit. They could not see us, but likewise we could not see whether Dave had come down the ramp yet.

After the last passenger stepped down from the bus, the driver took our bags and shoved them into the cargo hold. We hustled up the steps into the bus and went all the way to the back. We didn't take the very back seat—that would be too obvious if the cops came aboard looking for us—but sat in the next-to-last row, where we could duck behind all the people ahead of us.

From the bus window, we could see the Island Home. The ramp was now filled with people going onto the ferry and the three police officers were nowhere to be seen. Dave Jerome was, likewise, nowhere to be seen.

"Wonder how long Manny will make Dave stay," Al said.

"I can't imagine why he wants to question us about our statements," I said. "Everything that happened is right there in writing."

"Maybe he's just doing it to pull our chain. You know he doesn't appreciate our help."

"And poor Dave, who's never bugged Manny like we have, is the one who winds up paying the penalty."

We heard the bus engine start, but before the door closed someone in the middle of the bus yelled, "Wait, driver; there's one more dude running for the bus."

The driver kept the door open and soon the head of the running dude popped up at the top of the steps. Dave Jerome looked down the aisle, spotted us and waved. Then he came practically dancing down the aisle, said, *"hola, tres amigos,"* gave us each a high five and flopped into an open seat across the aisle from us.

The bus door closed with a whoosh of compressed air and we started to roll. Al and I recovered the ability to speak and did so simultaneously and rapidly, causing Dave to hold up his hands in self-defense. "Gimme a chance to talk," he said.

That shut us up, and Dave began to talk. "Like I said I would be, I was the last person off the boat. I was tucked up close behind two guys in suits, trying to look invisible and casual all at the same time. There were two blues and a statie at the foot of the ramp and I was hoping to somehow duck around behind the statie, using the two guys in suits for cover."

"And it worked?" I said.

"Not the way I expected. The three cops said something to the two suits, took them by the arms and walked them away. I saw the bus and started running across the parking lot. Got here just in time, as you can see."

"Those cops weren't after us?" I said.

"They were after those two in suits for something. Serves them right. Imagine wearing a suit on Martha's Vineyard."

"Your Martha's Vineyard lawyer sure can't imagine it," Al said.

"Anyway, here we are, all together and on our way home," Dave said. "The three musketeers ride again."

The flight from Logan to Minneapolis-St. Paul was routine and exceedingly boring, just the way I like flights to be. The greeting we received from three grinning women as we approached the baggage carousel was not at all routine and boring, which is also just the way I like wifely greetings to be.

After we'd finished hugging and kissing and had dragged our bags off the carousel, I asked if we were all going home in one car.

All three women laughed. “We’ve each got our own car and we’re each going to our own house,” Martha Todd said. “We’re not sharing rides with anybody tonight.”

She and I were barely in the door of our duplex on Lexington Avenue when she took me by the hand, towed me into the bedroom and showed me what she was willing to share. It was something I’d been missing for way too many nights.

39

A CASE OF JEWELLS

I was hazily aware of Martha's departure from our bed Wednesday morning, but I didn't become cognizant of anything outside my eyelids until after she had showered, dressed, eaten breakfast, put down food and drink for Sherlock Holmes and left for work. When my eyelids did finally part, I turned my gaze from Martha's vacant pillow to the digital clock on my bedside table. It said 8:11 a.m.

Instantly I was wide, wide, wide awake. Don O'Rourke had said he wanted to see me at my desk in the *Daily Dispatch* newsroom this morning. That usually meant being visible by 8:00. I'd barely been home for twelve hours and I was already in deep doo-doo at the *DD*.

I rolled out of bed and went looking for my cellphone. It was nowhere in sight. I had no idea where I might have put it during our single-minded scramble to get rid of our clothing in the bedroom. I gave up the search, rushed to the kitchen and punched the *Daily Dispatch* city desk number into our landline phone. We had talked about dropping the land line; I was glad at this moment that we hadn't.

The call was answered by Assistant City Editor Eddy Gambrell. I said hi, identified myself and asked to speak to Don.

"Hang on a sec, Mitch," he said. Then I heard him say, "Hey, Don, it's the vacationer from paradise. I guess his flight just got in."

The next voice was Don's. "I thought your flight left Boston yesterday afternoon. Did they take the Polar route and go over Russia on the way to St. Paul?"

"No, we had two-hundred mile-an-hour headwinds and had to stop three times for fuel," I said. "Actually, I overslept and I just got up. Travel is very tiring, you know." I pulled out a kitchen chair and sat down. The coolness of the wooden seat on my derriere called my attention to the fact that I was naked. Good thing we weren't on Skype.

"I'd heard it was broadening," Don said. "Are you fat as well as late?"

"As a matter of fact, I have put on a couple of pounds, thanks to one restaurant's cooking."

"So how soon can the broader, sleepier you be in this office?" Don said.

"I'll take a quick shower, throw on some clothes and scoot right down there. I can live without breakfast."

"Why don't you postpone the shower and get on the phone from home while you're eating breakfast? Make some calls and find out what's new on Martha's Vineyard; whether they caught the missing misses or not. Then email me a story like you've been doing for the last however many months it's been since we last saw your face in the newsroom."

"It's only been two weeks," I said. "Well, maybe two and a half. You know very well that I've been trying to get home."

"Well, now that you're here, get us some news from where you were. And be here on time tomorrow. Your twin made it in this morning, you know."

"I didn't know. But I will be Johnny on the Spot on the morrow."

"I'd rather you'd be Mitch on the desk on Thursday. Put some clothes on and start making calls today."

Did he know I was naked? More likely he thought I was in my jammies. Then again, he was a married man and he knew about homecomings after long separations. As I said, it's a good thing we weren't on Skype. And how did that dirty rat Al make it to work on time this morning? I was sure that his homecoming reception was just as vigorous and exhausting as mine had been.

I went to the bathroom, emptied my complaining bladder, wrapped myself in a bathrobe and returned to the kitchen. While I was spreading peanut butter on a piece of whole wheat toast, with Sherlock Holmes winding himself around my ankles, I heard my cell phone ringing. It seemed to be coming from the bedroom, so I hustled back there. Sure enough, the sound was coming from the pants that I had flung into one corner after their hasty removal.

By the time I dug the phone out of a pocket, the ringing had stopped. It told me I had missed a call from a 693 number. That was the Martha's Vineyard exchange. I tapped voice mail and there was a message from Alison Riggs: "Big news; call me ASAP." I did.

"Hey, Mitch, did I wake you up?" said Alison.

"Not quite," I said. "I was buttering a piece of toast and the phone wasn't in the kitchen. What's the big news? Did they catch the Jewells or are the nasty bounders still bounding?"

"As of an hour ago, the Jewells are in a proper setting. That being the Edgartown lockup."

"Where'd they catch them? Did they go to Rhode Island?"

"You won't believe where they were caught."

"Try me." I had gone to the room that Martha and I use as an office, and I now had pen and paper in hand, ready to take notes.

"Last thing the chief in Edgartown did yesterday was get a warrant to search the Jewells' house for evidence," Alison said. "They executed the warrant at seven this morning and what do you think they found in a little store room in the basement?"

"What?"

"Two very scared-looking redheads wearing nothing but their nighties, which, according to one of my police sources, were rather skimpy and a bit on the transparent side."

"Nice bonus for the cops. So how'd the twins get home without the Coast Guard seeing them?"

"They went almost all the way around the island. Instead of heading for the Cape or Rhode Island, they went around the western tip of the Vineyard, where the Gayhead light house is, sailed the length of the island along the south side, where nobody was looking for them, went around Chappaquiddick on the east end and managed to slip into Edgartown harbor, the only harbor not being watched, in the dark. They hung a blanket over the stern to hide the name of the boat, then they trotted on home, where apparently they planned to lay low for a while before trying to sneak onto a ferry or an airplane. They were mighty surprised to have half a dozen policemen charge in their front door before they were even out of bed this morning. They must have heard the cars drive up because they managed to run to the basement before the chief broke in the front door."

"How'd the cops find them so quickly in the basement?" I asked.

"They were in such a hurry that they left the door half open at the top of the stairs and left the light on when they got to the bottom of the stairs," Alisa said. "Cops noticed the open door, went down the stairs, saw a little room in the corner and yanked the door open. They had their guns in their hands, the cops I mean, which probably explains why Ima and Ura were described to me as looking very scared."

"Amazing. I can't believe they never thought about the cops searching the house."

"They thought they'd outsmarted everybody—which they had—but they also outsmarted themselves."

"So what's next? When will they be in court?"

"First thing tomorrow morning. You should come back and cover the arraignment."

"I'll be back soon enough when they go on trial," I said. "Meanwhile I'll settle for a phone chat with Chief Agnew in Edgartown. And I suppose I should call Oak Bluffs police, too. I'm not looking forward to that after skipping out on them yesterday. I'm sure they were very pissed at us."

"No, they weren't really pissed," Alison said. "But they were disappointed."

"We absolutely had to make that 9:30 ferry in order to get to the airport on time. And I don't see why they needed to talk to us about our statements anyway," I said.

"They didn't. That was just a cooked-up story to get you to come to the station. The chief was going to surprise all of you with written commendations for your help in solving the murder of Walter Jerome. I was there waiting to take your picture—the three stoo ... uh, the three musketeers, with Chief Benedetti and Detective Gouveia."

"Commendations? They chased us all the way to the Vineyard Haven ferry to give us commendations?"

"They didn't chase you to the ferry. They called you a second time and then just said the hell with it when you didn't show."

"But a Tisbury cop car came roaring up just as the ferry was pulling out. Wasn't he sent there after us?"

"No, silly, he was after two slick guys who'd been passing bad checks all over the island for a week. Caught'em, too, when they got off on the other side in Woods Hole."

Wait until the other two musketeers—oh, hell, *stooges*—hear that news, I thought, as I thanked Alison and ended the call.

Before I could punch in the number for the Edgartown PD, my cell phone rang again. This time the caller was ID'd as Martha Todd. "What's up?" I said.

"That's my question," Martha said. "Why aren't you at work?"

"Because you let me sleep until after eight o'clock, that's why. And when I called in, Don told me to stay home, make my calls and email a story. So, I ask again, to what do I owe the pleasure of this call, which, I might add, would have broken our ban on calls at work if I had been at work?"

"I was feeling kind of desperate for moral support and hoping you could take a break at 1:30. Judge Stoneface is going to announce his decision on my dad versus ICE at that time and I could really use a shoulder to lean on, especially if it goes the wrong way. I thought that was worth breaking the ban."

"You're right, it was. Sorry I even mentioned the ban. And seeing as how I'm not at the office, and that my story needs to be submitted long before 1:30, I'm sure I can meet you at the courthouse in time to hear the decision, which has got to go the right way."

"I hope you're right about all that. Okay, I'll see you there. And I'm sorry I didn't wake you up in time to get to the office. Or then again, maybe I'm not sorry. Whatever." She ended the call without the usual kissy sounds.

Whatever, indeed. I'd never heard Martha so discombobulated. It made me doubly glad that I'd made it home from Martha's Vineyard so I could be with her at the courthouse.

Edgartown Police Chief Morris Agnew was away from his office, and my call was transferred to Detective Aaron McGee, who was handling the investigation of the murder of Teddy Brewster. "What can I do for you?" he asked.

"You can fill me in on the status of the Jewell twins," I said. "Were you at the house when they were found?"

"Oh, yes, I was," McGee said. "And I'm glad I was. It was quite a sight. They were both in their nighties, which were both super short and sort of see-through. Best house tossing I've ever been on. Too bad you weren't there for the peep show."

I resisted the urge to tell him that I'd seen the twins wearing even less than their skimpy, see-through nighties. "Sorry I missed it," I said. "What's next? When do they go to court?"

"They'll be appearing first thing tomorrow morning. They've got a big shot lawyer coming down from Boston to defend them. They must have a lot of cash in the till if they can afford to hire this guy."

"Most of that cash was stolen," I said. "That big bucks lawyer might be disappointed when the Jewells' investment clients discover that their portfolios are empty and start filing suits to recover their money."

"With two charges of homicide and god knows how many charges of grand theft, those two are up to their cute little asses in doo-doo. Forensics should have a field day going through their business computers."

I asked McGee to describe the arrest and he told me a story almost identical to what I'd heard from Alison Riggs. He added that the Double Your Fun had been found and impounded, and that the twins were being held in separate cells in the Dukes County jail.

"I hope they're not still in their nighties," I said.

McGee laughed. "No, we let them put some clothes on before we took them out of the house. And we gave them some nice coveralls to wear when we checked them into their present quarters. They both look great in orange. Goes with their red hair."

"I'll bet. Can you email me some mug shots?"

"I'll send you their booking shots. Neither one is smiling for the camera."

"Be sure you ID them; I can't tell them apart."

"One of them is wearing an earring but I'm not sure which one it is. I'll look it up in my notes."

"Speaking of earrings, Ima told us that she lost one out at Teddy Brewster's campground. If you can find it you'll have physical evidence that she was there."

"Hey, actually they did find an earring when they scoured the ground out there. Be funny if it matches the one she's wearing in the mug shot."

I asked McGee for the prosecutor's name and office number. He said the people would be represented by Dukes County Attorney Lawrence Riggs and recited his phone number.

"Riggs," I said. "Any relation to a reporter named Alison?"

"Just her brother," said McGee.

"How handy for her."

"Her editor seems to appreciate the relationship. Have a nice day, Mister Mitchell."

My next call went to Detective Manny Gouveia in Oak Bluffs. He answered with his usual greeting, "Yeah? Gouveia here."

"This is your buddy Mitch Mitchell in St. Paul," I said. "I'm calling to apologize for skipping out on your surprise commendation show yesterday and to get your comments on the arrest of Ima and Ura Jewell."

"Yeah, well I didn't miss you guys all that much. The chief got carried away with that commendation thing and as far as I'm concerned it's just as well you weren't here. As for the Jewell sisters, they're in the pokey in Edgartown and we're continuin' with the investigation of the murder of Walter Jerome."

"Are you charging the Jewells with first-degree murder?"

"I ain't sure if it's first-degree, second-degree or manslaughter. You gotta talk to the DA about that."

"Were you present at the arrest of the Jewell sisters?"

"That happened in Edgartown. Why would I be there?"

"Just thought you might have been invited."

"That ain't my jurisdiction. I got enough problems right here, I don't need to go visitin' somebody else's territory. My job is to gather all the evidence I can about what those two did in Oak Bluffs, and that's what I'm workin' on today."

"Okay," I said. "I'll be checking with you regularly to see what's developing. And I'll be seeing you again when the Jewells go on trial."

"I can hardly wait," said Manny Gouveia. "You got any more questions right now?"

"Not at the moment. Talk to you later."

"Have a good day, Mister Mitchell."

Thinking about what might happen at 1:30, I hoped his wish would be granted, insincere as it was.

40

COURTING TROUBLE

I wrote my story, emailed it to Don and went back to my weight-reduction breakfast—peanut butter on whole wheat toast and black coffee. He responded ten minutes later with a couple of questions. I answered the questions and Don responded that everything was okay and that I should check with my Martha's Vineyard sources again in the afternoon for updates. I said I would do that and signed off.

After showering and putting on a white shirt and tie so I'd look respectable in court, I sat down with the morning paper. I didn't keep track of the passing minutes, and it was almost one o'clock when I checked my watch and realized I had to start moving immediately in order to get to the courthouse on time. I filled Sherlock's water dish, picked up my car keys and walked out to my Honda Civic, which was parked at the curb in front of the house. I'd dawdled so long that I had just enough time to drive downtown, park in the ramp on Kellogg Boulevard and hustle to the courthouse before the judge announced his decision.

I got into the car, closed the door, buckled up and turned the ignition key.

There was no sound other than the click of the key. I fiddled with the key, turning it off and then on again. Still nothing from under the hood. The car had been sitting in that spot since the night before we'd left for Martha's Vineyard, and apparently the battery had been bored to death during the nineteen nights and seventeen days of inactivity.

I sat for a moment, running silently through a string of curse words as fast as they came to mind. Then I asked myself, what could I do now?

Call a taxi was the answer. I pulled out my cellphone and Googled St. Paul taxis, chose one and called the number. "Be about five minutes," the dispatcher said. Good enough. That should have the driver dropping me off at the courthouse just in time. I went up on my porch, flopped into a wooden rocking chair and relaxed.

Time went by. Five minutes, six minutes, seven minutes. After eight minutes, I called the cab company's number again. "Driver had an accident," said the dispatcher. "Tangled with a pickup full of hay bales and the pickup won. I'm lookin' for another cab to send out your way. Be just a few more minutes."

More minutes ticked by. So many minutes that it was 1:24 when a cab came to a stop out front. I sprinted—well, trotted—to it, yanked the door open, threw myself into the back seat and said, "Courthouse, as fast as you can make it."

I'm sure there is a natural law that says when you're running late to a scheduled event everything that can possibly go wrong will go wrong. That law was in effect for this trip to the courthouse. At every intersection we either encountered a red light or were delayed by a car stopped ahead of us, waiting for oncoming traffic to clear before making a left turn. A trip that could have been completed in five or six minutes took an agonizing twelve. When at last we reached the courthouse, I handed the driver a twenty and jumped out without waiting for my share of the change.

I sprinted—well, trotted—up the courthouse steps, dashed through the door and was stopped in my tracks by a security guard. I was in the process of proving that I had no weapons or explosives on my person when a line of familiar figures exited the courtroom door in front of me. In the center of the lineup was Martha Todd. On her right was her mother, pushing her father in a wheelchair, and on her left was Triple-L—Linda L. Lansing. All three were smiling as they bore down on me.

"Where the heck were you?" Martha asked.

"Car didn't start," I said. "And cabs had a problem. Is it over already?"

"Took the judge thirty seconds to announce his decision against ICE and five minutes to rip their attorney and their representative up one side and down the other about the damn foolishness of their case against Dad," Martha said.

"He really gave them an ass-reaming about harassing an innocent man and wasting the court's time with a bogus immigration case," Triple-L said. "I've never heard a judge, let alone Stoneface, tear into anybody with that much force."

Dear old Dad just kept on smiling.

41

STAY IN TOUCH

I arrived at the *Daily Dispatch* at 7:58 a.m. on Thursday, but waited until 9:00 (which was 10:00 Eastern Standard Time) to call District Attorney Lawrence Riggs for a report on the court appearance by Ima and Ura Jewell. Of course he was not in his office and I left a message with his secretary.

Don O'Rourke was agitating for a quick story on the Walt Jerome case, so I decided to take a short cut and call the prosecutor's sister, who I was sure would have been covering it for the *Martha's Vineyard Chronicle*. She answered after two buzzes of her cell phone.

"Hi, Alison, your brother's out having a coffee break or something," I said. "How about an unofficial rundown on what happened to the Jewells in court this morning?"

"Who told you he's my brother?" Alison said.

"On a small island, with the same last name, I figured it had to be either your brother or your husband and I didn't recall seeing any wedding ring on your finger. A little birdie confirmed it and I'm not even on Twitter."

"Well, you'll have confirm anything I tell you with somebody bigger than your little birdie."

"My city editor is in a rush. If I get the report from you, I can have it in writing and ready to go by the time the bigger bird returns my call and chirps his official blessing."

"Well, okay, but don't cite me as a source. My lede will be that the Jewells came into court looking a bit tarnished, wearing classic orange jump suits and elegant prison-issue slippers with accessory leg shackles, at 8:35 Wednesday morning."

"I didn't know you had a flair as a fashion writer," I said.

"I have many talents that would amaze you. As for the rest of what you need, they were represented by Robert Fitzgerald King, of the Boston law firm of Benedict, King and Custer. Be sure you use his entire name when you ID him because there's another Robert King, whose multiple middle names are Franklin Delano, practicing law in Boston. Anyhow, Robert Fitzgerald King pleaded the defendants not guilty on all counts and requested that they be released on bail set at a reasonable amount."

"And what were all the charges?" I asked.

"They're each charged with two counts of first-degree murder, one count of fraud, one count of conspiracy, one count of grand theft, three counts of kidnapping involving the use of a deadly weapon—that was for grabbing you three musketeers, or whatever you're calling yourselves these days, at gunpoint—and one count of unlawful flight from authorities."

"And were they released on bail set at a reasonable amount?"

"Are you serious? District Attorney Lawrence Riggs pointed out that the defendants already had fled from police on one occasion, and District Judge Benjamin Newton ordered them held without bail. Robert Fitzgerald King said he was shocked at this curtailment of his clients' rights, but I think his shock was about as authentic as Louie's shock when he discovered that there was gambling in Rick's gin joint in Casablanca."

"So they're in the pokey until further notice."

"They will be honored guests of Dukes County for all the foreseeable future."

"So what's the next step in the procedure?"

"A preliminary hearing was set for one week from today. God knows when the trial will be held, but I'm sure you and your buddies will be invited to be guests of honor at the party when the time comes."

"With all those charges the party won't be held this year," I said.

"If you're lucky, it'll be next summer when the beach weather is the best," Alison said.

"I'll be sure to shop for new swim trunks. Meanwhile I'll be checking regularly with everyone, including you, for updates." My call-waiting alert sounded and I said, "I've got another call coming in. If it's your brother, should I say hi for you?"

"Better you don't mention talking to me. He's very touchy about that."

"Sibling rivalry?"

"Professional jealousy. Ta-ta, Mitch, have a wonderful day."

My new caller was, in fact, Dukes County Attorney Lawrence Riggs. I ran through the same rigmarole I had gone through with his sister and received identical information. Obviously Alison Riggs was a reporter whose accuracy could be trusted.

I thanked Lawrence Riggs and he said, "You're welcome. I'm sure you'll be having another Martha's Vineyard vacation with us sometime next year when this mess goes to trial."

"I'm looking forward to it," I said. "Can you make sure it starts during the prime beach weather?"

"I'll make that my priority," Riggs said. "Wouldn't want to drag you out here in the winter when it's windy, cold and damp."

"Don't need to go all the way to Martha's Vineyard for that. We get more than enough cold, wind and dampness in St. Paul."

"We'll let you know when we need you. Have a nice day, Mister Mitchell."

I wrote my story, emailed it to Don and punched David Jerome's cell phone number into my phone.

"Hey, Dave," I said when he answered. "Hang onto that house on Martha's Vineyard. We're gonna need a place to stay next summer."

The End

CPSIA information can be obtained
at www.ICGtesting.com
Printed in the USA
FFHW020022021118
49212976-53431FF

9 781977 204813